IMOGEN'S STORY

Book one of **The Book Club** novels

IMOGEN'S STORY

ALI FISCHER

HYPERBOLE PUBLISHING

DEDICATION

I dedicate this book to Swati and Gemma.

And to my husband, thank you for being my inspiration
on what a great male lead character should be. And thank you
for putting the kids to bed and cooking the dinner while I tap
away furiously at my keyboard. Your support has
been invaluable. I love you dearly.

PLAYLIST

Here is a playlist for you to listen to while you read. Each song has been picked to match the mood and emotions felt.

Chapter 1: *I've Gotta Be Me*, Paloma Faith

Chapter 4: *Better Luck Next Time*, Kelsey Ballerini

Chapter 11: *Take You Dancing*, Jason Derulo

Chapter 13: *Losing Me* (Piano version), Gabrielle Aplin & JP Cooper

Chapter 15: *Starving* (feat. Zedd), Hailee Steinfield & GREY

Chapter 16: *Hold My Girl*, George Ezra

Chapter 17: *Bird Set Free*, Sia

Chapter 18: *Close* (feat. Tove Lo), Nick Jonas

Chapter 20: *Run For Your Life*, The Beatles

Chapter 21: *The Last Time*, The Script

Chapter 23: *Wicked Game*, Grace Carter

Chapter 29: *Feels Like Home*, Hannah Grace

Be Brave
to let go of the past.
And fight
for the present that you deserve.
A better future is always yours.

When you know why you like someone,
it's a crush.
When you have no reason or explanation,
it's love.

PROLOGUE

Imogen heard the letterbox rattle, followed by the soft thud of the post landing on her doormat. The floorboards were cool beneath her feet as she tiptoed out of her bedroom and across the small apartment. She dipped to collect the post and flicked through the items, discarding the junk mail in the bin as she reached the kitchen.

She held an A4-sized envelope in her hands. It was thick, thicker than a rejection letter would be. Imogen allowed herself to feel excitement and hope—she was sure this letter would provide her with a safer and happier future. She held her breath while listening to make sure Mark wasn't awake and then slid her thumb along the fold of the envelope. Knowing she didn't have long before he would want to know where she was, she pulled the covering letter out halfway.

Dear Miss Taylor,

We are pleased to inform you that Spencer & Black Associates would like to offer you the position of Senior Designer reporting directly to James Spencer. Enclosed you will find two copies of your employment contract—please sign them both and send one back in the supplied envelope. If you have any queries or concerns, do not hesitate to call me.

Imogen took a deep breath, slid the letter back into the envelope, and tucked it into her laptop bag, hidden under paperwork. She would have to wait for Mark to leave before she could read through the contract but knew she would sign it without hesitation and post it on her way to the office on Monday. That gave her two days to plan her letter of resignation and start the process of moving out of London. She was doing this—she was really going to escape Mark and find freedom.

'Imogen, what are you doing?' She was startled out of her daydream, the feeling of hope replaced with panic.

'I'm just making a cup of tea. Do you want one?' She filled the kettle and flicked it on.

'Yes, please, I'll have it in the bedroom. I want you again before I need to head off, so hurry up.'

A feeling of nausea washed over her. She was going to have to carry on as usual right up until the last minute, which meant servicing Mark whenever he demanded it.

While stirring the tea, she made a list in her head. Sell the flat, find a place to live, somehow pack belongings worth taking into my Mini and disappear. 'Good luck Imogen, you're going to need it with that exit strategy,' she said under her breath.

'Here's your tea.' Imogen placed the cup on the bedside table before returning to her side of the bed. She put her own cup down with a shaky hand.

'Thank you, sweetheart—what would I do without you? Thankfully, I'll never need to find out as I don't intend to let you go.' Mark reached over to Imogen and wrapped his hand around the back of her neck, pulling her down onto him.

'Now, kiss me before I do all sorts of naughty things with that mouth of yours.'

Imogen closed her eyes and imagined her happy place, walking under trees with nothing but the sound of leaves crunching underfoot.

CHAPTER 1

Song choice: I've Gotta Be Me (Paloma Faith)

Imogen looked up at the building, shielding her eyes from the sun as it reflected off the windows. It seemed bigger this morning than it did when she came for her interview a little over three months ago. She figured that was because it was now filled with her hopes and dreams for a brighter future. Adjusting the handbag on her shoulder, she made her way to the security cabin.

'Hi, I'm Imogen Taylor—it's my first day today with Spencer and Black Associates.'

'Good morning Miss Taylor, I'm Sam, Sam Briggs, and I'm in charge of the security for the site. If you need any help with anything, give me a shout. You can normally find me out here. If you don't mind, I need to take a photo to add to our file and your access card. You need to keep this card on you and visible at all times—a lot of the internal doors won't open without it.'

Imogen was relieved that she had made an effort with her makeup today and doubled up on concealer. The last few months had been rough, evidenced by the dark circles under her eyes. She'd grown her chestnut brown hair to shoulder length to reinvent herself. For most of her life, she'd had the same chin-length bob—now seemed like a good time to try something new.

Imogen took the tree-lined path to the office with her new security pass in hand. She took a few deep breaths before swiping her card at the door and stepping in.

The reception area was as impressive as the first time she'd seen it. The bright morning sunshine bounced off the polished porcelain floor tiles. Lush green foliage spilt out of large oak planters, adding flashes of colour to an otherwise white reception area. Her black patent heels clicked as she made her way to the reception desk.

'Good morning, Imogen. Sam called through to say you were heading in—I'm Sarah Wright.' Imogen shook the outstretched hand and took in the striking woman before her. She was envious of the cascade of wavy hair falling to her shoulders with the colour of a shiny copper penny. 'I was on holiday when you came in for your interview—it's great to finally meet you. James has been very excited to have you on board. I'll let him know you're here.'

'Thanks, Sarah, it's lovely to meet you too. I'm excited to be here.'

Imogen straightened out her black pencil skirt, tucked in her cream silk blouse and double-checked that the buttons weren't gaping open. She struggled to get blouses to fit, one disadvantage of a more voluptuous figure. She chastised herself for deciding to wear something that could release the puppies on her first day.

'If you'd like to take a seat over there, James will be down soon, and Imogen, if you need anything, give me a shout. Welcome to Spencer and Black Associates.'

'Thank you, Sarah. I appreciate that. I'll have to buy you a coffee soon so you can fill me in on all the insider info.'

'In that case, I'll have a skinny latte with an extra shot, and I'll tell you anything you want to know.'

Imogen felt at ease here—the place had a relaxed vibe. As she took a seat, she checked her phone for messages since she wouldn't look at it until the end of the day. It wouldn't make a great impression for her to be checking it too much at work. She noticed one new unread message and clicked on it. She wished she hadn't bothered.

Take me back, Imogen. I can't live without you, and I don't want you to live without me. I will find you and make you see you need to be with me.

Imogen's blood went cold, a shiver running down her spine. She didn't need this today. She turned her phone off and stuffed it back into her bag as James walked into reception.

He wore tailored stone-coloured chinos, dark brown leather shoes and a light blue shirt with the sleeves rolled up to his elbows. He looked casual but well put-together. The cut of his shirt showed off his trim figure and broad shoulders. He had green eyes and strawberry blonde hair cut short around the sides but longer on top and styled to one side. He came across as effortlessly well-groomed.

'Good morning, Imogen. How are you this morning, ready and raring to go, I hope?'

Imogen took some deep breaths and composed herself as she stood up, straightened her skirt again and put a smile on her face.

'I'm good, thank you, Mr Spencer—I'm looking forward to getting stuck in. Thank you so much for giving me this opportunity.' Imogen couldn't believe her luck when offered the role at Spencer and Black Associates. They were getting quite the reputation for being one of the best property development and interior design businesses. They had exceptionally high standards and treated their staff well. This was the calibre of company she wanted to work for.

'That's great to hear, and call me James—we're a relaxed family around here, no airs or graces in this place. I'm looking forward to finally getting some help—our client base for interior design is skyrocketing. Your CV turned up on my desk at the right time.'

James' energy was infectious, and the unpleasant text message was soon out of her mind as she walked through into the main offices.

'Right, let's get you settled at your desk before we grab a coffee and take you on a tour of the office.'

'Sounds good.'

The office space was impressive and spanned two floors. An open space in the middle went up to a glass roof. The walkway on the ground floor had the same greenery as the reception area, and taller trees were growing out of huge concrete planters, reaching for the sky above them. Imogen appreciated the perfect balance between the warmth of the oak and the industrial feel of the concrete.

She stopped walking and noticed the seating areas stationed in between the trees. Lining the walkway were three beautiful sofas. They were breathtaking, with sweeping lines and covered in luxurious deep blue velvet. She recognised them.

'James, are they what I think they are? Are they the Divino Vamp sofas?'

'They are indeed. Usually, you see them in white, but I commissioned them in our signature blue. Do you like them?'

'They're beautiful. I have a great deal of respect for Fran Divino—she's a real inspiration.'

'I'll have to arrange for an introduction next time she visits. You're undoubtedly aware that she only sells through a select few interior designers? We're fortunate to showcase some of her products here.' It impressed Imogen—this must be a sign that she was in the right place.

James led her up a broad staircase to a mezzanine, which joined the two sides of the upper level. Ample comfortable seating adorned the area and was already bustling with people having their morning coffee. There was an intimidating coffee machine at the far end of the mezzanine, and a fridge stocked full of fresh juices. A display of lovely-looking pastries grabbed Imogen's attention—they would end up going straight to her hips if she indulged, but they looked like they were worth it.

'This'll be our first port of call once you've ditched your bag—I'm very much in need of a caffeine hit. Right, here's our office.' James indicated a set of large glass doors. He swiped his card over a reader and the door unlocked.

He held it open for Imogen as she walked into the spacious office. She was struck by how bright and fresh the office felt. The floor-to-ceiling windows ensured that the space was flooded with natural daylight but was tempered by the navy-blue carpet underfoot. There were six workstations set up to the left of the room. Each station had a white desk and an oversized comfortable-looking chair in bright colours. Opposite each desk was a drafting table. Behind the workstation area and along the natural brick wall stood a large oak shelving unit and a hanging rail made of oak and black industrial metal pipes.

'This is where you can store your handbag and coat if you want. Most of our designers like an organised workspace and prefer to declutter as much as possible, but it's entirely up to you—as I said, we're a relaxed bunch. You'll get to meet everyone soon—as you can see, the place is like the Mary Celeste this time on a Monday morning.'

Imogen left her bag in one of the cubes of the shelving unit. She needed it out of sight, so it did not tempt her to reach for her phone. James walked her over to her workstation.

'You should have everything you need already set up here. If you want anything else, give Sarah a shout, and she can sort that out for you. She's a star—she keeps us all organised. If you take her a coffee now and then, she'll look after you well, and you'll have a friend for life. You'll also get the nice stationery.'

Imogen thought about how she could do with a good friend right now—she'd have to work out how to use that coffee machine pronto.

'My office is over there in the corner, perks of being the boss. I've always wanted a fancy corner office—you should see the way I can get the glass to frost up. It's cool. My door is always open, unless it's closed, in which case it's always best to knock first.' At that, James gave Imogen a quick wink and a laugh.

Imogen was shocked and had to stop herself from laughing out loud. Did he just wink at her? Perhaps James was a bit of a Casanova. That would certainly keep her days entertaining. James carried on with the tour.

'Next to my office is our meeting room—we like to meet there every Monday morning after we've all fuelled up and prepared for the week ahead. We keep everyone up to date on where we are with our projects and work collaboratively. A problem shared is a problem halved, so never worry about discussing any issues you may be facing. We've all had those tricky clients that are hard to read, so lean on us whenever you need to.'

James clapped his hands together. 'Come on then, let's get that drink, and I'll show you around.'

'What's your poison, Imogen? Do you like coffee, or are you more of a tea person? We have a tea caddy over there full of all sorts.'

'I'm in camp coffee for sure—I prefer my tea to be of the Long Island variety.'

'I like your style. I think we're going to get along just fine.'

James pushed a few buttons, pulled a lever, and a glorious rich aroma was in the air within a few seconds. She could see a steady stream of silky-looking coffee flowing into a cup.

'How'd you like it, Imogen? Espresso, Americano, Cappuccino? You name it, and I'll try my best to make it. If I were you, though, I'd stick to an Americano as that's all I'm good at. If you're after fancy latte art, you need to time your visit here for when Cameron's making one.'

'Americano's great, thank you.' Imogen was overwhelmed

with the facilities—she just hoped she'd memorised the buttons and levers correctly to make a coffee next time. James made himself a drink while Imogen added milk to hers. She took a sip and closed her eyes. The coffee wasn't at all bitter—it was smooth and nutty, with a hint of fudge. This was one of the best coffees she'd ever had, and she'd had a lot.

James and Imogen took their drinks with them on their way back to the ground floor. He pointed out the facilities, the shower block and a gym. Imogen's thoughts went back to the pastries in the kitchen—a pre-work visit to the gym would allow her to have a guilt-free croissant and a coffee. She could even cancel the overpriced gym membership that she barely used. Perfect.

'Right, let me introduce you to the team—I think they're all in now. I can take you over to the architects' office later to meet Cameron.'

They made their way back to their office, and James led Imogen into the meeting room. The walls were all glass, and the table in the centre of the room was another piece by Divino—it was stunning. James spoke as if reading her mind.

'Yep, another Divino piece. We bring clients in here for meetings, so we want to show them everything we can offer, and these tables are a work of art.' James turned to everyone in the room.

'Good morning. How are we all today? I hope you had a great weekend. I'd like to introduce our newest member of the team, Imogen Taylor. Take a seat, Imogen, and we'll do some introductions.'

Imogen sat on another beautiful plush velvet chair in navy blue. This office was better furnished than her home. That wasn't hard to achieve, though—she'd only had a few days to settle in. It was something she hoped to rectify once she climbed the ladder and earned the big commissions.

'Introduce yourselves, everyone. Let's start with you, Lucy.'

'Hello. I'm Lucy Steele. I've been here for a year, but it feels like I've been here for a lifetime—in a good way. My workstation is next to you, so I'm sure we'll become great friends. I also like to bake, so you'll need to use the gym if you don't want to expand too rapidly.' When Lucy gave Imogen a big smile, she could tell they would get on well.

The rest of the team introduced themselves. Imogen made a mental note of their names—Chris, Ade and Karen.

'Thanks, everyone. It's great to meet you. I've recently moved out of Central London, so I'm new to the area—and local knowledge is gratefully received.'

The meeting went ahead as usual, with everyone sharing what they worked on. Imogen found it helpful to learn what projects were currently in progress. It was a great insight into how they worked together. When the meeting was over, they all headed to their workstations. James asked Imogen into his office to take her through her first project.

As she expected, it was designed in line with the rest of the building—clean lines, minimalist, and bright flashes of colour introduced by the soft furnishings. They sat down, and James explained the help he needed with his latest client. It was a large build for office space, and there was a lot of work to be done to get it finished in the tight timescales they were working to. It was for a multinational company, so it could open the door to work worldwide if they proved themselves on this job. Imogen was to take over sourcing the furniture for the reception area and meeting rooms. And was given a budget that she could work with.

'Right, here are your login details, and I've already emailed you links to all the files you need. If you have any questions, just shout. Have a great day, Imogen.'

Imogen sat at her desk and logged on, ready for a day's work. She was excited to get stuck in. She could see the direction James wanted to go, and she liked it.

CHAPTER 2

Imogen was so engrossed with getting up to speed that she didn't notice Sarah standing at her desk.

'Hey you—fancy grabbing some lunch?'

'Oh, hi Sarah, is it that time already? Yeah, lunch sounds good. Where did you have in mind, as I've no idea what's around here?'

Sarah told her about a coffee shop a five-minute walk away.

'It's lovely—they do the best mac 'n' cheese you've ever eaten, and walking there and back gets your step count up.'

'Well, if I wasn't convinced before, I certainly am now. Let's go.'

Imogen grabbed her bag, and they headed out.

The office was in a rural business estate on the outskirts of the larger town. It was a beautiful setting, surrounded by large trees, manicured gardens and even a small maze. Behind the estate, there was a large wood. It was a far cry from the hustle and bustle of London, but still close enough that she could stay in touch with her family. Some calm and space to breathe and grow were what Imogen needed in her life right now. She felt clichéd thinking about it, but she needed to find herself. She'd spent so long living under the cloud of her ex-boyfriend that she had lost sight of who she was.

As they stepped outside, the last of the summer sun warmed their skin. Imogen stopped and tilted her head to the sky with her eyes closed while taking deep breaths.

'You all right, chick?' Sarah asked with a hint of good humour in her voice.

'Yeah, I'm all right, thanks. Just enjoying the fresh air. It's still a novelty to me—I'm used to exhaust fumes and smog.'

'Oh, that's right, you're from London, aren't you? What made you move to somewhere that's—how should I put this—less glamorous?'

'That is a long story, but let's just say that there was a man involved.' Imogen wasn't ready to share her demons with anyone just yet. She felt that if she told people about her past, it would continue to haunt her. Her best chance of moving on was to rein-vent herself, which meant keeping her old self hidden.

'Say no more—I've dated some right tosspots in my past, too. We'll have to get together one evening, and I can regale you with my stories.'

'I'd like that. I've only moved here recently, so I haven't ven-tured out anywhere—unless you count the local supermarket.'

'Easy tiger—you're living the high life. Are you local? I'm just down the road in Oundle. I persuaded my parents to invest in a flat and rent it to me. Well, when I say rent—I use that term in the loosest form of the sense, of course.'

'I'm in Oundle too. I was lucky enough to enquire at a local estate agent just as a ground floor maisonette came to market, so I snapped it up—it's a big financial commitment, but I get so much more value for money than anything I could afford in

London. I even have a garden. I thought that was awesome until I realised I'm not green-fingered at all. My mum tells me it will come—like it's some sort of Jedi power.'

Laughing together, they turned the corner and were at the coffee shop. On Sarah's recommendation, Imogen ordered the mac 'n' cheese. Sarah added a side order of sweet potato fries, claiming they count as one of your five-a-day.

'Oh my goodness, that is delicious—it's like a hug in a bowl,' exclaimed Imogen.

'I'd say almost as good as sex,' added Sarah with a loud groan as she consumed another mouthful.

'I don't remember the last time I had good sex, so this is the most satisfaction I've had for ages.' Imogen blushed at the admission. She felt so at ease with Sarah she almost forgot that she'd only just met her.

'Well, my lovely, we need to sort that out asap. You know, you should join my book club. Well, I say club, but it's just my friend and me at the moment. We started our own exclusive club, as the local book clubs are too cultured. We don't want to read the latest bestseller or tear-jerker. We want to read about hot men, not pre-war feminism. Every Tuesday night, we meet at the Local for a drink and talk about our latest read. You can come along tomorrow and meet my friend. Give me your mobile number, and I'll message you the link to the book we're reading at the moment. We only started it last week, so you aren't too far behind to catch up.'

Imogen gave Sarah her number and reached into her bag to turn her phone on so she could programme it in. As soon as she turned it on, it beeped.

```
Imogen, you can't ignore me forever. I'll find you and
make sure you know how much I love you.
```

Then another beep.

```
Oh, I see, you're playing hard to get. Treat 'em mean
and keep 'em keen. I like it. It's turning me on.
You're making me hard, and I can't even see you. This
is why we're perfect for each other.
```

Imogen threw her phone back in her bag—she thought she
was going to throw up. She took a few deep breaths to steady
herself—her heart was racing, and she could hear a rushing in
her ears.

'Chick, are you okay? You look like you've just seen a ghost or
something. What was on your phone?'

'Oh, nothing, just a text message from someone I thought I'd
heard the last from. Sorry, I'll be okay in a minute.'

'Was it the dickhead ex-boyfriend? Do you want me to poke
him in the eyes for you?'

Imogen forced a laugh. 'No, it's okay, but I appreciate the offer. I tried changing my mobile number, but he got hold of it.
He's persistent—I'll give him that.'

'Why don't you just block him?'

'It sounds weird, but I feel safer seeing his messages. They all
say he wants to find me and prove his love to me—I take comfort in the fact that means he hasn't found me yet.'

'That doesn't sound so bad—he must love you?'

'Trust me, his idea of love is not normal. He's the sort of person you don't want to end up with. I had to leave London in

secret overnight just to be in with a chance of getting away from him, and now he keeps harassing me.'

'That is seriously fucked up, chick. Look, I know we've only just met, but I reckon you need a good friend, and I'm your gal. You can talk to me, and I'll be here for you, just remember that. In the meantime, I'll take you out and get you drunk and introduce you to the world of hot men without the hassle of having to deal with them long term.'

'Okay, I'm up for that. Thank you, Sarah. You're right—I could do with a friend right now.'

They finished eating and went back to the office. The walk helped take away some of the guilt of eating that decadent lunch. It also gave Imogen some time to get over the grotesque messages she'd received.

She stowed her bag and decided to grab a fresh fruit juice and a coffee to see her through the rest of the day.

As she walked up to the coffee machine, she noticed that lovely smell again and could see that someone was already making a drink. She went to the fridge and picked out a juice while waiting for the machine to be free.

'Hi, I won't be a sec and then it's all yours.'

Imogen looked up at the man talking to her and stopped in her tracks. He was tall with dark brown, almost black hair cut short around the sides and back but was longer on top and styled to look perfectly messed up. It looked so shiny and soft she wanted to run her fingers through it. He had a beard that was barely more than stubble. He was the epitome of tall, dark and handsome, wearing a well-tailored white shirt rolled up to his elbows and unbuttoned at the collar. Imogen thanked the warm late summer weather for that—it enabled her to see that he had powerful forearms, dappled with more dark hair. His skin was a golden olive tone. His shirt was tucked into a pair of dark blue, perfectly-fitting jeans. She noticed another aroma in the air, and it wasn't the coffee. She couldn't put her finger on it, it didn't smell like aftershave, but it was doing something to her.

She could feel herself heat up and could tell that a flush was rising on her skin. She told herself to get a grip and took a deep breath.

'That's okay—I'm watching you in the hope I can work out how to use this thing.'

'Ah, you must be Imogen. Hi, I'm Cameron. James told me you were starting today.' He put his cup down and turned to shake her hand.

The delay was just a nanosecond, but it finally registered with Imogen to offer her hand. As soon as his hand connected with hers, she felt the flush rise further. Her heart was racing for the third time that day, but she didn't feel sick this time. She felt something unfamiliar but altogether more pleasant. Imogen was aware of a beeping noise. It was her smartwatch alerting her to something. She pulled back the sleeve of her blouse to look at the display.

`Heart rate high. Take a deep breath.`

She covered her watch with her sleeve, hoping that Cameron didn't see the message. The smile on his face told her she wasn't quick enough. He coughed and offered to make Imogen a drink.

'I'm a coffee nerd—I was adamant that we'd have a proper barista machine installed. James wanted one of those pod machines for ease, but I think he's glad I got my way. Here, watch me. I'll take you through it.'

Imogen watched as Cameron made the espresso, steamed the milk to glossy perfection and poured it into the coffee. The only problem was that she didn't look at how he did it, her gaze never leaving his forearms, mesmerised by his muscles flexing as he prepared the drink. Before she knew it, he was handing her a latte with a perfectly-crafted heart pattern in the delicate milk foam.

'I've only mastered the heart so far—not the most masculine of latte art when making a coffee for my builders, but there you go. Enjoy.'

Cameron handed the hot drink to Imogen. It was the best coffee she'd had, for more reasons than the drink alone. She took a sip and closed her eyes—the groan was inescapable as it left her mouth.

When she opened her eyes, Cameron was staring at her. Their eyes met for just a moment, but that was all that was needed for Imogen to know she'd need to avoid him if she was going to be able to function.

'Thanks for the coffee, and nice to meet you. I'd best get back to work.'

Imogen didn't wait for a response—she knew she needed to get away to hide the flush working its way up to her face. Realising too late that her pass was in her handbag, her escape was halted when the glass door to the office refused to open. She felt a jolt go through her. It was like someone had flicked on a switch inside her, and a heat spread throughout her body. She could feel Cameron standing behind her. He reached around and swiped his card across the sensor.

'Here you go, I'll swipe you in. You need to make sure you

keep your pass on you at all times. Otherwise, you might find yourself locked out.'

She turned to face him, took a steadying breath and tried to sound as normal as she could.

'Yep, safe to say I've learned that lesson now, thank you. It's very security-conscious around here, isn't it?'

'I'm afraid that's my doing. I want my staff to feel safe at work, and sometimes we work late. I don't want anyone to access any offices without a pass. You never know who's out there.'

'I certainly appreciate that. It's good to know I can feel safe here.'

'Well, have a great afternoon and see you around, Imogen.'

Imogen walked back to her desk in a daze but remembered to get her access pass from her bag. She hung it around her neck with the lanyard—she wouldn't forget that again in a hurry.

'Hey Lucy, how are you?'

'Oh, hey Imogen, I'm good, thanks—just putting the final touches on a proposal. How was lunch? Did Sarah introduce you to the mac 'n' cheese?'

'Oh my God, she did, and it was amazing. I'm going to have to limit how much of that I eat.'

'I reckon I put on about half a stone when I started here thanks to Sarah and her mac 'n' cheese, oh, and not forgetting the sweet potato fries. I see you've met Cameron from the look of that perfectly-made latte.'

'Yes, I timed that well, didn't I? James mentioned that it's best to get one when he's there.'

'I can tell from your blushing that you appreciated what you saw too—wink-wink, nudge-nudge.' Lucy laughed and gave Imogen a shove.

'OMG, it was so embarrassing—I felt like such a dweeb. I just stood there and stared at him for ages, and then my bloody watch announced that my heart rate was too high. Total cringe.'

'Oh God, that is so funny. Don't worry, Cameron is a cool guy. He's probably used to it. His aura is like some sort of superpower—he must be used to women drooling all over him all the time.'

'That doesn't make me feel any better, Lucy.'

When the giggling subsided, they got back to work, just in time for James to appear at Imogen's desk.

'Hey, how are you getting on? Is it a good time for me to take you over to the other side of the office and show you where the architects are?'

'Yeah, sure, that's good timing as I just finished catching up on the client files.'

'Super, let's go.'

James took Imogen over to the other side of the mezzanine floor and once again swiped his card at another set of glass doors. Whilst this half of the building had the same floor-to-ceiling windows and blue carpet, the furniture was darker. Dotted around the open-plan office were oak desks with black-metal fixtures. It felt more masculine, but not in a harsh way. The only similarity was the storage unit on the back wall and the coat rack full of rigger boots and high-vis jackets.

James called out to the few men stationed at their desks and announced that Imogen had started and that they should make her feel welcome.

'I'll let you get to know this rabble when you see them around the office—otherwise, we'll be here all day while I listen to them chatting you up.' James rolled his eyes and directed Imogen to an office in the corner.

He knocked on the open door.

'Hey, James—what can I do for you?'

'I wanted to introduce you to Imogen. She started today, so I'm here to conclude the grand tour.'

'Ah, we meet again. Hello Imogen, how was your coffee?' Cameron fixed Imogen with a smile that turned her insides to mush.

'Amazing, thank you. The best I've ever had.'

'Wow, I'm glad to hear I'm the best you've had.' Cameron held eye contact for a little too long.

Imogen's inner monologue was screaming at her to keep it together and breathe. James' eyes darted between the two, clearly confused by what was occurring. He swiftly moved the conversation along.

'Right, anyway, we'd best let you get on—I know you're busy. See you later for drinks?'

'Yeah, sure thing. See you later. Nice to see you again, Imogen. If you ever need a coffee, you know where to find me.' There was that smile again. Imogen wondered if anyone else had noticed the temperature rise or if it was just her.

'Yes, thank you, bye.' A flustered Imogen needed to get out of this office before she combusted in front of Cameron.

The rest of the day continued without further heart-racing incidents, which suited her just fine. She walked down to see the HR manager and picked up some company literature and her employee handbook, which she'd no intention of reading that evening. She'd a date with a gin and tonic and a steamy novel as she had some catching up to do. Imogen tidied up her desk, grabbed her bag, said goodbye to her new teammates, and headed downstairs.

'Oh, hey Imogen, how was your first day?'

'Hey Sarah, it was great, thank you—apart from embarrassing myself in front of Cameron. You could have warned me he was mega hot.'

'It's a rite of passage around here. I think every female—and some of the male staff members—have fallen foul of his hotness. On Lucy's first day, she blurted out "Wow" in his face, but you didn't hear that from me.'

Laughing, they said their goodbyes and Imogen went to her car.

She gave herself a pep talk as she strolled along the path, swinging her bag like she didn't have a care in the world. 'Well done. You've survived the first day of your new life. Just take each day as it comes. You've got this.'

For the first time in a long time, she felt happy and could see a brighter future in front of her.

CHAPTER 3

Imogen pulled up outside her house and parked on the street. While walking along her pathway, she took a moment to admire the front of the house. She'd fallen in love with the place. It was fate that she'd called the estate agent that day. If she'd left it any longer, the ground floor maisonette would have been snatched up. She was sure of that.

As soon as Imogen was inside the house, she locked the door, took off her shoes and left her bag on the small console table that stood in the hallway. She left her phone in her bag for now. She'd put it on charge later, but at that moment, she wasn't ready to look at it again.

After getting out of her work clothes and grabbing a light dinner, Imogen fixed herself a large gin and tonic. She settled down on the sofa, ready for an evening of reading.

Johnny pinned Melissa up against the wall, her hands over her head. He bent his head down and sucked seductively down her neck and along her collarbone. Melissa let out a groan and begged for Johnny to take her.

'I can't wait any longer, Johnny. If I don't feel you inside me soon, I'm

going to go crazy.' Her heart rate was racing, and she was covered in a sheen of perspiration. Her body was longing to feel Johnny—it felt empty without him. Johnny lifted her with ease and carried her through to the bedroom. She was on her back across the bed in one swift movement, and he'd lifted her dress above her hips.

Melissa heard a ripping noise, and her lacy knickers were on the floor. Johnny was all over her, devouring every inch of her. He looked into her eyes and licked and sucked her in the most intimate way.

Imogen was taken aback by how quickly the book of the week had escalated to a hot sex scene. She wasn't sure if it was the gin or Johnny, but she was feeling a tingling sensation from her core that she hadn't felt for a long time. Imogen decided that a date with BOB was called for to finish her day. She turned the lights out in the living room, ensured the doors and windows were all secure and took her reading into the bedroom.

Five chapters in and two orgasms later, it was time to sleep. An early night was required since she wanted to use the gym before work. Almost as soon as her head hit the pillow, she was asleep with a smile on her face.

'No, get off me, please. I don't want to tonight.'

'You don't know what you want, and you can't say no to me. You'll enjoy it once I start—you always do.'

'I'm exhausted. I just want to go to sleep.' Imogen felt his fingers groping her all over. They slid down her body and pulled her underwear down. She knew it was pointless fighting it—it just delayed the inevitable.

'I'm serious, Mark, please not tonight.'

'Are you telling me you don't like this?' he said as he thrust two fingers inside her. It was so forceful it hurt. He mistook her groan for pleasure instead of pain. Before she could push him away, he was over her and pushing his cock into her. Thankfully, it only lasted a few minutes before he grunted and came. She could feel his sticky warmth dripping out of her, synchronised with a tear rolling down her cheek.

Imogen awoke with a start. Sweat coated her body, and tears were running down her face. She felt like she was going to throw up. Her watch was beeping, telling her to breathe again. Turning on her bedside light, she sat up, rubbed her face and gave herself a minute to calm down before going into the bathroom. She needed a hot shower to remove the sticky residue of her nightmare. She hoped that moving away and starting a new life would help her forget her demons, but that didn't seem to be the case.

When she came back into the bedroom, it was 6 a.m., so she got into her gym kit, packed up some work clothes and toiletries, and went to the office. She could be there before anyone else and take her time figuring out how the equipment worked. She needed to work off some anger without being watched.

There were only two other cars in the car park. That was one perk of being awake early—she had the pick of the spaces. She smiled to herself at that thought—she was always trying to find the silver lining.

Imogen was at the office so early that Sam wasn't in the security cabin, so she walked to the main entrance. Her access card allowed her in the front doors out of hours, so that wasn't a problem. She went straight to the changing rooms to dump her stuff, grab a towel and bottle of water and hit the gym.

As she entered the gym, she could tell that whoever had equipped it knew what they were doing. The equipment on offer was impressive. It could rival any commercial setup. She was going to cancel her gym membership today, that was for sure. She started on the running machine, her preferred method to pound out her frustration. Ten minutes later, she was sweating and ready to move on to something else as the door opened. Cameron walked in wearing shorts and a form-fitting T-shirt and glistening with sweat. She nearly fell off the running machine when she saw him.

'Oh, hey Imogen, you're here early.'

'Hi, I couldn't sleep, so I came here to do something useful. I figured I'd have the place to myself at this time.'

'Well, don't worry, I've been out for a run around the woods, so I'll only be doing some weights at the other end. I won't bother you. If you need help with any equipment, just give me a shout, though. I don't want you hurting yourself.'

'Cheers, will do.' Imogen was grateful that her breathlessness could be down to her workout and not the impact of seeing Cameron.

He strolled to the other end of the gym and sat astride the bench, ready to lift some weights. Imogen found a rowing machine and took a seat. She could see Cameron and couldn't take her eyes off him. As he leaned back under the bar, she saw his thighs tense—they were impressive and not too big and chunky so that he couldn't walk properly, but big enough that you knew he had some power in his legs. The shadow of her nightmare was gone, and Imogen's thoughts were on Cameron. She imagined scenes from last night's book, but Cameron was between her legs instead of Johnny. She started rowing faster to bring her attention back to her gym session and burn off some energy, but then he lifted the weights. With every lift, his stomach visibly hardened under his top.

Imogen imagined herself straddling him. She wanted to lift his T-shirt and run her fingers over his washboard abs. Her desire to lick along his muscled ridges and breathe him in was overpowering. She imagined taking hold of his shorts and pulling them down, feeling the heat coming off his skin.

'Hey, are you okay?'

His voice pulled Imogen out of her daydream with a start. She realised she'd stopped rowing.

'You've been sitting there looking dazed for a while. Are you feeling okay?'

'Oh yeah, I'm fine', she stuttered, 'I was just wondering which piece of equipment to tackle next.' Imogen had to stop the smile, and the blush, from spreading. She knew exactly which piece of equipment she wanted to tackle, or rather, whose equipment.

'They can look a bit daunting, can't they? I recommend you give the pec deck a go. You've done all the leg work so far, so you should give them a rest. Here, I'll give you a hand and set up the weights for you.'

Cameron led her to the equipment, and she sat down.

'Right, I assume you've used something like this before?'

'Yeah, I have. My gym has something similar, but you had to change the weight by putting the pin in the one you want. I haven't seen an electronic one before.'

'Okay, do you remember what weight you used? I can select that to start with and see how you get on.'

'I can't remember. I used to just put the pin in a little under halfway.'

'Okay, trial and error it is.'

Cameron pressed a few buttons and asked Imogen to let him know how it felt. After a few tries, he found the right weight. She pulled the handles together in front of her chest and opened her arms to return to the start position. This time it was Cameron's turn to forget himself and stare. With every repetition, Imogen's chest heaved with the resistance from the weights. She could see the effect it was having on him. She felt the chemistry forming between them, and the flush rose on her skin. His eyes connected with hers, and she was sure she saw passion in them. He blinked and looked away—breaking the spell.

'I think you've got the hang of that, Imogen. I need to get ready for work. Next time you use the machine, you can enter your name, and it'll pull up the last saved settings.'

'Wow, that's fancy. I appreciate your help, thanks.'

'No worries, have a good day.' With a final look, he smiled and walked away. With a sharp exhalation, Imogen realised she was holding her breath. She should get back on the running machine and then have a cold shower.

CHAPTER 4

Song choice: Better Luck Next Time (Kelsea Ballerini)

Imogen finished getting ready for work and went to the mezzanine for a coffee and a pastry. While she was there, she made an extra drink for Sarah to thank her for the book recommendation.

'Good morning, Sarah. How are you this morning?'

'Morning Imogen, I'm good, thanks, Is that coffee for me, by any chance?'

'It is indeed. I've been doing it wrong. Apologies if it tastes like dishwater—I'm a coffee-making virgin. To be honest, after reading some of that book last night, I think I might be a straight-up virgin.'

'I'm glad to hear you're enjoying it. You can tell us your thoughts tonight at the pub. We meet at seven thirty prompt so don't be late.'

'No worries, I'll be there, and I'll get the first round in.'

'Music to my ears.' Sarah paused for a moment and gave Imogen a quizzical look. 'You have a lovely glow today, was the book that good or did you have a sweet evening with BOB?'

'The book is good, yes, and what I do with my battery-operated boyfriend stays between him and me, at least until I've had a few too many to drink.'

'Well, I can see I'll have to get the second and third round in tonight to get all the juicy gossip.' Sarah laughed but was interrupted by the phone ringing, so Imogen waved goodbye and went back up to the office to start her research of local designers.

It was a productive morning. She'd lined up a meeting to see the work of a local carpenter who made amazing furniture out of rustic slices of wood and coloured resin. She'd a quick meeting with James to update him on her progress.

'Oh, I forgot to say yesterday that we all plan to go to lunch on Friday to celebrate you being here for an entire week. Are you in because it'll be pretty pointless if you don't come along?'

'That sounds like it'll be fun. Of course, I'm in.'

'Excellent—I'll buy you a Long Island Ice Tea while we're there. I remember that's how you like your tea. We may end up staying for a while and turn it into a session, so prepare to get a taxi home—on our account, of course.'

'I made the right decision working here.'

When Imogen got back to her desk, Lucy had come in from her client meeting.

'Hey Lucy, how did it go this morning?'

'It went well, cheers. I think they'll go ahead with the plans, which is great as I love them. I'd happily live in their house after I've finished with it. How are you settling in?'

'That's good to hear—well done, Lucy. I'm doing great, thanks. I've worked out James' filing system and have got up to speed. Sarah's invited me into her book club, and we're meeting tonight. So for the first time since moving here, I have a social life.'

'Oh, nice one. They tried to get me into their book club. It wasn't for me, though—I get too embarrassed reading those books. Enjoy it—it'll be fun.'

'So, tell me about yourself, Lucy. Do you have a significant other in your life, or are you young, free, and single?'

'I'm single, but not for want of trying. I'm just not very confident, so I don't put myself out there.'

Imogen thought Lucy was beautiful with her long wavy dark brown hair. The curls were bouncy and shiny—she could have worked in shampoo adverts. Imogen didn't understand her lack of confidence. She was going to have to work on that.

'Maybe the two of us should go out on the prowl one night soon. What do you reckon? You can show me the sights, and I can be your wingman?'

'Great idea. I could do with getting out of my flat. I love Doris, my cat, but I think I may need to spend more time with other humans.'

'I think you may have a higher success rate with men if you left your cat occasionally.'

'Yeah, you're probably right. Let's do it soon.' They decided to get a date for a decent night out one weekend into the diary.

The rest of the day was uneventful. By late afternoon, Imogen's mind wandered back to her gym session that morning. Imagining Cameron on his back was helping the rest of the day fly by. She realised she hadn't bumped into him since then. Part of her was relieved, but the other part felt bereft. She hoped he wasn't avoiding her and was just busy. Imogen knew there couldn't be anything between them as he was the co-owner of the company she worked for—but seeing him had reawakened a flame in her that her ex had dampened out. It gave her hope for the future. She felt ready to get back out there and trust again. She had mentally checked out of her relationship with Mark a long time ago, so it didn't surprise her how quickly she was moving on. Her heart and her body were craving some passion and normality.

Before long, it was time to go home and get ready for her night out. She was excited—it was nice to have something to look forward to.

'See you later, Sarah, seven thirty on the dot. It's the pub in Market Place, isn't it? The Rose and Crown, I think it's called?'

'Yep, that's the one. I'm looking forward to it.'

When Imogen got home, she grabbed a quick dinner and a shower. She was going to make an effort tonight. Since moving, this was her first evening out, and she wanted to make it count. Imogen curled her hair, having seen a video on YouTube about using hair straighteners. The thought confused her, even so, she had to give it a go. Thirty minutes and two tired arms later, the outcome pleased her. She'd curled her hair into soft waves that fell to just above her shoulders, and she loved it. She was finding her inner self.

Mark didn't like her making too much effort when she went out. When they started dating, he used to go to her place beforehand. He said it was because he wanted to see her and give her a lift, so she didn't need to travel alone. At first, she thought he was caring until he started commenting on her outfits and makeup. Then, it progressed to him asking her to change, telling her she didn't look good in what she had chosen to wear. When she realised he was selecting outfits that had long sleeves, higher necklines and longer hemlines, she tried to argue about it. He'd resort to emotional blackmail—claiming it was disrespectful to have her body on display to other men.

It didn't stop there.

'Let me pick you up, Imogen. I can't stand the thought of something happening to you while you're trying to get home. You can't trust the late bus or taxi drivers nowadays.'

He'd tell her the time and place where he would pick her up. She thought he was such a caring boyfriend, but it wasn't until much later that she realised it was his way of controlling what she did and where she went. By dictating when he'd pick her up, he decided when her evening would end, and he made sure she'd be going home with him and no one else.

Imogen withdrew from her friends. It was too much hassle to go out anywhere without him. The invites became less frequent until she almost lost touch with everyone in her life that wasn't a mutual friend. Without realising it, Imogen had lost any identity of her own as she was either with Mark or with his friends. She wore what he had approved. She was isolated and alone since she had nobody she could trust to talk to, and she couldn't understand how she got to this point. She hated herself for feeling so dependent on him but couldn't find the courage to leave. That was the old Imogen, though, and she was long gone.

She went with natural-looking makeup. Her eyes were her best feature, so she always invested in a good mascara to make the most of her lashes. A light dusting of bronzer and a clear lip gloss, and she was ready. While deciding what to wear, she could still hear Mark's comments in her mind when she looked through her wardrobe, but tonight she was going to ignore him. She chose an A-line summer dress that stopped just above the knee. It had a boat neck and capped sleeves and was a beautiful green, like the colour of grass. She paired the dress with some peep-toe slingback wedges in navy blue.

She grabbed her denim jacket and handbag and checked her reflection in the hall mirror on her way out. She saw herself and not an image of someone else's ideal. With a smile on her face, she set off for the pub.

Imogen was a few minutes early, so she ordered drinks from the bar. She looked around. The pub wasn't what she'd expected. She thought Sarah might prefer something more modern and stylish—however, this pub was old-school. The furniture was dark wood and had seen better days. Imogen felt a little over-dressed but decided that it didn't matter, as she was wearing what she wanted. The bar was at the back of the room. There was an open archway that led to another room to the left. This one had a pool table, dartboard and a large flat-screen television on the wall. From the look of the people in there, it attracted a younger crowd.

'Hello, what can I get you?' Imogen's attention was drawn back to the bar and the man behind it. He was young, with long hair tied in a bun on the top of his head and the makings of an impressive beard. She thought he would fit in well in Shoreditch, which made her feel at home.

Imogen scanned the shelves behind him. This was always the tricky part, knowing what she wanted to drink. One of her favourite gins caught her eye. With a buzz of excitement, she ordered.

'Please, could I have three gin and tonics, with the Isle of Harris gin and the Fever-Tree light tonic? Oh, and make them doubles, please.'

'You most certainly can—good choice, I might add. Would you like lemon, lime, or pink grapefruit to garnish?'

'I think pink grapefruit, please. Thank you.'

'So, I assume you're meeting people here and aren't just really thirsty? I don't recognise you. Are you new around here?'

'Yep. I moved here recently and haven't been out and about yet. I'm meeting some friends in a minute. The name's Imogen, by the way.'

'Well, welcome to the area. I think you're going to love it, especially if you keep drinking in here. I'm Seth. If you need anything, just shout.'

'Cheers, Seth—will do.'

Imogen paid for the drinks, carried them to a table near the window, and waited for Sarah and her friend to arrive.

'Yo! Imogen, you made it.' Sarah called from the doorway. 'And I see you've got the drinks in, nice one. Imogen meet Jess, Jess meet Imogen.'

Jess was taller than Imogen, but only by a couple of inches. She was slender but still had curves in the right places, and her hair was a perfectly-styled blonde bob. Her skin was golden. She looked like she'd just got back from a long holiday in St. Tropez. While her clothes were simple—jeans, a T-shirt and some flip-flops—you could tell they were the best that money could buy. Growing up and living in London, Imogen could spot when someone had money but didn't need to dress to flaunt it, and this was the vibe she got from Jess.

'Hey Imogen, Sarah told me all about you on the way here.

She said you're enjoying the book so far.' Jess didn't have any sort of regional accent and was softly spoken.

'You could say that. It's certainly proving to be very educational.'

Within minutes, they were laughing and discussing Johnny in sordid detail. Imogen was having a great night and had no pre-approved home time—she felt free. She fitted in with Sarah and Jess, and it felt like they'd been friends for years. She wondered if the volume of gin they were drinking was also responsible for her feeling so happy and content.

'Hey Seth, can we get another round over here, please, Mr Lovely Barman?' Sarah was keeping her promise to keep the drinks flowing. Imogen felt she was reaching capacity, though. She wasn't used to extensive drinking sessions anymore.

'Here you go, ladies. It sounds like the book club's going well tonight, judging by all the laughter. Your new recruit is fitting right in.'

Seth gave Imogen a wink, and she laughed and winked back—or at least she tried to. It came across more like a slow blink.

'Last orders, I'm afraid. I'm going to be cleaning down and locking up soon. Are you all okay getting home, or do you need a taxi calling?'

'We're okay. Cheers, Seth. We're all within walking distance, I think. You're near, aren't you, chick?'

Imogen nodded while taking a long sip of her drink. She leaned back in her chair and smiled.

'Thank you so much for tonight, girls—I've had the best time. I can't remember how long it's been since I last went out and had fun. You two should join Lucy and me for a night out we're planning. You up for that?'

'Absolutely. You're game, aren't you, Sarah?'

'Yep, count me in. I reckon it might be time to go home now, though—I don't think Imogen can keep her eyes open. We'd better walk her home, Jess.'

They finished the last of their drinks, said their goodbyes to Seth and headed out into the cool night air.

'Right then, ladies, I'm just five minutes down there. Are you sure you're okay walking me home? I'm okay if you want to just head home yourselves?'

'No, it's cool. I think you're near us, anyway.'

A few minutes later, they were outside Imogen's place. She said thank you and goodbye. The other two waited until she was in and the door was closed before going home themselves.

Imogen leaned against the closed door and took a moment to enjoy the feeling. Then she was aware of another sensation that would make her suffer tomorrow. She got a large glass of water and two painkillers and put herself to bed.

CHAPTER 5

The alarm was an unwelcome interruption to her sleep. Still, Imogen rolled out of bed and got into the shower. She had a dull headache but felt like she'd got off lightly. Last night was a big session, by her standards.

Today, she wore something more casual, fitted dark blue jeans and a silk top. She paired it with some tan leather flat shoes and a spritz of her favourite Chanel perfume, primarily to hide the smell of gin coming out of her pores.

Realising that she hadn't been near her phone for over twenty-four hours, Imogen looked at the screen. Thankfully, there were no more messages from Mark. A feeling of relief washed over her—she didn't think she could hold anything down this morning if he sent her something. Relief was soon overtaken with annoyance at how a simple and everyday act like checking her phone made her feel anxious. She threw it in her bag and finished getting ready for work.

After finding one of the last empty parking spaces in the car park, Imogen went into the office. Her first stop was for a coffee and a pastry, and perhaps some fresh orange juice would be a good idea too this morning.

Sarah wasn't at her desk. Imogen hoped she was okay and not at home with her head in the toilet. She made a mental note to check in on her later.

After getting her laptop up and running, she noticed that the glass to James' office was frosted over, and the door was closed. With her elbow on her desk and her head in her hand, she tapped a finger on her lips as she muttered to herself, 'Intriguing.' She had a tough decision to make, grab a coffee and risk missing who came out, or sit and wait without caffeine? It didn't take long to make her mind up. She'd grab a coffee and hope she was quick enough to see who left.

'I missed you in the gym this morning, Imogen.' Cameron was behind her, standing so close she could feel the heat coming off his body. She noticed that all-too-familiar flush rising on her skin, and she hadn't even seen him yet. Just hearing his deep voice was enough to turn her legs to jelly.

'I had a night out and wasn't up for a gym session this morning. I didn't realise I'd be missed.' Imogen turned around to face Cameron, and their eyes met. There it was again, a feeling like being hit by lightning. She wondered if anyone else could hear her heart beating.

'Sounds like you need one of my extra strong lattes. Move aside and let the pro in.' Cameron took hold of her hips and moved her. She wished he hadn't let her go.

He handed her the drink and recommended one of the green juices from the fridge.

'The taste is questionable, but I swear by them. They get me through the day after a night out with James, and he's a party animal. If you feel up to it, I could take you for a walk around the woods at lunchtime? That'll help clear your head and give you a second wave to get you through the afternoon.'

'That sounds like a good idea. I'd like to go while it's still dry. Autumn is fast approaching.'

'Great, I'll call you when I'm leaving. See you later.'

Imogen watched as Cameron strolled back to his office. She took two pastries back to her desk. She was going to need the energy.

James' glass was still frosted, so she hadn't missed who was in there with him. She didn't have to wait for long. A few minutes later, the door opened. Imogen tried to look busy while keeping an eye on it. She couldn't control the sharp intake of breath when she saw Sarah coming out.

'Okay, James, I'll get that ordered for you and sort out the finer details.'

'Thanks, Sarah, keeping me organised as ever.'

Imogen noticed Sarah had a notebook and pen with her, so maybe she just had an early meeting with James. She didn't have long to compose herself before Sarah was at her desk.

'Hey you, how are you feeling? I wasn't too amazing when I woke up, that's for sure.'

'I'm okay, cheers. Slight headache, but Cameron has sorted me out this morning,' she pointed to the coffee sitting on her desk. 'What was going on in there? Early morning meeting?'

'Oh, that?' Sarah looked at James' office. 'Just a mid-week catch-up and getting the weekly orders sorted for the kitchen. Nothing to see here.' Sarah fidgeted with her hair. 'I must get back to work—I've loads to do today. Catch you later.'

The morning dragged by. Imogen kept having hot flushes from

the hangover and needed some fresh air. The green juice had a kick of ginger in it that made her feel better, though—she'd have to remember that tip. Working for a party animal and having a friend who loved a drink made her think more hangovers were looming in her near future.

Imogen's desk phone rang. 'Hey, I'm heading out now. Shall we meet in reception?' Hearing his voice did crazy things to her. Imogen steadied her breath as she answered.

'Sounds good—see you in a minute.'

She patted her back pocket to check that she had her phone and popped a mint into her mouth.

'I hope you aren't going to the coffee shop without me. That would be so uncool.' Sarah was alone, with no sign of Cameron yet.

'Of course not—I'd never do that. Cameron has offered to show me around the woods to get some fresh air. I'm looking forward to it—I love walking underneath the trees. It's going to be awesome in autumn.' Imogen could tell she was rambling. She was more nervous than excited.

'Yeah, I'm sure that's why you're excited. It's got nothing to do with the hotness that is Cameron. Oh, speak of the devil— here he comes.'

'Hello, ladies. Who's the devil? Not me, I hope.'

'Of course not, Cameron. You're an angel, aren't you?' Sarah couldn't contain her smirk.

'Cheeky. Shall we get going, Imogen?'

'Yep. I'm looking forward to getting some fresh air.'

As they left, Cameron held the door open for Imogen and put his hand on the small of her back. It felt so right and so natural. The warmth radiated through her. She felt safe.

The conversation flowed easily. It was a refreshing change for Imogen to be with a man that showed genuine interest in her. They reached the woods in no time, and Cameron showed her where the path started.

'I don't know what your sense of direction's like, but I recommend sticking to the well-trodden paths around here. It's easy to get turned around when you get deeper in.'

Cameron saying "Deeper in" sent shivers through Imogen's body. She chastised herself. Jesus, get a grip, girl.

The surrounding scenery soon distracted Imogen. It was beautiful. The sun was lower at this time of year and was breaking in through the changing-coloured canopy of the trees in shades of green, yellow and red. Birds were singing, and Imogen heard the rustling of fallen leaves beneath her feet. She felt calm and safe with Cameron. The rush of emotions was almost too much for her to cope with.

'Are you okay, Imogen? You look upset about something.'

'I'm okay, thank you. This is just such a lovely place, and for the first time in a long time, I feel so happy and at ease. Thank you for bringing me here.'

'I know we've only just met, so I don't want to come across as over-familiar, but James told me you'd moved out of London in less-than-ideal circumstances. I wondered what you'd been through to drive you away from your life. You don't have to tell me, but I'm here for you, whatever you need.'

Cameron stopped walking and was facing Imogen and gazing into her eyes. Placing his hands on her shoulders, he repeated, 'Whatever you need, Imogen, you only have to ask.'

The air around them crackled, and Imogen's heart beating out of her chest replaced the sound of birdsong. She lifted her chin to bring her lips closer to his. Her body gave all the right signals. She hoped they were being received loud and clear.

As if biding his time while contemplating what to do, Cameron released his hands from her shoulders. He brought one to her face while the other slid down to the small of her back. His thumb gently dusted over her bottom lip. 'Can I kiss you?' His voice was soft and laced with desire.

'Yes.'

He released a low groan as he kissed her softly, tentatively. She had never been kissed like this before—it was so gentle and felt so right. She brought her hands up to grasp the back of Cameron's head and neck. His hair was like velvet, just as she had imagined. She could smell his scent again, and it ignited a desire inside her she didn't realise she was capable of. Her moan of pleasure encouraged him, their tongues now dancing and exploring each other's mouths.

Cameron's hand moved from the small of her back to the curve of her arse. He squeezed and encouraged her to rub against him. She could feel his arousal through their jeans, adding to her desire to give herself to him there and then under the trees. She didn't care that anyone could see them. The feeling between her legs was one of immense impatience, the throbbing almost unbearable. Abruptly, Cameron broke away from the kiss.

'My God, Imogen, you're driving me crazy. I'm scared I won't be able to stop myself.'

'I don't want you to stop. Please don't stop.' Imogen rested her hands on his chest. She felt his heart beating and heard his ragged breath. She leaned her forehead to his. 'Please, don't stop.'

Suddenly Imogen was up against a large oak tree. The bark pressed into her back as Cameron lifted her. She wrapped her legs around his waist, and he ground himself against her. The friction from their jeans was almost too much to cope with. Imogen groaned and rocked her hips into him as he nibbled on her earlobe. He kissed along her jawline and took her in a deep and passionate kiss that sent her over the edge. She felt the intense release from her core spread as she tipped her head back with a gasp of pure ecstasy. Cameron continued to hold her, peppering her with kisses while she came down from her high.

A vibrating in her back pocket brought Imogen crashing down to earth. She released her legs and staggered. The shift in her mood was clear.

'I'm sorry, did I take it too far?' He ran his hand through his hair. 'I don't know what came over me. This isn't how I normally behave around women I've only just met. Are you okay?'

'It's fine, please don't be sorry, I just have to check my phone.' She looked down at the screen and froze.

Did you think I had moved on? I haven't. I could never move on from you, Imogen. We're meant to be together, and I will do whatever it takes to make you see that. I will love you always x

Imogen couldn't believe how quickly the most perfect moment could be ruined so wholly. She leaned against a nearby fallen tree trunk to steady herself. The combination of a mind-blowing orgasm and an unwelcome reminder of her past left her legs weak and nearing collapse.

'What's going on, Imogen? I want to, no—need—to help you.'

She released a deflated sigh. 'It's my ex. He's the reason I moved out of London. It took everything I had to leave him, and it's safe to say he didn't take it well. He won't leave me alone. I just need to wait it out until he moves on and gets bored.'

Cameron clenched his fists. 'Give me the dickhead's number. Let's see how big his balls are when we match him with someone his own size.'

'No, I don't want you getting involved in this mess. It'll be okay—I'll be okay. Mark doesn't know where I live or work, so he can't hurt me.'

Imogen didn't want to go into detail about her relationship. She didn't want to ruin today by letting Mark take over. She felt so stupid to think she could move on or that anyone would want her, especially Cameron, who was technically her boss.

'I'll understand if you don't want to take things further. You don't need to get mixed up with someone with baggage. We'd better get back. Don't worry, I won't tell anyone about this. No one should know. I have to go.'

She turned to leave, but Cameron reached out to her, wrapping his arm around her waist.

'Imogen, wait. You don't need to run off. I'm worried about you.'

She pulled herself away with a look of panic in her eyes. 'Please, let me go.'

'My God, what did he do to you?'

'Cameron, please, I have to go. I don't want to get into this now. I can't.'

'Okay, but I'm walking you back. I'm not about to leave you on your own after what just happened.'

CHAPTER 6

Imogen avoided Cameron for the rest of the day and was grateful when it was time to go home. Sarah stopped her to ask how her lunch break went on her way out of the office. She couldn't escape the grilling forever, she supposed.

'It was okay, thank you, but I got a message from my dickhead ex, which cut the walk short. I think I'm going to have to change my phone number again. Not that it matters—there are only a handful of people who have my number nowadays.'

'Imogen, I'm sorry to hear that. Are you okay? Do you want me to come over tonight and keep you company?'

'It's all right, hun. I'm going to go home, grab a salad and crash. I'll see you tomorrow though—have a nice evening.' With that, Imogen left the building and relaxed a little.

'Hold on, Miss Taylor, wait for me.' It was Sam, calling her from his security cabin. 'I'm under strict instructions to walk you to your car each evening.'

'Oh, hi Sam, why is that?'

'Mr Black didn't go into detail, but he wanted to make sure you get to your car safely—something about protecting what's important. It's my pleasure, though.'

'I don't suppose I can talk you out of it?'

'Nope. Let's get going, shall we?'

Imogen didn't know how she felt about it. On the one hand, it reassured her that Cameron cared enough to sort this out. Still, it made her worry about her safety and made her situation more real. She felt like she hadn't found freedom after all. She would have to take it up with Cameron when she saw him next. There was no point in dragging Sam into the debate.

'Here we are, Sam. this is me. Thank you for walking with me.'

'As I said, Miss Taylor, it's my pleasure. It's not often I get to walk with a fine young lady like yourself. You get home safely now and have a lovely evening.'

The following day Imogen woke ready to get on with the rest of her new life. Today was another day, and Mark wouldn't keep her down. She'd had years of his abuse, and she wouldn't have another day of it. Early arrival in the office meant Imogen could have another session in the gym. She was going to do some strength work to make sure she was in condition to fend for herself if need be.

After ten minutes on the pec deck, her arms were sore and felt like jelly, so she went to the mat to do some squats.

'Well, that's something I'm happy to see in the morning.'

Cameron was standing behind her admiring the view as she was mid-squat.

She spun around to face him, her hands on her hips. 'I have a bone to pick with you. Why are you asking Sam to walk me to my car? Do you think I can't look after myself or something? I'm sick of men trying to control me.'

'Jesus Christ, Imogen, I'm sure you're very capable, and I'm not trying to control you, but I'll be damned if anyone hurts you under my watch. I have a duty of care to the people that work here. If anyone else came to me and told me someone was harassing them, I'd do the same. If Mark came for you now, I don't think you'd be able to fight him off. Here, I'll show you.' In a quick movement, Cameron came up behind Imogen and wrapped his arm around her throat. 'Now, try to get out this, Imogen.'

She froze in terror for a minute before struggling out of his hold, but she couldn't move his arm.

'You might think you can handle yourself, but I need to know that you can.' In an effortless movement, he took Imogen's legs out from under her and caught her in his arms before she hit the ground. He had her pinned to the floor, his whole body in contact with hers. Her heart rate rose—not because of fear, but because this was turning her on. The look in his eyes said he felt the same.

'I could do anything to you right now. Anything.'

'I'd be okay with that.' She was breathless and felt her nipples straining against her crop top. If he didn't kiss her now, she'd explode.

He gave her a quick kiss on the tip of her nose and jumped up. The sudden loss of his body heat left her feeling cold and exposed.

'Well, I'd better go for my run—I have a lot to get through today. See you later.'

And he was gone, almost as quickly as he'd appeared. Imogen lay on the mat, waiting for her breathing to return to normal. A feeling of anger swelled inside her. Why was she letting him get to her so much? She'd just started her new life, which was necessary for her to escape from a man, and now her life was being turned upside down again by another. She saw the punch bag and decided she needed to punch something this morning.

CHAPTER 7

It took all of Cameron's restraint to pull himself away from Imogen. He could see how aroused she was lying beneath him on the mat. Her body looked amazing in her leggings and crop top, and she wasn't wearing a bra—her nipples were straining against the fabric of her top. He could have taken her right there, but that wasn't how someone in his position behaves, and it certainly wasn't how a gentleman behaves.

The feel of her body underneath his awakened a need so strong he had no control over it. His pulse quickened as his blood rushed to his groin. Memories of yesterday's kiss flashed in his mind, how it felt to hold her in his arms as she came for him. Then he remembered what had ruined the moment. The hold this man still had over her was worrying. She was vulnerable, and he didn't want to add to her troubles. He suspected she wasn't in the right frame of mind to be getting involved with someone else so soon. But then again, who was he to say what she was ready for?

His shorts strained against his growing erection. He knew he had to leave before he got to the point of no return. It was time to cool off and consider if taking this further was a good idea. This was unfamiliar territory for him as he'd never met a woman that had got under his skin so completely and so quickly before. It was an arsehole move, leaving her lying there, but he didn't have a choice.

Diverting through the changing rooms would give him time to calm down and reach a point where he could be decent in public—he didn't want to run outside while his cock was standing to attention. He hit his stride and was soon back in the woods, the place where he could clear his thoughts and find calm.

Since the walk there yesterday, though, all he saw were reminders of that kiss. He could hear Imogen's gasp when she climaxed in his arms. It made him feel amazing that he could induce that reaction from her while they were both still clothed. He couldn't help but fantasise about all the things he could do to her and the ways he could worship her body if they ever made it to a bedroom. This was going one of two ways. He was either going to scratch that itch and see where it went or walk away now before he risked hurting her. His mind was spinning. He had an overwhelming need to protect her, but perhaps staying away was best for her. His last relationship ended badly, and he didn't need to put himself through that again. But he couldn't help but think she was special, that she was the one for him.

He shook his head to clear his thoughts and concentrated on the rhythm of his feet pounding the earth beneath him. Cameron was going to play it cool and let Imogen set the pace. If she was interested, she could make a move. He'd back off and give her the space to move on from her ex and hope she found him when she was ready.

CHAPTER 8

Imogen had worked out her frustrations on the punchbag and was standing under the shower, her mind replaying the last few days. Cameron was driving her crazy. She was confused and didn't know how to play it. She barely knew him but couldn't deny the chemistry between them. All sensible thoughts went out the window when he was near. She would never, and had never, got so personal with a man in public as she had in the woods. What was happening to her? Her brain was telling her to stay away from him—for now, at least. Rebuilding her life and establishing herself in a job she loved should be her priority. She couldn't risk it all for a man. She had ambitions to head up her own team one day, and no man was going to get in the way. Why did everything have to be so complicated?

As the warm water washed the shampoo suds down the drain, she made her mind up. Until she'd spent some time on her own, discovering what she wanted for herself, she couldn't start something with Cameron. She hoped he would be patient with her and wait, but part of her knew that was too much to ask. He could have the pick of women, so he didn't need to wait around for damaged goods.

When Imogen got to her desk, Lucy was already there and concentrating on some designs.

'Hey Lucy, how are you getting on?'

'Hi, good, thanks. I'm putting in the finishing touches, and then I'm done. Which is perfect timing, as we won't get a lot done tomorrow.'

'Oh yeah, tomorrow—I'm looking forward to that. I haven't been out for ages, and then I go out twice in the same week. My body won't know what's hit it.'

'I'm bringing muffins in tomorrow. We'll need to line our stomachs. We try to go out every few months, and James and Cameron are massive party animals, so expect a wild night. They aren't like normal bosses—we don't see it as going out on a work night. It's more like a big group of friends having a great time. You'll love it.'

'Sounds awesome. I'll make sure not to have breakfast tomorrow so I can fill up on muffins.'

Imogen found it easy to avoid Cameron for the rest of the day as she had a meeting with James at their client's offices in the town centre. He was driving, so they left together after lunch. As they were heading out, Sarah called to her.

'Imogen, shall I walk round to yours in the morning so we can come in together? That way, you can leave your car there overnight, and I can drive you in on Saturday to pick it up.'

'Good plan—I'll see you in the morning.'

It was great to get out of the office and see how James managed his clients. The meeting went well. Imogen talked them through her plans for the reception area and the meeting rooms and displayed her image boards featuring the wooden furniture. On the drive back, James congratulated her—she was impressive. He dropped her off at her car as he didn't see the point of her going back to the office for the few minutes left of the working day. He suggested she get a good night's sleep as tomorrow would be wild. She wondered if she could keep up with everyone.

Imogen was looking forward to an evening of pampering. Tomorrow would be a chance for her to let her hair down and become reacquainted with her pre-Mark fun self.

Soaking in a hot bath, she slathered herself in her favourite salt scrub. She wanted to remove all traces of her old self, so she worked it in until her skin tingled. The cooling water encouraged her to drain the bath and carry on with getting ready. Tonight, she would paint her nails a deep scarlet. Mark discouraged her from drawing attention to herself, so her colour choice was a sign that she wasn't the shrinking violet she once was. When she was ready for bed, she stood in front of her wardrobe, considering her options. She needed to choose something sexy but suitable for work in the morning before they went out. She chose a pair of skinny-fit dark blue jeans, her favourite patent black stilettos and a black silk top with an open back. It stayed up with well-designed cap sleeves, leaving her back totally exposed. She could wear a jacket at work to cover herself as she didn't feel comfortable showing so much skin in the office. The top demanded she wore the sexiest underwear she had, a bodysuit with straps that went over her shoulders. They looped back and connected to the sides to wear backless tops without showing any straps. Going braless wasn't an option when she had to go into the office first.

CHAPTER 9

Imogen curled her hair again since she had time—Sarah wouldn't be at hers for another hour, and she thought the fun waves captured her mood.

Instead of natural makeup, she went with smoky black eyes and black eyeliner. She had watched a YouTuber explain how to do it last night while she soaked in the bath, and the result was good—it was an almost-vamp look. She finished the rest of her face, going heavier with the bronzer than usual, and spritzed it with setting spray. A black and grey beaded-cuff bracelet added some drama and completed the outfit. The finished look was outside her comfort zone, but it felt right. She grabbed her nude liquid lipstick, mints, phone and black jacket and was ready to go. She was sitting outside on the garden wall when Sarah arrived.

'Wow, Jen, you look fucking awesome. I love the smoky eyes. Are you making such an effort for anyone in particular?' Sarah gave her an overly-dramatic wink.

'Thanks, Sarah. I'm trying out a new look, and no, I'm not trying to impress anyone. This is all for me. I love Jen. I haven't been called that for ages. You look great too—are you trying to impress someone in particular?'

Sarah went coy. 'Who on earth would I be trying to impress? I'm just making an effort in case Mr Right is out later.'

Imogen wasn't so sure. She was certain that James' demeanour changed when he talked to her yesterday. She was going to keep an eye on them tonight.

She parked her car at the top of the multi-storey car park.

'Oh crap, we've got to walk down all these stairs in our heels. We should've brought flats for this.' Sarah wasn't amused. Her shoes were new and reminded her of it with each flight of stairs they descended, which she voiced several times on the way down.

When they got to the office, at last, Sarah went to her desk to dig out some plasters. 'What kind of idiot wears new shoes to an all-day bender? What a muppet.'

Imogen laughed. True to her word, Lucy had baked a vast assortment of muffins. The scent of freshly-baked goods and great coffee filled the air. Today would be a good day—she was sure of it.

'Wow, Imogen, you look sexy as hell.'

'Cheers Lucy, you scrub up well yourself.' Imogen felt self-conscious. She had either overdone it, or she looked less than on par every other day. Maybe she should make more effort going forward? It was lovely seeing everyone dressed and ready for a brilliant afternoon out. A buzz of excitement in the air made the morning fly by. James came out of his office at twelve o'clock sharp and announced pub time.

The team headed to the two people-carriers were waiting to take everyone to the local for lunch. James' team was first, so they went ahead of the others.

They got to the pub, and James opened a tab—the drinks

were on him. Now Imogen understood why everyone was getting ready for a big session. As promised, a Long Island Iced Tea was thrust into her hand.

'Cheers, James, I'm concerned that starting with a hard cocktail might not be a good idea.'

'You'll be all right—we'll look after you. Don't worry, no man is left behind.'

They went into a back room set with two long banks of tables. It would be theirs for the afternoon. She noticed Cameron hadn't arrived with the others. The thought that he might not join them left her with a sinking feeling in her gut. As if reading her mind, Sarah turned to her.

'Don't worry, he's been held up on site this morning and will be coming straight here as soon as he can.'

'What? Who? Oh, you mean Cameron? I'm not worried, Sarah—I don't know what you mean.'

'Yeah, okay. Jen, you can't fool me. I can see it in your eyes— and he's no better. If you two don't end up doing a Johnny and Melissa tonight, I'll eat my metaphorical hat.'

Imogen blushed, whacked Sarah on the arm and told her to sod off. The cocktail went down well, and before she had eaten her starter, her glass was empty.

'Right, there are empty glasses on this table. Who needs a refill?' James was already calling the waitress over before anyone could reply. Within minutes, the waitress delivered trays of drinks.

Cameron didn't make it until the main course was served. He ordered food, as James had already got him a pint in. Sitting at the end of Imogen's table, he was told to down his drink to catch up. He obliged without argument.

Imogen tried not to look at him, but she couldn't help it. He was deep in conversation with James, but it was as though he sensed her looking. He turned his head, and their eyes locked. She saw a flicker of something in his. He gave her an appreciative smile and returned to his conversation with James.

She felt like someone had punched her in the stomach. It wasn't that she expected him to run over and take her over the carbonara, but more of a reaction would have settled her nervousness around him. She was confused—it was driving her crazy.

At the end of the meal, they mingled, chatting. It was an excellent opportunity for Imogen to get to know the other staff, especially the guys from Cameron's side of the office. They were mostly younger male architects, and skilled tradesmen were kept on staff. They were good fun—the laughs kept coming, along with the drinks. She felt light-headed, and her confidence grew with each sip. Imogen, Sarah and Lucy were chatting away, mostly trying to determine if any of the team's male members had caught Lucy's eye when a young, dark-haired man came over.

'Hello ladies, are you going to introduce me to your new teammate?'

'Scott, meet Imogen. Jen, meet Scott. Scott is the electrician, so if you ever need a lightbulb changing, you know where to go.' Imogen noticed that Sarah didn't seem too impressed with Scott.

'Nice to meet you, Imogen.' Scott leaned over and kissed Imogen on each cheek. His hands lingered too long on her shoulders. 'I hope you're settling in well.'

'Yes, thank you. I feel like I've been here for ages already. Everyone is so friendly. Nice to meet you, Scott.'

Sarah stared at him. She was sending the message that he

should probably leave now, but he didn't catch on.

'We're heading over to the Voodoo Lounge in Stamford. Are you up for it?' Cameron had joined them, much to Imogen's delight.

Lucy and Sarah agreed it was a great idea and explained to Imogen that it was a unique club under a restaurant.

'It's quirky and has loads of live acts, from poetry readings to comedy and up-and-coming awesome bands. You'll love it.' Sarah's mood had improved at the mention of moving on.

'You ladies are sharing a cab with James and me. Scott, you can go with the others.' Scott looked disappointed but took the hint and moved away.

'Sorry if he was bothering you three. You can't blame the man, though, can you?' He said the last part directly to Imogen. Cameron made that clear from the way he focused his eyes on her alone.

When the taxis arrived, the group piled onto the street. Lucy got in first and sat on the fold-down seat with her back to the driver. Sarah sat opposite, then James and Imogen got in, leaving Cameron on the other fold-down seat opposite Imogen. There wasn't a lot of room, so Cameron had to fit his legs around Imogen's. As his legs brushed up against her, she felt the sparks. The only way Imogen would survive the journey was to keep her gaze fixed on the scenery outside the window. Play it cool, Imogen, she told herself.

CHAPTER 10

It annoyed Cameron that there were issues on site this morning, but he sorted them out quickly. He freshened up at the office and got to the pub in time for the main course, and James had saved him a seat on his table. He played it cool but wanted to be near Imogen. His eyes found her as he walked into the back room. She took his breath away—she looked sexy as hell—and he wished he could go and kiss her. This was going to be more challenging than he thought.

'So, James, tell me, how's Imogen getting on?'

'She's great, an excellent addition to the team. She's got a lot to add, and I love her design ideas. I don't mind how she looks either, to be honest.'

'Hold on there, mate, you can't talk about her like that.'

Cameron's blood was boiling. He'd known James for a long time and knew that he liked the ladies, but he wouldn't get his teeth into her. Not if Cameron had anything to do with it.

'Why not? I won't do anything that would make working with her awkward, but you can't deny she's hot. Come on, Cam, admit it—she's hot.'

'She's beautiful.' Cameron turned to sneak a look at her. It's like she knew they were talking about her as their eyes locked. A strong desire for her hit him, and a rush of heat shot through his veins. He took a deep breath to steady himself.

'Cam, come back to me, mate,' James said with a laugh. 'I was winding you up to see your reaction. I had a feeling you liked her.'

'Sorry, what did you say?'

'Oh my God, Cam, you've got it bad, haven't you? Well, good luck. I have a source that tells me her ex is a psycho, so you might want to ask her what you'll be getting into. You get hacked into little pieces by some madman, and I can't run this company without you, mate.'

'Thanks for the heads-up. I'm playing it cool and letting her set the pace. You know I'm not really into relationships, and I don't want a fling with someone I have to work with.'

'Whatever you reckon, Cam.'

'Maybe we should talk about you and your latest conquest?' That silenced James pretty fast.

Cameron avoided talking to Imogen for most of the afternoon. He and James wanted to move on to the Voodoo Lounge. It gave him the perfect excuse to rescue Imogen from Scott. He could see him trying to charm her, and he didn't like it.

CHAPTER 11

Song Choice: Take You Dancing (Jason Derulo)

They pulled up outside the club, and Cameron paid the taxi driver. As they got out, he held out his hand to help Imogen. She was on edge after having their legs touch for the whole journey, and holding his hand was too much. As she stood up, their faces were almost touching. Time stopped as Imogen imagined leaning in and kissing him, but then thoughts of being hurt came flooding back and closed her down.

'Come on, you two, move out of the way. Some of us need a drink.'

'All right, Sarah, keep your pants on.'

'Or don't, Sarah,' James laughed. That earned him a slap on the arm.

Taking the lead, Cameron took Imogen's hand and guided her down the stairs to the club. The simple gesture sent shockwaves through Imogen, but he left her side to order a round of drinks. She felt his residual heat on her hand, and it made her want more.

'Come on, girls, let's dance.' Sarah was up for a great night out. She said the alcohol had calmed the pain in her feet.

It was still early in the evening, so it wasn't busy. They only had to share the small dance floor with a few others. After a couple of songs, James and Cameron arrived with the drinks. The bar was renowned for its cocktails, and they didn't disappoint. Imogen's Mojito quenched her thirst, but it was gone too quickly.

'I'm going to have to get another—that was delicious. Who's in?' Sarah shook her empty glass with a smile on her face.

'I'll have whatever you have, Jen—buyer's choice.'

Imogen made her way back to the others with a drink in each hand, but a sleazy-looking drunk man stepped into her way, blocking her path. He'd come straight from the office and was still in his suit, his tie loose around his neck.

'All right, sweetheart, is one of those for me?' He slurred his words and staggered on his feet.

'No, it isn't. Can you move out of the way, please?'

'Oh really? What? Aren't I good enough for you? I'll just grab what I can then.' Before Imogen could stop him, he'd grabbed her breasts. With her hands full of drinks, she was defenceless against his advances.

His sense of timing was perfect. Cameron chose that moment to turn around and check on Imogen. He could see the sleaze bothering her, and how he furiously stalked over to them showed that it bothered him, too. A determined Imogen stopped him in his tracks as she thrust two glasses into his hands.

'Take these for me, please?' She turned back to the suit,

bringing her face close to his. The smirk on his face turned into a pained expression as she grabbed his balls and twisted. An involuntary yelp escaped his mouth. 'Touch me again, arsehole, and I'll rip these off, do you understand?' Nodding, he hobbled away.

'Bloody hell Imogen, you should have let me deck him. Are you all right?'

'I'm fine. Contrary to popular belief, I can look after myself.'

'No shit.' Cameron had a look of pride on his face as he let her lead him back to their group.

Refreshed and buzzing from their drinks, Sarah and Imogen went back to the dance floor. Imogen felt alive and liberated. She closed her eyes and let the beat of the music control her moves until her hair clung to her damp skin. She had lost all sense of time.

She felt the warm pressure of hands on her hips. Someone was pushing themselves into her back, but she knew it wasn't Cameron behind her even before opening her eyes. Her body hadn't come alive for this man. Imogen scanned the dance floor, hoping she would find a sign of what she should do. Her mind was racing with questions, should she go with the flow or make her excuses? There was a time when she would have let it happen—this guy wasn't unattractive, and he was a good mover, but Imogen had a feeling in her gut that she'd learned to listen to.

Her eyes found what they were searching for and settled on Cameron. His back was to the bar, leaning on it with one elbow, staring straight at her. He nodded along to whatever James was shouting in his ear without turning to face him. Imogen looked at him, willing him to come and take over.

She watched as Cameron turned and said something to James,

downed the rest of his drink and came to the dance floor. James followed him. A gentlemanly pat on the shoulder and quick word in his ear, and the stranger stepped aside. Cameron's hands were on her hips, and it felt right, their bodies moving in sync with the music. Imogen sparked to life as she felt the warmth of his breath on her neck.

'I'm hoping I correctly interpreted the pleading in your eyes and haven't just cock-blocked you?' Without waiting for a response, he turned her around and splayed his hands across her exposed back. The heat from his palms was almost burning her.

'I approve of this top, by the way. It's very sexy.'

As if someone had flicked a switch, the heat coursing through her veins turned to ice. 'For your information, I don't need your approval on what I wear.' Imogen pulled away and walked off, leaving a confused Cameron to follow. He caught up in a quieter room and touched her arm, careful not to grab her.

'Hey, I'm sorry. I didn't mean it like that. Look, we need to talk.'

Imogen closed her eyes. Her mind was racing, and the alcohol made it difficult to think.

'You're right. I'm sorry, too.' The resignation was clear in her tone and deep exhalation. She sat at a nearby table.

'What did he do to you to make you so defensive? You know I'm not like your ex, don't you?' He dragged his chair closer so that his knees were on either side of hers.

'Now isn't the time to go into it—it's a long story. I guess your choice of words hit a nerve that is still exposed. I'm sorry for my overreaction. That's something I need to work on.'

'Don't be sorry, just tell me when something triggers you. I don't want to upset you. I don't know how you feel about me, but seeing you dancing with another man tonight made me so jealous I could've thrown that man out of here. It took all I had to explain that you were with me and he should walk away. Sorry if that overstepped the mark. I realise you're a free agent, but I couldn't stand and watch any longer.'

'I'm so confused. From all the mixed messages you've been giving me, I thought you weren't interested, and I don't want to jump straight into another relationship. I'm not sure I'm ready for that. There is chemistry between us, and it's like nothing I've ever felt before. I'm willing to wait and see what happens naturally rather than rush into something. I need to settle into my job and find my feet, and I don't want you pulling those feet from under me.'

'I get what you mean, and I can see why you've been getting mixed messages. I've tried to keep my distance as I don't want to mess things up for you and your career, but I have feelings for you I'm not used to.' Cameron moved his hand up to Imogen's face and stroked his thumb across her cheekbone, his eyes staring deep into her soul.

She understood that look—it told her to make the first move to show him she was ready for that much, at least. Closing her eyes and tilting her face towards him, she rested her forehead against his. The music stopped, everyone around her faded into the distance, and all she was aware of was his lips on hers. He parted her lips with his tongue, deepening the kiss until they were both close to losing control.

'I think it's time I took you home, don't you?' Imogen's reply was barely audible, but Cameron got the message.

'What about Sarah?'

'Don't worry, James is with her. He'll take care of her and

make sure she gets home. I'm sure of that.'

'Okay, let's get out of here.' Imogen tried to contain the urgency in her voice.

They grabbed their jackets from the cloakroom and hailed a taxi. One was nearby, waiting for customers, and they were quickly on their way to Imogen's. Cameron put his arm around her and pulled her close to him. He stroked her leg as she rested her head on his shoulder. She felt safe in his arms. She looked into his eyes as he kissed her on the forehead, breathing in the heady mix of his aftershave and the scent that was unique to Cameron. It was driving her crazy. If he stroked his hand up any further, she felt she would orgasm right there.

'If you could just pull over here, that would be great. Thank you.' They reached Imogen's house.

'Are you sure you want me to come in?'

'I need you to come in, Cameron. The way I'm feeling—I don't think BOB will cut it tonight.'

'Fuck, we need to get in the house then.' He paid the driver while Imogen got her keys ready. After giving him all the reasons why she wasn't ready—now she was going to show him how much she was.

CHAPTER 12

As soon as the front door was closed, Cameron pinned her against the hall, just as he did in the woods, wrapping her legs around his waist. His hands were all over her, stroking her thighs and squeezing her rear. Their breathing was heavy and filled with lust, their kisses increasing in passion and desperation. Imogen rested her forehead on his to catch her breath.

'The bedroom is down the hall,' Imogen hoped he got the hint that she needed him. He carried her, stroking her back and without breaking their kiss. She undid each button of his shirt, desperate to touch him skin to skin. Kicking the door open, he laid Imogen on her back in the middle of the bed. He slid each shoe off and dropped them to the floor, his attention now focused on undoing her jeans. As he lifted her hips to pull them down, he saw the bodysuit she was wearing.

'Oh God, that's so hot. It's a good job I didn't see you wearing it earlier—otherwise, we wouldn't have made it out of the club.'

He pulled her jeans off and lifted her top over her head.

'Keep your hands up. I want to see you spread out. You're so beautiful.' Cameron took off his shirt while Imogen admired the view. She bit her lower lip to stop the appreciative moans from escaping her mouth. She was enjoying the strip show.

'Wait! You're fulfilling my cowboy fantasies. Let me look at you in just your jeans—it's when men are at their sexiest.'

Cameron had the most beautiful olive-toned skin, his shoulders were broad, and his pecs were incredible. Dark hair covered his chest that looked soft and inviting—Imogen wanted to run her fingers through it. She was desperate to get her hands on him. He was perfectly toned—rugged but not overly muscular, and his abs were solid. The anticipation of what was inside his jeans was driving her mad. Surely there had to be something wrong with him, just one flaw?

Cameron undid his leather belt. He opened his top button and then stopped, taking his time. He looked down at Imogen and parted her legs.

'Would it turn you on if I went down on you in nothing but my jeans?'

'Like you wouldn't believe.' Imogen heard the distinctive popping noise of her bodysuit being undone. Cameron moved the loose sections to the side and licked across her sensitive bud. She whimpered. His touch was driving her crazy. It was soft but enough to send her close to the edge. He dipped his tongue deep into her, and she didn't know how much more she could take. She closed her eyes and grabbed the bars of her headboard. She was getting so hot she ground her hips into his face, begging for more.

Cameron slid a finger into her while expertly licking and sucking on her clitoris. Imogen was aware of a new sensation—his wet finger was pressing against her rosebud. The unfamiliar experience caused her to lie still. Cameron carried on gently, looking up to check she was okay with his foreplay. She relaxed into it, curious to see where it went.

He pressed a little firmer, and she felt the urge to bear down on him. The tip of his finger dipped inside her opening while his tongue was inside her sex. It was too much. The onslaught of stimulation sent her over the edge. She gripped the pillow, ground her hips into his mouth, and groaned. She closed her eyes, riding the waves that kept on coming with every lick of his tongue and press of his finger. Heat radiated from her core, and all her tension melted away.

Cameron pulled away, undoing his jeans. Before taking them off, he removed his wallet from his back pocket. Imogen could see his erection straining against his boxer shorts. Any doubt about his size was gone. He pulled his boxer shorts down, retrieved a condom from his wallet, and climbed onto the bed.

'Are you all right?'

'Absolutely, I've never felt better.'

He slid the straps off her shoulders, pulled the bodysuit off, and dropped it on the floor.

'I don't want to risk upsetting you, but feel free to wear that underwear whenever you want. Just be sure to let me know.' He bent his head, this time taking her nipple in his mouth. He sucked hard, and it stole her breath away. She grasped his hard length. It felt thick in her hands, and she could feel the slickness caused by his pre-cum. A desire to lick it came over her, shocking her. Pressing her hands on his chest, she pushed him onto his back. He looked at her with raised eyebrows. Imogen directed her kisses from his collarbone down to his nipples, where she could feel his heart pounding. And then continued down to his navel. Now it was her turn to dish out some pleasure.

She looked up at him from her position between his legs with an expression that was pure sex.

'Take it slow, Imogen. I don't know how long I can hold on.'

She gave him a mischievous look and took as much of his shaft as she could into her mouth. She swirled her tongue around the tip and licked his length. Her breasts grazed his thighs as she moved on him. He groaned, clutching the bedsheets. She could tell he was trying not to lose control and needed to slow down before it was over too soon. She wanted the first time to last all night.

'I can't take much more. I need to feel myself inside you now.'

He deftly moved her to her back. She didn't know where this passionate side was coming from. It must be down to the chemistry she felt with Cameron. Seeing how crazy she had driven him made her feel empowered and in control.

He was over her and kissing her. He was taking his time, covering every part of her with his lips. She had never felt so worshipped before. Usually, she felt used, like a piece of meat, but this was different. She wanted to please Cameron, and he certainly delighted her.

'Are you ready?'

'Yes, I've never felt more ready for anything in my life.'

He nudged her legs open with his knee and put the condom on. Resting on one elbow, he guided himself into her with his free hand. He took it so slowly that Imogen felt every inch of his impressive shaft entering her. He kept eye contact with her, encouraging her to keep her eyes open when all she wanted to do was close them and let the sensations take over.

He withdrew just a little and then pushed in harder—he was

deep inside her. She wouldn't have been able to take anymore. She had never felt so full and taken over. He possessed every part of her. With every thrust, she could feel the ripples of pleasure spreading through her body like skimming stones. It wouldn't be long before she reached her climax. She'd never had an orgasm from penetrative sex before. Her ex had never put her needs first and didn't make her feel this way—and he wasn't as lucky in the size department.

Cameron was on his knees. Sitting on his heels, he lifted her hips and wrapped her legs around him so that her feet rested on the mattress. This changed the angle, and he stroked his cock along her sensitive nerve endings. She assumed this must be the elusive G-spot. That was the end of her. She felt intense waves of pleasure, like an earthquake. She gasped and begged Cameron for more. He bent down to kiss her and slowed his pace. He kept up the same tempo until she came back down from one of the most intense orgasms she'd ever had.

'So, did I hear that you have a BOB? Ever had a threesome with it?'

'I do, and no—how would that even work?'

Cameron smiled, 'You are about to have a treat. Where do you keep it?'

All Imogen could do was point to her bedside cabinet. Cameron leaned over, still deep inside her and on his knees. She couldn't help but stare. He was magnificent, stretched out before her, and she thought she'd found the perfect man.

'Ah, here it is. This is perfect for what I want.' Cameron held up her power bullet, 'I'm pleased to see it's only a small one. I'd feel inadequate next to a twelve-inch shaft.'

'I don't think you've anything to worry about there. What are you going to do?'

'I'll show you.' He turned the vibrator on and placed it on Imogen's clit as he thrust harder and deeper.

'Oh my God.' She rocked her hips in time with his thrusting, eager for more. Cameron teased the vibrator around her clit, careful not to touch it directly. Her urgency was clear with every hungry push of her hips. He responded by increasing his pace. They were going to climax together. Within seconds, Imogen was breathing hard and moaning out his name.

'Fucking hell, this is too good.' Cameron groaned while he climaxed with force. His final few thrusts ensured Imogen had reached the end of her orgasm. Still deep inside her, he slid her legs down and nestled himself on top of her, leaning on his elbow to support his weight.

'You are amazing. Are you all right?'

'I don't know how I am. That was hands down the best sex I've ever had. It was also my first threesome. I'm up for that again if you are?'

'Anytime, you can count on that. I'm glad you enjoyed it. I'll just dispose of this. Don't go anywhere.' He slid his firm length out of her and removed the condom.

It was a fine sight as she watched Cameron walk out of her room. It was the first time she saw his arse in all its glory, and it was perfectly formed—the word peachy came to mind. She made a note to bite those cheeks at the first opportunity. Within minutes, he was back, holding two glasses of water.

'I thought you might need some hydration.' He got back in bed and pulled Imogen into a big hug. At that moment, she felt loved. She realised that was ridiculous so soon, but she couldn't remember ever feeling like this. Maybe it was just post-orgasm endorphins. She snuggled her face into his neck. His scent was so strong after what they'd done—it was like a drug to her. She wished she could bottle it.

'You smell amazing. Do you use a fancy shower gel or aftershave?'

'Nope, maybe it's just my pheromones, baby. You can't resist my animal magnetism.' Cameron grabbed her roughly and kissed her neck. They laughed before snuggling down and drifting off.

'Do you mind if I stay? I don't think I can pull myself away now.'

'I'd love it if you stayed. You have to promise to spoon me, though.'

'Consider it done.' They fell asleep in each other's arms, exhausted but satisfied.

CHAPTER 13

Song Choice: Losing Me (Piano Version) (Gabrielle Aplin & JP Cooper)

Cameron woke up to the sound of pleading. At first, he couldn't figure out what was happening, then he realised something was wrong with Imogen. She was in his arms, but she was hot and sweating and fighting against him.

'Imogen baby, wake up. You're having a nightmare.' He tried to wake her gently by stroking her hair.

'Get off, you can't hurt me anymore, get off me.'

Cameron sat up with Imogen in his arms, holding her and begging her to wake up. She stirred and looked around, confused.

'Imogen, you were dreaming. You're safe. You're safe now.' He rocked her in his arms. Her panicked breathing calmed down as she shook her head and ran her fingers through her hair.

'Shit, sorry I woke you.' Her voice was ragged from her cries.

'It's okay. I'm worried about you, though. Do you want to talk about it?'

'I need a shower—I feel gross.'

This frustrated him. He wanted to know what he was dealing with—or rather, who he was up against. He wanted her to open up and felt very protective of her.

'Do you want to join me in the shower? I don't want to be on my own.'

Cameron didn't need any further encouragement. He picked Imogen up in his arms and carried her to the bathroom. He set her down on the edge of the bath, turned on the shower, and checked the temperature. He took her by the hand and helped her in. She looked beautiful with a hint of sleep on her—her hair was messy from their antics, and he could smell himself on her skin. Usually, he showered on his own after dating and looked for the quickest exit. This was different, and it scared him. He felt an ache in his heart and wanted to protect her from everything.

Taking her shower gel, he lathered it in his hands. He wanted to wash away her nightmare and help her forget, then he was going to cover her with his scent again. The animal in him wanted to mark her and let the world know she was his. He worked on her shoulders, rubbing her tension away. She groaned with appreciation while he caressed her back before cupping her breasts. He used to joke that anything bigger than a handful was a waste, but he thought Imogen's full breasts were perfect. He worked his hands down to her stomach and held her close, kissing her neck. She whimpered, and Cameron felt the blood flow to his manhood, but he had to keep it together. Imogen needed to be cared for. She needed a connection that was more than physical.

Imogen turned to face him. She held him in her arms, and her breathing returned to normal. Cameron took her face and kissed her with the warm water flowing over them.

'Are you ready to tell me about your past, Imogen? I need to know what I can do to protect you.'

'I think it's time. It's only fair you know what you're getting yourself into. I won't hold it against you if you walk away.'

She wrapped herself up in the softness of her fluffy bath towel and went back to her bedroom.

'What we need is a cup of tea. My mum tells me it cures all evils—I'm hoping that's the case for hangovers too.' Cameron left Imogen lying on the bed and went to the kitchen to make the tea.

When he came back, he paused in the doorway to admire her. She looked adorable, snuggled up in the sheets. He wanted to pounce, but not now. First, he had to listen.

CHAPTER 14

Imogen's heart was racing. She couldn't be sure if it was the result of Cameron's shower or the fact that he looked so fuckable with just a towel around his waist. She was about to show him how weak she could be. She took a breath.

'I guess I should start at the beginning. About five years ago, I was coming out of a relationship. It wasn't anything serious, but I was young, and it was the first proper relationship I had. I needed my friends around me and kept busy going out all the time. Mark was a mutual friend—we ran in the same circles, and he stepped up and looked after me. He was there for me on the nights out when I got too drunk to look after myself. I ended up relying on him, and I felt safe going out if he was there. One thing led to another, and we just sort of fell into dating. He was caring and very much the alpha male. I liked it. He was Tarzan, I was Jane, and London was our jungle. For the first twelve months, I didn't see it for what it was. Maybe if I was more experienced with relationships, I would have spotted the warnings signs sooner, but I didn't. He was attentive and insisted on driving me into town if I was going out without him. Then, he would come over and help me choose what to wear. It soon escalated into him approving my outfits before I could leave—that was when I was allowed out.'

'I see why my comment earlier upset you. Sorry about that.'

'No, really—it's my issue, not yours. I would hate for Mark to change you. Please, just be yourself around me.'

Cameron finished his tea and rested his arm on Imogen's leg, 'Carry on, beautiful.'

'His need to drive me around got worse, so he would tell me where and when he would pick me up. At first, I just thought he was caring. Unfortunately, he was just controlling. It got to a point where I lost touch with my friends. I only went out with Mark and our mutual friends—it was easier that way. He was kinder to be around when he controlled what I was doing.

'He was insanely jealous. He used to lose his cool with me if I mentioned anyone was good-looking.' Imogen paused for a moment to take a steadying breath.

'Anyway, behaviour like that became the norm. He had a high sex drive too.' Imogen looked at Cameron and didn't know how much to tell him.

'It's okay, you can tell me everything. I'm an actual man—I can take it.'

'All right, if you're sure. At first, it was great. We were a young couple, and you're at it like rabbits, right? Well, it carried on—he wanted it all the time. If I ever said no, he would badger me until I gave in. In the end, it progressed to him taking what he wanted. He didn't care if I said no. One time—the last time—I woke up with him in me. We'd had a big drinking session the night before, so I guess I slept heavier that night.'

'For fuck's sake, Imogen, tell me where I can find him. I'm

about ready to kill the bastard.' Imogen could tell that Cameron was losing it. She needed him to know that he shouldn't get involved.

'Mark is a dangerous man, Cameron—I don't want you anywhere near him. He used to threaten me, telling me he would come for both of us if I left him for someone else. There was a song he used to sing along to in the car. It was our song, apparently because it matched how he felt. The lyrics went on about how he would rather see his girlfriend dead than be with another man. It still gives me chills now.

'I know you must think I'm weak and stupid to stay with him for so long.'

Cameron sat up and turned to face her.

'I don't think you're weak, Imogen. I know how it works with people like that.' He held her tighter.

'By the time I'd worked up the courage to tell him it was over, he was unstable. He didn't take it well. I couldn't go to any of our friends because he would find me there. He'd turn up, hammering on my door and shouting that I had to take him back. You know, the usual "I'm sorry. I'll change,"—all that crap. I guess I wanted to see if he could change and hoped that things would get better. In the end, he wore me down.

'It was at that point that Izzy, my sister, and I fell out with each other. She was the only person who saw him for what he was, and I stupidly ignored her. I don't understand why, but I was adamant that things could be better.

'At first, they were. He was kind and attentive again, like he was when we first got together. Now I realise he held me to him under a false sense of security. After a few months, his behaviour changed again. I didn't feel strong enough to tell him it was over because by then, I was terrified of him and what he would do if I walked away. I knew I wouldn't be able to finish it—it didn't work the first time, and it wasn't going to be any different.

'In the end, I needed a clean break, so I moved my home and job. It wasn't too hard. I had already lost a lot of friends over the years, anyway.'

Imogen took a deep breath. 'So, there you go. That's my sordid past. I've changed my number, but Mark found it somehow, which freaks me out. But as long as he doesn't find me, I'll be all right. I just keep telling myself that he'll move on soon. For now, I just have to put up with text messages reminding me he's still thinking of me. I don't block him because I might be pre-warned if he drops over the edge and comes for me.'

She looked at Cameron and waited for him to end things between them—he shouldn't have to deal with this. He took her by the hands and looked into her eyes.

'We'll sort it out, Imogen, you and me together. While I'm around, you don't have to worry. Do you hear me? You're safe now. On the other hand, he is very much on a dangerous path.'

'Is it twisted to say that everything you just said has turned me on? Can you make me forget, even if it's just for tonight?'

Cameron made her forget—twice.

CHAPTER 15

Song Choice: Starving (feat. Zedd) (Hailee Steinfeld & GREY)

Imogen couldn't believe what she was waking up to. She rolled to her side to admire the view. Cameron was asleep, lying on his back and looking gorgeous. The duvet covered his manhood but left enough on show that she could see that sexy v shape like it was pointing to the goods. She couldn't resist it—she reached over and gently stroked the hair on his chest. It was so soft, and she wanted to snuggle into it and never leave.

'Good morning, gorgeous. How did you sleep?'

'Oh, sorry, did I wake you again? I must stop doing that. I'm good, thank you—well, better than good, to be honest. How are you?'

'I'm all good, and I don't mind waking up from being stroked by you, although I have other body parts that are partial to a good stroking.' Cameron gave her a wink and blew her a kiss.

'You're an animal, Mr Black, but I like it. Keep it up.'

'All night, baby, I can keep it up all night.'

'Oh my goodness, Cameron, stop it.' Imogen couldn't stop laughing.

'Come here and kiss me—it's the only way to shut me up.' His kiss was gentle and yet filled with passion, and it took Imogen's breath away.

She moved to sit astride Cameron, and she felt the urgency in her core—she needed him, and she needed him now. She rocked against him and felt his cock growing hard beneath her.

'Fuck me, Cameron. I want it now, and I need it hard.' Cameron was like a drug to her. The more she had, the more she needed.

'Shit, I would love nothing more, but we're out of condoms. Are you sure you don't have any stashed away?'

'I don't, but I've had the contraceptive injection, so we're covered in that respect.'

Cameron ran his fingers through her hair. She could tell he was considering his options. 'As a rule, I don't ride bareback, but I trust you. Do you trust me?'

'I do. I don't know what's got into me, but I crave you so much right now.'

'Do it.' The urgency was back. Imogen didn't pause for thought as she got on her knees and positioned herself over him. She took hold of Cameron's hard cock and lowered herself on him, inch by inch.

'Fuck.' Cameron bit his bottom lip.

Imogen rode him, grinding against him to increase the friction. His hands encouraged her to go faster, and their hips moved in synchronicity. He went so deep she was on the verge of pain.

'I need you to fuck me, Cameron. I need it harder.'

Cameron rolled her onto her back without breaking their intimate connection and kneeled before her. He wrapped her legs around his hips, allowing him to give her what she needed.

She felt the tremors spread, and her breath quickened—she felt like she was going wild.

'I'm going to come, Imogen. Are you ready?'

'Yes, Cameron, oh yes.' Imogen moaned and grabbed the pillows under her head. She arched her back, closed her eyes and let the sensation take over. Cameron was thrusting hard, and he exploded with a loud groan. Imogen felt herself throbbing around his firm length. He gave her one more thrust that rocked through her like an aftershock.

Cameron kissed her and whispered in her ear, 'Was that what you needed?'

'That was exactly it. I think I need a few minutes before I can consider walking.' Imogen was panting and struggling to form the words.

'We've got all day, baby. Take your time.'

They lay in each other's arms in a comfortable silence until a thought came to Imogen.

'Oh no. Sarah is picking me up to get my car. What time is it?'

'It's ten-thirty. Did she say what time?'

'No, I'll check to see if she's been in touch.' Imogen looked at her bedside table, where her phone was usually on charge.

'Hang on, where's my phone? Have I left it in the hallway?'

'I'll get it for you. I don't want you to fall over, jelly legs.' Cameron kissed her on his way out.

'We can take a taxi to get our cars later. Drop her a text to say not to worry—she's probably still in bed, anyway.' Cameron handed Imogen her phone.

'Good plan. She's not messaged yet.' Imogen texted Sarah, explaining that she'd get the car herself later and not to worry about picking her up.

'Sorted. What's the plan then?'

'Well, I reckon we could do with another shower for a start, then some breakfast. I'm starving—you've worked me harder than my trainer.'

'I'm a hard taskmaster. I hope you can keep up.'

'Challenge accepted. I don't suppose you have a spare toothbrush, do you?'

'I've a spare head for my electric toothbrush—we can call that yours if you like?'

'Perfect.'

After showering and getting dressed, they strolled into the centre of the market town and stopped at a cafe for a cooked breakfast. The conversation flowed. Cameron told Imogen about how he and James grew up together. After a few years of working in their respective fields, they started Spencer & Black Associates.

'Did you argue over whose name came first?'

'I never like to come first, Imogen, you know that.' Cameron winked and laughed, 'but no, not really. It just sounded better that way round.'

Imogen was silent as she thought about work.

'I don't know what this is between us, even if there is an us, but would it offend you if I asked that we keep it low key and not public knowledge in the office? I've just started and don't want people knowing I'm sleeping—or have slept—with the boss.'

Cameron ran his hands through his hair and leant back in his chair.

'I understand what you're saying, Imogen. I'm happy to keep it under wraps, but for the record, you are sleeping with the boss, not have slept with. Do you understand what I'm saying? I want more of what we had last night and this morning. I can't promise I won't try to have you over my desk, though. Just thinking about it is making my blood rush to all the right places.'

'Down, boy. I guess we ought to get our cars. I'm sure a man like you has a busy weekend planned.'

'I've not got a lot on. I try to keep some weekends free, especially after a night out with James. We could do something tonight if you fancy it. Would you like to come to mine? We can grab a bite to eat at my local.'

'That sounds lovely. Are you sure?'

'Yep, let's get our cars. You can drop yours off, grab what you need, and then we'll head over to mine. I can drop you back home tomorrow.'

Cameron ordered a taxi on his app while they finished their drinks. He walked Imogen to her car.

'You go back home, and I'll be following behind. My car's on the ground floor, so I'll be a few minutes behind you.' Cameron kissed her before she said goodbye and drove away.

Imogen couldn't believe what was happening. She wasn't sure if she was ready for a relationship but was happy to go with the flow. As long as it wasn't public knowledge in the office, it would be easier to cope if it fell apart. Cameron made her feel amazing. In the few days since she met him, she felt alive again—even if it didn't last long, she could take that away. He reignited her fire, and she wasn't going to let any man extinguish her flame again.

When Imogen got home, she packed an overnight bag. She

put in her sexiest nightwear, not that she intended to wear it for long. A few minutes later, the roar of an engine outside filled her stomach with butterflies. The excitement she felt seeing Cameron again was ridiculous—it had only been a few minutes. She grabbed her things and went outside to meet him.

'Wow, that's a nice car.' Cameron walked up to Imogen's front door as she came out of the house. The car was perfect for him. It was big, sporty and very sexy.

'Thank you, you are a lady of good taste.'

'Is it an X5? I've never seen one so sexy.'

'It is, indeed. I feel like Batman when I drive it, but don't tell anyone I said that—I'll deny it. I need a practical car for when I'm on-site, but I like a car that growls and knows how to move, so the M50i was a good option. I had the custom frozen black paint job too.'

'Well, I reckon you need to take me for a drive in it, Batman— let's see what it can do. I'm a bit of a petrol head, so I appreciate a powerful engine.'

'Now you're talking my language. Let's hit the road.'

Cameron put Imogen's bags on the back seat and opened the door for her.

'Here you go, m'lady.'

'Why, thank you, sir.'

Cameron got in the car and opened the windows.

'So you can hear the engine. If you like cars, you'll love this.'

He pressed the ignition button, and the engine roared to life. He was right when he said it growled. Vibrations rippled through Imogen's body. Cameron closed the windows and drove off with a smile on his face.

She watched as he handled the car with ease. With

every movement he made, she could feel herself getting hotter. Transfixed, she watched his forearms flexing as he turned the wheel. Cameron caught her gazing at him.

'You all right there?' He asked with a grin.

'It turns out that your driving turns me on, and your forearms are off the scale. I have a thing about forearms now too. It's relentless.' Imogen threw her hands up in the air in mock frustration.

'I thought you looked flushed. Maybe we ought to try out car sex soon? I'm up for adding that to my schedule.' Cameron reached over and rubbed his hand on Imogen's thigh. It felt natural and right. Her heart ached with desire.

A few minutes later, they drove into a beautiful village. Trees lined the roads, and the large houses and cottages were mostly sandstone. Cameron took a remote control out of the centre console. He pressed the button and drove through two black wrought-iron gates. The car crunched over the gravel driveway as Cameron pulled in and came to a stop.

'We have reached our destination, m'lady—I shall grab your bags.' He grabbed Imogen's things while she got out of the car.

His house was beautiful and not what she expected. It was a large sandstone house built in an L-shape. The place looked as if he had built it recently, yet it blended in with the older country cottages around it.

'Your house is stunning.'

'Thank you. It's probably not what you expected. It's not your typical bachelor pad, but I'm a country boy through and through, so this feels more like home than a townhouse or penthouse apartment. James thinks I'm weird. He lives in Stamford and enjoys being close to the action. I stay at his when we go out, so I get the best of both worlds.' Cameron opened the front door and showed Imogen in.

As expected, Cameron's home was perfect inside. She could see that the oak accents in the office came from him, as the flooring was oak throughout the house. It felt light and airy but homely too. She felt at ease here.

'Right, I need a change of clothes. I'll be down in a minute. Make yourself comfortable, wander around and help yourself to anything you can find in the kitchen.'

Imogen had a look around downstairs before going to the back of the house to find the kitchen. It was the entire width of the house, with a boot room and utility room on one end. The kitchen had enormous bi-fold doors along the back wall that opened to a large patio area, and then all she could see were fields. It was breathtaking. She poured two glasses of orange juice and took them to a large tan leather sofa that created an informal seating area with a television on the wall. She imagined Cameron coming home from work and sitting here with a drink, watching sport on the TV while his dinner cooked.

'I see you've found the best seat in the house. I don't know why I bothered building the rest—all I need is this kitchen.' Cameron sat next to Imogen and picked up the orange juice. She gave him an appreciative look and wondered how it was possible for a man wearing something as simple as dark blue jeans and a crisp white t-shirt could look so supremely hot. He'd forgone a belt, so his jeans sat lower on his hips. She started a conversation before she got too heated.

'Do you enjoy cooking?'

'Yeah, I do. It's how I wind down in the evening. I love it when I have friends over for dinner too. That's when I can flex my culinary muscles. I can cook you dinner tonight if you'd prefer to stay in?'

'Oh, that sounds great, but only if you're sure. I don't want to be a bother.'

'It would be my pleasure. Do you like steak?'

CHAPTER 16

Song choice: Hold My Girl (George Ezra)

Imogen found it fascinating watching Cameron prepare dinner. He put on some music in the background, opened an expensive bottle of red wine and told her to sit on one of the wooden stools at the island while he did all the work. He insisted that she just kept him company and wasn't to lift a finger. She thought she could get used to this. Even though he was at home in the kitchen, he looked like a professional from her chef programmes. He was slicing shallots as he chatted to her. She thought he would cut his finger off, but he chopped them in no time.

'Are you trained? You look like you've been a chef for years.'

'No, but I'm obsessed with watching cookery on TV, always have been. When I was at uni, I was the one that cooked for everyone. I guess my passion grew from there.'

While Cameron finished the meal, they compared opinions of the latest round of contestants on *Masterchef*, in between Cameron giving her tips on cooking the perfect steak.

'You need a hot, heavy-based pan to start with, then finish it with some smoked butter and garlic in the pan. It makes all the difference.'

'So, is there anything you can't do well? There must be something wrong with you. What's your weakness, Superman?'

'My weakness? I think it might be you, Imogen.' She stared back at him, lost for words.

'That, and I sometimes leave the toilet seat up. Right, dinner is served.' Realising what he'd said, Cameron felt the need to move the conversation on. Imogen took a moment to enjoy the food, closing her eyes and inhaling the delicious aroma. Cameron couldn't take his eyes off her.

'Oh Cameron, this is delicious. It's better than any pub steak I've had, thank you.'

'You're very welcome. I'm glad you're enjoying it. So, would you say that my meat's the best you've ever had too?' Cameron tried to keep a straight face but failed miserably.

Imogen replied with a roll of her eyes and a slap on the arm, but she thought that—actually, yes—his meat was the best she'd ever tasted. She was thinking of sex again, and from the way he was looking at her, so was he, she guessed.

He slid the empty plates along the island and leaned over to kiss her.

'I'm afraid I have nothing for dessert. Will I do?'

'Do I get to cover you with whipped cream?'

Cameron turned to a device on the island. 'Alexa, add whipping cream to my shopping list.' He looked at Imogen. 'Not this time, but I'm sure we can work around that.' He bent in for a kiss and held Imogen's face in his hand. She wrapped her arms around his neck and stood between his legs. He tasted of red wine—she wanted to drink him in. His hands slid down, cupped her arse and gave her cheeks an appreciative squeeze. He groaned, and the sound set Imogen off. She deepened the kiss and bit on his lower lip while pulling the hem of his T-shirt up, making her intentions clear.

She admired his form. His shoulders were broad, and he was tall enough that she could wear her highest heels and still not be at eye level with him. She ran her hands down his chest and traced the lines of his abs with her finger. She bent her head and sucked on his nipple. Cameron was breathing hard, which encouraged her. She undid his button fly.

'I need to give you your dessert,' Cameron ran his hands up her thighs and under her skirt until he reached the waistband of her knickers. He lowered them until they fell to the floor and kicked them to the side. Butterflies fluttered in her stomach with the anticipation of what was to come.

He lifted her onto the edge of the oak-topped island. His kisses were more forceful, he only stopped to whisper in her ear, 'Wait here.' He went to his American fridge-freezer and pressed a button, returning with an ice cube. With his other hand, he encouraged Imogen to lie back. The surface felt hard against her back, but she didn't care. Cameron put the ice cube in his mouth, gave Imogen a look and then bent his head to her sex.

Keeping the ice cube in his mouth, he sucked on Imogen's clit. The ice-cold sensation was like nothing she had experienced before—the shockwaves it sent through her awakened her every sense. She squirmed beneath him, and he took hold of her hips to draw her closer. The melting ice cube was dripping down her opening, adding to her desperation to feel him inside her as she pulsed with need. She wasn't sure how long she could stand it. Cameron crunched the ice before reaching for his red wine. He took a swig from his glass held it in his mouth for a few seconds before swallowing slowly, never taking his eyes off Imogen.

He licked around her opening and circled his tongue over her delicate mound. In stark contrast to the ice, the wine warmed her and left her tingling. Cameron increased the pressure with his tongue and dipped two fingers inside her. Within seconds, Imogen's climax was ripping through her. She arched her back and gasped with every breath.

CHAPTER 17

Song choice: Bird Set Free (Sia)

Imogen inhaled and closed her eyes. The heat from the sun-warmed her face and burned away the morning dew hanging in the air. The view from Cameron's balcony was heavenly. She used to love the high-rises of the London skyline, but in the end, they made her feel trapped and alone. Now, there was sprawling countryside as far as she could see. The feeling of freedom was overwhelming.

'You look deep in thought. Is something troubling you?'

She hadn't heard him come up behind her but felt the warmth of his arms as he wrapped them around hers.

'I'm enjoying the peace. It's so quiet—just listen to that birdsong.'

'Have you heard anything from Mark? Is he bothering you?'

'I haven't heard from him since the other day. I'm hoping it means he's given up and moved on.'

'Promise to tell me if he bothers you again. I'm here for you. You know you aren't alone with this now?'

'Thank you, Cameron. I appreciate that. I don't want him to come between us.'

He held her closer. 'He won't if we don't let him.'

Imogen was overwhelmed again. How was it possible that she'd found someone like Cameron so soon? Was she even ready to get into another relationship or read too much into it? She changed the subject. Mark had dominated too much of their time already.

'Do you have a lot on next week?'

'I do. I'll be out of the office for a few days on-site, getting the final fixtures and fittings sorted. That was the problem on Friday. The crew read the schematics wrong and put the wiring in the wrong place. It was a nightmare, but we got it sorted. Do you have much on in and outside work next week?'

'I'm nicely busy at work—I feel like I've hit the ground running. I've got the all-important book club on Tuesday night, but other than that, my evenings are free.'

'Book club? Tell me all, it sounds cultural.'

'Ha, Well, it's not. Sarah and her friend Jess introduced me to erotic fiction. It's eye-opening, but I'm not complaining. We meet in the pub on Tuesday nights, although this time I won't drink too much.'

'Well, if you ever want to act out any of the scenes, you know where to find me—I'm more than willing to oblige in any way you see fit.'

'Deal. But I don't think there's much left for us to try.'

'Oh, you'd be surprised—I've only just started. And don't

forget car sex. Although, if my car feels like something has hit it, it sends a dash-cam recording to my phone to alert me. That could be a new way of making home movies.' Cameron laughed while nuzzling into the crook of Imogen's neck. She was grateful he couldn't see how much she was blushing.

Cameron pulled up outside Imogen's house and turned off the engine. He unclipped his seatbelt and turned to face her, delaying her inevitable departure. He felt the sparks between them, the air was heavy with desire. Acting on impulse, he leaned over the centre console, pressing his lips to hers. He didn't think he'd ever tire of what her kisses did to him. They filled him with nervous anticipation, like a schoolboy experiencing his first kiss. The strength of his feelings for her had thrown him. He was relieved when she asked if they could keep their relationship private. Could they even call it a relationship? Cameron had no idea what to call it at this stage, but if it ended, he would rather not have to deal with the whispers from the office. Until they knew what was going on between them, he was okay with it being between them.

'Wait there gorgeous, I'll get the door for you.' Cameron grabbed her bags from the backseat before opening her door and helping her out. As she got out, she rewarded him with a parting kiss. He broke away first, stroked her cheek and said his goodbyes.

'I'll see you in the office. In the meantime, you can read your book and take notes.'

He watched her walk to the front door, and when he saw she was safely inside, he got back in the car.

She closed the door and leaned her back against it as she heard him start his engine. Previously, that sound had filled her with anticipation and butterflies—this time, it filled her with emptiness and longing. She needed to keep busy. It was the only way to get him out of her mind.

She unpacked her bag and sorted out the laundry when she realised her phone needed charging.

She was in the kitchen when she heard the familiar noise telling her she had a message. Another ping followed it. With a feeling of excitement, she almost skipped to her phone. She assumed it was Cameron and couldn't wait to see what he had to say.

```
Hello Imogen, did you think I'd given up? I hope you
haven't moved on. I'll never give up on us.
```

Imogen felt both panic and bile rising in her throat. She clicked on the second message.

```
I imagine by now you've turned a few heads. Don't
forget, anyone looking at you might lose their head.
I don't want to have to teach you a lesson, so don't
be a naughty girl. Be strong, Imogen, and resist
temptation until I come back to you.
```

She dropped her phone and ran to the bathroom to throw up with such force it took the air out of her lungs. Gasping for breath, she sat on the bathroom floor and cried. Did he know she'd moved on? Had he found her, or was he playing mind games?

Standing up, she washed her face and spoke to herself in the mirror. 'Fuck off, Mark. You're not holding me down any longer. I won't have it. You can't hurt me anymore. I have friends around me, and I have Cameron. There's nothing you can do to me. I'm safe.' She knew he couldn't hear her, but saying the words aloud added conviction.

Imogen decided to keep the messages to herself. She didn't want to get Cameron mixed up in her mess or, worse, get hurt. She'd carry on ignoring him. Eventually, he'd get bored with terrorising her and would leave her alone. The best thing was to pretend he didn't exist and carry on with her new life.

She spent the rest of the day gardening as a new means of distraction. It wasn't until she felt her stomach growl in protest that she realised she hadn't eaten all day. After changing, she sat in front of the TV with a bowl of soup, ready to catch up on some missed episodes of *Masterchef*. Her mind wandered to Cameron. Was he watching too? She rubbed her chest as she felt her heart ache at the thought of him.

Ping.

A feeling of panic washed over her, replacing the heartache. She checked to see who the message was from with a sideways glance. She saw it was from Cameron and breathed a sigh of relief.

Hey, sexy, this guy on *Masterchef* is crap. Did you see what he did to that poor piece of fish? Despicable. Anyway, just wanted to say I'm thinking of you. Call me later if you get horny after reading your naughty book x

Imogen wanted to phone Cameron now and ask if she could stay with him but didn't want to admit defeat. She needed to be strong and didn't want to scare him off. She was going to come across as too clingy, or she'd look like she was too much trouble to be with. Keeping her issues to herself was the best plan. If Cameron couldn't help, what sense was there in bringing him into it?

Hey you, I agree. He did a terrible job of it. If he gets through to the next stage, there's something dodgy going on. I'll be going to bed soon, armed with my book, so keep your phone handy x

As promised, Imogen took her phone and her book to bed with her after texting Cameron. Three chapters in, and Johnny and Melissa were up to all sorts of kinky shenanigans. In her head, it was her and Cameron, and it made her hot.

'Hey you, am I interrupting anything?'

'Nope, not a thing. To be honest, I've been watching some rubbish on TV in bed and waiting for your call. What's going on in the book?'

'Well, Johnny and Melissa have been at it like rabbits. I don't know where they get the energy from. The last time was pretty hot, though.'

'What did they do?' Cameron's voice had grown huskier.

'They were working late. Johnny has an office, and Melissa asked him to sign some documents. Then they had loads of sex on just about every surface.'

'Give me the details. Talk dirty to me. What did Johnny do to Melissa?'

'She walked in, and he got up and closed the door. They were kissing, and he lifted her skirt, slid his fingers into her and then asked her to bend over his desk.'

'Did that make you hot? Are you hot and ready for it now?'

'Yes. I imagined it was you doing everything to me in your office.'

'Have you got BOB with you?'

'Yes.' Imogen was breathless. She hadn't done this before. She felt nervous and unsure but was so turned on that she was willing to give it a go.

'Turn it on, Imogen, and place it gently on your clit. But don't hold it on there for long. Do exactly what I say. Do you understand?'

'Yes, I've turned it on,' Imogen sighed down the phone when her vibrator touched her clit. She was more turned on than she had realised.

'Now take it away and stroke it over your nipples.'

Imogen did as she was told. She imagined it was Cameron doing it to her.

'Circle it around your clit. Imagine I'm doing it to you with my tongue. Now dip it inside you, coat it in your delicious cream. Are you getting hotter, Imogen?'

'Yes, I'm close.'

'Circle your clit again, but this time I want you to imagine me spreading your legs wide and entering you. Can you feel me thrusting into you, Imogen?'

'Yes, Cameron, oh God, I'm coming,' Imogen was breathing hard and gasping with each spasm of her sex.

'Are you still there? I wish I could fuck you right now.'

'I'm here. I wish I was with you, too. That'll keep me going until I see you again. Thank you, Cameron.' Imogen fought to get her breath back.

'I'm glad to be of service. Next time we're in my office late at night, you can thank me in person. I like the sound of that. Goodnight Imogen, sweet dreams.'

CHAPTER 18

Song Choice: Close (feat. Tove Lo) (Nick Jonas)

Imogen had mixed emotions as she walked into the office on Monday morning. She worried about the messages Mark sent her. Was he watching her, or was he nowhere near finding her and getting desperate? She was determined not to let him get to her. She had a man that knew how to treat her, and she felt safe in his arms and craved him. Her fear of the past and her hope for the future were battling against each other in her mind. Was she too dependent on Cameron? She shouldn't be falling for someone so soon, and could her heart take it if he didn't feel the same? Cameron was used to women falling at his feet. Why would he want a relationship with someone like her? She wished she could talk to someone about it—maybe she could open up to Sarah.

'Hey Imogen, how are you? Did you have a good time on Friday? Did you shag Cameron? Did you hear about Lucy going home with a hottie? So many questions, so little time.' Sarah's face was beaming. It was full of hope for fresh gossip.

'Morning Sarah, I'm good, thank you. I had a great time on Friday, and I won't discuss such matters in the office. Lucy pulled a hottie? No, I didn't know that. Can you do me a favour? Keep anything you saw between Cameron and me under wraps. We can talk about it on Tuesday, but I don't want it coming out in the office.' Imogen was whispering.

'Got it. Consider your secret safe with me.' Sarah tapped the side of her nose with her finger. 'See you and Lucy at lunchtime for a debrief. We need to get the info on her new chap.'

'Oh yes, I can't wait to hear about that. I'll see you later.'

Once settled at her desk, Imogen saw an email from Cameron.

To: Imogen Taylor
From: Cameron Black
Subject: Something has come up.
Good morning gorgeous,
I couldn't get to sleep last night after our phone call. In the end, I had to take matters into my own hands. Anyway, I just wanted you to know that I'm on site all day, so I won't see you. I'm out with James tonight, but if you need me, just call.
Don't forget to walk back to your car with Sam. Have a great day.

Thinking of you

Cam x

To: Cameron Black

From: Imogen Taylor
Subject: RE Something has come up.

I'm glad to hear you handled the situation well. I wish I was there to assist. I hope you have a good day on-site and survive a night out with James.

I shall be a good girl and walk with Sam.

Thinking of you too, which is a distraction.

Imogen x

The team meeting and chat about Friday filled her morning. Before she knew it, she picked Sarah up for lunch with Lucy. They reached the coffee shop in record time, eager to get the gossip.

'So, Lucy, you need to tell us about the mystery man you pulled on Friday.' Sarah would not let Lucy off. Their backsides barely touched the seats before Sarah pounced.

'Okay, I won't keep you in suspense.' Lucy was excited to share her news.

'While I was in the queue for the ladies' room, this hot guy came up and started chatting with me. He said he'd noticed me on the dance floor but was too intimidated to come up and talk to me in front of you guys. Then when he saw me in the queue, he decided to go for it.

We chatted until I got to the front—side note, I was grateful for that because I was so desperate for a wee, I thought I was going to pee myself. Anyway, he said he'd wait for me to come out, which I thought was crap. I was sure he'd walk off and leave me—but sure enough, he was waiting. We went into the quieter room to talk. He lives and works in London but said he was in the area to visit a friend.' Lucy took a deep breath and sat back in her seat, ready to hear what the others thought.

'Wow, Lucy, that's great. What's he like? Is he a considerate lover?' Sarah said with a wink.

'OMG, Sarah, you're terrible.'

'It's all right, Lucy. She's living her life vicariously through you now, but we need the details. Come on, girl, spill the beans.'

'Okay, so we went back to my place since he thought it would be rude to take someone back to his mate's flat. He was a perfect gentleman, you know, not all hands-on in the taxi—I hate it when men go straight for these.' Lucy gestured to her breasts.

'We talked and had some wine. He was interested in listening to me and asked loads of questions. It was like he was genuinely attracted to me as a person and not just trying to get me into bed. He kissed me, and one thing led to another, and you know, we did it on the sofa.' Lucy looked scandalized. Imogen thought it was sweet, and Sarah giggled.

'Please tell me he got you off, Lucy. I'm hoping he's not all talk and no trousers.'

'Sarah!' She covered her face with her hands before being encouraged to continue. 'It was very nice, thank you—you won't hear me moaning about it.'

'If you're not moaning, then he's doing it wrong.' Sarah laughed.

Imogen smacked her on the arm. 'Come on, leave her alone, Sarah—it's obvious she had a marvellous time. It's not always about screaming orgasms.'

That earned Imogen a scornful look.

'All right, it is mostly about screaming orgasms, but maybe he was just too drunk or nervous?'

'Anyway, it was great. He's going to come and stay at mine this weekend, and I can't wait. He's making all the effort for me, but I won't get my hopes up. I do like him so far, though.'

'I'm pleased for you, Lucy. You deserve to be happy.'

'Thanks, Imogen, we still need to organise that night out soon. Maybe we can do it in a few weeks? We could head to London, then I can stay over for the weekend with Paul and kill two birds with one stone.'

'Sounds like a plan.'

Imogen worked until six o'clock, deadlines were looming, and she wanted to get ahead. She packed her gym kit that morning, intending to stay late and work out. Her stamina needed working on if she was going to keep up with Cameron. It was playing on her mind that she should build some strength in case the worst happened. Imogen said goodbye to the last of her colleagues as they left for the evening. She powered down her laptop and went to the changing rooms. As she walked across the mezzanine floor, she saw Cameron coming across from reception. Her heart stopped. He looked sexy as hell, wearing rugged work trousers, a once-white T-shirt covered in brick dust, and chunky work boots. He didn't see her, which gave her longer to admire the view. The way he walked with such confidence—each stride hinting at the power of his legs—was enough to raise her heart rate. Reaching the stairs, he pounced up them two at a time until he saw Imogen and came to an abrupt halt.

'Hey you, what are you doing here so late?'

'Hi, getting some stuff done then heading to the gym. Thought I'd work on my stamina.'

'Is there anyone up there still?'

'I don't think so, not in my office, anyway. I don't know about your side.'

Cameron looked around, took a few more steps, and stopped just short of the top. He was at eye level with Imogen and couldn't pass up the opportunity for a quick kiss.

'God, I missed this. Do you want to come to my office? I need to pick up some drawings as I'm back on site tomorrow.'

Imogen felt her heart rate increasing as the memories of their late-night phone call came to mind. Her body remembered the sensations—it craved the sexual high again.

Imogen saw they were alone as they went through the glass doors. She wondered if Cameron thought the same, or did she have it bad?

He led Imogen by the hand to his office. For the first time, she looked around, taking it all in. The office was set up similarly to James' but with the same leather sofa he had at home. The furniture was all-natural wood and black metal. It oozed masculinity and warmth. She wanted to touch the surfaces, to feel the wood beneath her fingers.

'I see you have a thing for that sofa.'

'Handy, as I have a thing for you on it.'

Imogen had been so distracted by looking around that she didn't notice he'd closed his door and the glass walls were now opaque. She had enough time to drop her bags before he closed the gap between them. His lips collided with hers with such force it knocked the air out of her lungs.

'I haven't stopped thinking about taking you in my office all day. It became—how should I put it—problematic more than once.' Cameron lifted Imogen's skirt. She came alive every time he touched her. He ignited a flame—his touch was oxygen, breathing life into her. Her core was pulsing, aching to feel him in her, and desperate for the release.

She reached under his T-shirt and ran her hands along the curves of his muscles. Breathing in his intoxicating scent, she undid the button of his trousers. Cameron's breath became shallow with anticipation. He cupped her sex with his hand, moved her underwear to the side, and slid his finger inside her.

'Oh, Imogen, you are so ready. I need you now.'

Imogen pulled down his zipper and released his straining cock.

'Fuck me then. Take me any way you want me.'

Cameron didn't need to be asked twice. He turned her around and encouraged her knees onto the sofa, her hands grabbed the back. He leant over her and kissed her nape while pulling her underwear down to her knees, with the waistband restricting how far she could spread herself. Cameron moved her skirt up and stroked her cheeks, then parted them. She was ready to take him. He took his erection and rubbed it over her entrance, coating his tip with her arousal, then he inched in.

Imogen felt stretched and packed to capacity. She was sure she had taken him all, but he held her hips and pulled her onto him even further. The sensation was out of this world. They both let out loud groans, unable to control themselves and their carnal desire. Cameron pulled out to his tip, then thrust into her with force. She pushed against the sofa to brace herself.

With one hand holding her shoulder and the other at her hip, he pounded into her, eliciting groans that spurred him on.

'You're hot and tight around me, Imogen—you're perfect. I want to feel you come on me and feel your pussy clenching, milking every drop from me.'

Cameron rubbed his hand against her clit. She cried out with pleasure. She didn't care if anyone heard—she'd lost control of herself and was chasing her climax.

'Oh God, Cameron, please. I need to come. Fuck me hard—now.'

He was now thrusting as hard and as fast as he could, all the while rubbing her clitoris. Within seconds, she was crying out his name. He felt her sex pulsating around him—it sent him over the edge, and his orgasm ripped out of him with a moan. He collapsed over her back, panting and kissing her hot nape.

'Christ, that was amazing.'

Imogen's legs struggled to hold her up. Cameron supported her as she went weak. Wrapping his arms around her waist, he helped her pull her underwear up and guided her to sit on his lap. He took her into his arms and kissed her. Taking a moment to catch his breath, he stroked her hair out of her face and looked into her eyes with concern.

'Is there something wrong?'

Imogen's reply was barely a whisper. 'I've never had it so good, Cameron. The connection we have scares me—what we have, whatever it is—I don't know if I'm ready for it.'

'It's hit me hard, too. I've never spent the day with a semi in my trousers. Let's just take each day as it comes and see where we end up? I can't make any promises of everlasting love, but I'm not sure I can stop this either. Are you okay?'

Imogen nodded in response. She felt better for getting that off her chest. 'Well, I guess I don't need to work out tonight.'

'Give me a sec to get changed, and I'll walk you to the car. I'm not around much this week. Do you want to do something together on Friday night?'

'What did you have in mind? Not that it matters, the answer will still be yes.'

CHAPTER 19

'**G**ood evening ladies, here are your drinks—enjoy.'
'Cheers, Seth—perfect barman, as always.' Sarah handed the drinks to Jess and Imogen.

'Right, first things first, the book club can come later as we have more pressing matters to attend to. Imogen, did you and Cameron do it, or what?'

'You're not going to let me keep it to myself, are you? Can you promise not to disclose this information to anybody? To be honest, I need to talk to someone about it as it's doing my head in.'

'What happens in the book club stays in the book club, Imogen, rule number one. You have our word that you can tell us anything, and we won't tell a soul. Isn't that right, Jess?'

'Absolutely. Your secret is safe with us.'

Imogen told them almost everything, only leaving out the recent office antics.

'I can't believe I'm talking to someone who's bagged, Cameron. I'm surprised you can still walk, to be honest. He's like the perfect man—sexy AF, strong, and you know from his job that he's good with his hands. He's funny and caring but gives off the aura that he'll fuck your brains out.'

Imogen nearly spat her drink out. 'You're too much sometimes, Sarah. You're right, though. I'm glad of a night off. He's a talented man, that's all I'm going to say on that front—oh, and that he's an excellent cook.

'We're just going to see if it goes anywhere. I'm not sure it's what I need right now, but I can't stop craving him. Anyway, Sarah, I think it's time you told us what's going on with you and James.'

'What? Me and James, are you still hooked on that idea? It's nothing, just some innocent flirting. You know what he's like. We both have a similar sense of humour and dirty minds. It's nothing more than that, honest.'

'I'm not sure I believe you. I'll be keeping my eye on you. Now, what do we think about Johnny and Melissa? They're at it like rabbits.'

Friday soon came around again. The week had given her some breathing space from Cameron, with the added bonus of no communication from Mark. Her head was clear. She felt excited about her weekend. The roar of Cameron's engine announced his arrival and triggered a flutter of butterflies in her stomach. After the last check of her hair and a smooth of her dress, she opened the door before he made it up the path.

'Hello sexy, how have you been?'

Imogen gave Cameron an appreciative once-over. As expected, his clothes fit him well and showcased his body to perfection. He looked gorgeous in his dark blue jeans, a light blue shirt, and a navy-blue fitted blazer. The blazer enhanced his broad shoulders. Her outfit choice, a navy wraparound dress and matching peep-toe wedges, complimented his. They looked like the perfect couple.

'Good, thank you. Do you want to come in, or are we heading straight out?'

'I think it's best we go straight out—otherwise, we won't make it out of the house tonight. I reckon I could get you naked in seconds with one pull of that bow.'

'You could so keep your hands off. Are you going to tell me what the plan is, or are you keeping me in suspense?'

'I figured I couldn't go wrong with the classic dinner and a movie. A drive-in cinema is showing Casino Royale, and I'm a sucker for a Bond movie. I haven't gone down the romance route. I hope that's okay.'

'Oh, me too. I've never been to a drive-in, but it's my favourite of all the Bond movies, so it gets a thumbs up from me.'

'Well, I hope you love it. We can snuggle in the back—it'll be like kissing in the back row of the cinema.'

They pulled up outside the restaurant in a quaint village tucked away and hidden behind trees.

'Good evening, Mr Black. We've got your favourite table ready. Come on through.'

Imogen raised her eyebrows at Cameron.

'What? What's that look for?'

'He knows you by name, and you have a favourite table? Is this where you bring all your dates?'

'You are the first date I've brought here. No, it's not where I bring my dates. I just like this place, and I come here a lot with my family and friends. That, and I co-own it.' He gave her one of his charming smiles.

'Oh. Well, obviously you co-own it. Why didn't I think of that in the first place? Is that why you're so interested in cooking?'

'Yeah, partly. My cousin runs it day-to-day—I don't think he's working tonight, but I'll bring you back when he's here so you can meet him. I think you'll like him—he's a good guy.' I'm more of a silent partner, but I like to know what I'm talking about and what standards we should be setting.

'I'd like that.' Being introduced to his family so early on felt like a big step, but it pleased her.

As they sat down, a waiter came over and asked what they'd like to drink while they read the menu.

'Would you like a glass of champagne, Imogen, or do you fancy something else?'

'Champagne would be lovely, thank you.'

'I'll just have half a pint, please—designated driver duty.'

'So, what do you recommend? It all sounds delicious.'

'I think you should go big or go home. If you like lobster, then I'd highly recommend that.'

'Lobster, I love it. You're spoiling me. I could get used to this.'

'I intend for you to get used to it.' He fixed her with a piercing stare.

Her heart skipped a beat. Before she said anything, the waiter was back to take their order. Imogen was looking forward to her meal tonight. They decided on the bread and olives to share, and both ordered the lobster.

'I've always been rubbish at getting the meat out without making a mess of me and the table. How do you do it so effortlessly?' Lobster juice trickled down her fingers.

'Here, I'll do it for you. It's all about breaking the air seal in the main claw first. Once you've done that, the meat slides out, see?' Cameron fed Imogen the claw meat. 'Then you're best off sucking hard on the individual legs—that way, you get all the meat and juice out of them. It's deliciously sweet—plus, I'll enjoy watching you.'

'I'd best make sure I'm doing it right then.'

'Oh, you do it right.'

'Are we still talking about lobster, or have you moved on?'

'I'm in a different place entirely.'

Imogen laughed. He wasn't your stereotypical wealthy businessman, and she loved that. She felt at ease with him.

'Tell me all about you, Cameron. I feel there's so much I don't know.'

'There isn't much to say. I grew up near here, and my family was in the trade too. My dad was always working on the next project. He's left his mark in many communities around here, but he didn't want me to work for him. He said I should make my own way in the world and make my own decisions. I thought it was because he didn't trust me to run his business, but now I understand he wanted me to earn what I had and do things my way. He's always there to support me, though. He encouraged me to study architecture. I'd already learned most of the building trade skills working for him during the school holidays. Still, he wanted to make sure I had more options. I'm very grateful for that. The rest, you know.'

'What about your mum? What's she like?'

'She's great. She taught me how to be a gentleman.' Cameron smiled. 'She's tough as nails, though. Cross her, and you'll know about it. She spent most of her time on-site with Dad getting stuck in, so she had to learn to hold her own with the tradesmen. She's the only person I know who can tell my dad off. You'll get on with her.'

They pulled up at the drive-in, and Cameron went to the booth for popcorn and refreshments. He came back with his arms full of treats.

'I couldn't decide. It was like being a kid in a sweet shop, only it was a grown man in a sweet shop. I got you some Prosecco. They'd run out of the little bottles, so I went big—I hope that's okay.'

'Yep, great. Apologies if I get pissed and make a fool of myself.'

'Just don't puke on my leather interior, sexy.'

They settled down to watch the movie. The combination of the film, drink and Cameron nearby was getting her hot. But she was content to be on a date with a man that cared for her in all the right ways.

'Do you think we can see the movie okay in the back seat?'

'Yeah, I reckon.' And with that, he climbed over the seats. Imogen followed him after taking her shoes off.

He put his arm around her and pulled her in tight. Too occupied with kissing each other like teenagers at the movies, they didn't notice they couldn't see much of the big screen. The tinted windows afforded them some privacy, which added to Imogen's increasing feeling of bravery.

She reached down and undid his jeans. He fixed his eyes on her with a look of passion.

'Sit back and enjoy the movie, Cameron.' She pulled his boxers down. He lifted his hips to help her out, and his cock sprang to attention in Imogen's hand.

'Could you pass me my drink, please?' She took a large sip of her Prosecco and handed the glass back. She bent her head and took his tip in her mouth. When she was sure the drink wouldn't spill out, she took more of his erection.

'Oh God, that is so good. It's almost too good.' Cameron threw his head back and gasped.

Imogen moved her head up and sucked the tip while swallowing the drink. She topped up and repeated the process.

'Imogen, I'm going to come soon. Do you want me to warn you?' Even in the middle of the best blow job she'd ever given, he was still thinking about her. Imogen didn't bother to answer—instead, she wrapped her hands around the base of his erection, stroking his length while she sucked on the head. She increased her tempo until she could hear Cameron breathing hard and felt him thrusting his hips to encourage her to take more.

'Ah fuck.' Cameron was coming hard. Imogen felt her mouth fill with his hot release. She swallowed it down as it mixed with the Prosecco.

'You can thank Melissa for that.' Imogen drained the rest of her glass.

'Bloody hell Imogen, words fail me. Give me a minute to recover, and I'll repay the favour.'

'No need. That was for you.' She had a triumphant grin on her face. His kiss said it all—she had blown his mind. He wrapped her in his arms, and they snuggled up to watch the rest of the movie in comfortable silence.

CHAPTER 20

Song Choice: Run for your life (The Beatles)

'**A**re you sure you'll be all right this weekend? I don't want to think of you sitting alone and pining for me.'

Imogen laughed. 'It's fine. I've already messaged Sarah to see if she fancied meeting up at the pub tonight. Have a great time with your mates, and don't get too drunk watching the game. I'll see you in the office on Monday.'

'Same to you, then. Don't get too drunk. I don't like the thought of you being incapacitated without me there to look after you.'

'I promise. I'll be good—ish.'

'Maybe I should make sure the office stocks up on green juice. Thanks for a great night—it's the best viewing of Casino Royale I've been to, that's for sure.'

'You're welcome. It was my pleasure.'

'I'll see you soon. Take care, beautiful. Bye.'

'Bye, babe.' Imogen hung up the phone and smiled to herself. Cameron had only dropped her off five minutes before calling her to check-in. A few months ago, that behaviour would have left her feeling controlled, but now she felt elated and alive. A night out with Sarah would keep her mind occupied. Thoughts of the men in and out of her life needed to be kept to a minimum. If anything was going to work with Cameron, she had to make sure she didn't fall too fast.

Standing in front of her full-length mirror, she checked her reflection. She dressed casually in jeans, a white boat-neck top and tan leather flats. She made an effort with her hair and make-up before grabbing a jacket and heading out.

Sarah was waiting for her at the bar and chatting with Seth.

'Hey you, I've got you a G&T. Seth told me which one you like best, so I went with that. I also invited Jess—she'll be here any minute.'

'Perfect. Oh, here she is. Cheers, you.'

'Hello ladies, I see you started without me. Do I have to play catch up?'

'Hey Jess, don't worry, I've only just arrived too. Here's your drink—we're only on our first.'

'Good, I was worried I missed some gossip. Let's sit down, and you can tell us all about it. Sarah tells me you had a date with the hunk last night.'

'I'm going to need to down this, then. I'll get us another round while you grab a table.' Imogen joined the others at their usual table, already onto her second gin.

'Spit it out. Jess and I are desperate to know all the juicy details.'

Imogen took a sip of her drink and rested her elbows on the table. 'Cameron took me on a perfect date. We had dinner at the restaurant he co-owns with his cousin. Then he took me to my first drive-in movie. He even picked my favourite film.'

'That's great and everything, but we want to know about the juicy details.'

'Sarah's right. Skip to the good parts.'

'Flipping heck, you two are insatiable. Cameron bought me a bottle of Prosecco to drink in the car. Okay, so, you know that thing that Melissa did to Johnny with the champagne? Well, I gave it a go.'

Sarah choked on her drink. 'No way, was it amazing? Did he love it?'

'He said it was the best he'd ever had, so yeah, I reckon he loved it.'

'That's amazing.' Jess clapped her hands with glee.

'You're such a minx. I love it. Now I need to find someone to try it out on.'

'How about James?'

'Oh God, will you quit with that? I don't think there's anything there, although I would like there to be something if I'm honest. I fancy him. There, I said it.'

'Right. Well, let's formulate a plan to get you two together. The first stage in getting help is admitting you have a problem.' All three of them were laughing.

The plans to get James and Sarah together became more elaborate as they consumed more alcohol. Sarah ended the conversation by waving her empty glass in Imogen's direction. 'Come on, chick, it's your round.'

'On it. Like a car bonnet, as they say.' An unsteady Imogen

made it to the bar carrying three empty martini glasses.

'Do you want a tray for those?'

'Nah, I'm all right. Cheers, Seth—I got this.' Imogen took hold of the three glasses filled with vodka and cranberry juice and made her way back to the table. She froze when she heard a song playing on the jukebox. The next sound she heard was glass smashing and then the cold sensation of the drinks splashing her feet. Panic set in, and her heart rate increased—ready for the fight or flight instinct to kick in. The song playing was the same one that Mark used to play to her. He sang the lyrics to her, about rather seeing his girl dead than with another man. His unmistakable message put the fear of God in her. She scanned the room as she was sure Mark must be here to play the song. Sarah was by her side in seconds.

'Imogen, are you all right? What's wrong?'

'That song—Mark used to play it to me all the time. It's how he threatened me. I need to get out of here now.' Imogen was in full panic and couldn't control her body. She was shaking. Seth came out from behind the bar to check on her and see what was happening.

'Seth, can you walk us back to Imogen's house? We need to get her out of here. Did you see who played that song on the jukebox?'

'I didn't see anyone. I'm sorry. I didn't even know we had that song on there. I'll walk you home. Let me just get someone to cover the bar and clean this up.'

'I'll wait outside.' Imogen realised that the pub had fallen silent, and everyone was looking at her. She needed to get out and away from prying eyes.

'When we get to yours, unlock your door, and I'll look around, just to make sure the house is clear, okay?' Sarah brought Seth up to speed on the walk home about why Imogen had freaked out. He was concerned that Mark may have broken in.

'All clear—no broken windows, and your back door is secure. Are you going to be okay?'

Imogen was shaken, but she was determined not to stop living her life. 'Yeah, don't worry, I'll be fine. It's probably nothing. I'm just overreacting. Thanks for everything, and sorry about the mess.'

'Don't worry about it. Sarah, you have my number, so if you need anything, call me.'

'Cheers, Seth, will do.'

Imogen locked the front door as soon as Seth left.

'So, this Mark, is he dangerous? Should I be worried about you more than I am already? Do I need to call Cameron to come over?' Sarah's face was full of concern.

'Yeah, Imogen, he sounds like a dangerous weirdo. Do you want to move into mine for a bit? I have plenty of space.' Jess' arm was still around Imogen.

'No, it's okay—but thank you, I appreciate your concern. Mark was never hugely violent. I would describe him as more forceful. I don't think he'd hurt anyone. He has too much to lose. He's got a top job in the city, and I don't think he'd risk that to come for me. I think I just overreacted—it's the first time I've heard that song since I left him, so it hit me hard. I'm fine. You can go home if you want to. I'm so exhausted I'd like to just go to bed.'

Sarah looked at Imogen with concern on her face and then looked at Jess for her input.

'I'll lock the door when you leave, and I'm in a neighbourhood watch area, so I'm safe. If I change my mind, I'll call you, I promise.'

'Okay, but I don't like it. Call either of us if you need someone.'

'Cheers, Sarah. I promise I will if I need you.'

'I'm calling us a taxi. I don't fancy walking home.' Jess looked out of the window while they waited for the taxi to arrive.

After an uneventful Sunday, Imogen got to work early on Monday morning and went to the gym. She took out her frustration about being such an idiot on the punch bag. She'd made such a fuss over nothing. That Mark hadn't been in contact with her confirmed it was a coincidence. Imogen glanced at the door every few punches, hoping to see Cameron come in. Still, by the end of her workout, he hadn't made it, so she finished up, got ready for work and went to her office. As she got to her desk, an envelope in front of her monitor caught her eye. Being crimson red, it wasn't hard to miss. A smile crept across her face—perhaps Cameron had left her a love letter before going to the site. Nausea wiped the smile from her face as she opened it, the rush of excitement gone.

Dear Imogen,

Did you like the song on Saturday night? I played it for you. I see you've been cheating on me, tut-tut little slut.

I'm willing to give you a chance, though. End it with him, or I will make him lose his head.

I can't wait to have you in my arms.

126

All my love now and forever.

XXX

Imogen dropped the card onto her desk and took some breaths, so she didn't vomit. She studied the envelope, hoping to find a clue as to where it came from, but there was no stamp or postmark and only her first name on it.

'How the fuck did you get this on my desk, Mark?' She whispered, running to the reception area. She hoped Sarah would know how the envelope ended up on her desk.

'Hey Imogen, how are you? Anymore contact from you-know-who?'

'Hi, Sarah. You didn't leave an envelope addressed to me on my desk, did you?'

'No, why? Have you received a love letter?' Sarah wiggled her eyebrows as she spoke.

'Oh no, nothing like that, not to worry. I must get back to work. Speak to you later.'

Imogen didn't want to tell anyone. She was frantic with fear and couldn't think straight. The card was at the back of one of her drawers. Something told her to keep it—just in case she needed it as evidence.

She sat through the morning meeting but had no idea what was discussed. She kept thinking about what she should do. It was going around in her mind, but she kept returning to the fact that the safest thing was to end it with Cameron while she worked out how to get Mark out of her life.

When she returned to her desk, Imogen noticed her phone flashing, telling her she had a voicemail.

'Jen, it's Sarah. Come downstairs as soon as you can.' Sarah's urgent message left Imogen concerned. She rushed down the stairs.

'Oh my God. Have you heard the news?' Sarah blurted out before she'd even reached her desk.

Imogen's heart stopped. Instantly, thoughts of Cameron getting hurt came to mind. 'What is it, Sarah? Spit it out.'

'Someone attacked Seth yesterday. A bloke jumped him as he closed up and told him to stay away from his woman. He's okay. He needed a couple of stitches over his eyebrow but he's all right.'

'Shit, I feel terrible. Does he know who did it?'

'No, the coward attacked him from behind. He hit his head on the way down. The police took a statement, but there wasn't a clear image on the CCTV footage and no witnesses, so they don't think it'll go anywhere.'

'Bloody hell, why is the world so full of dickheads, Sarah? Will you keep me posted if you hear anything?'

'Yeah, of course.'

Imogen returned to her office, deep in thought, and a feeling of dread spread through her. She knew it was Mark—he was sending her a message. It broke her heart, but she decided she had to end it with Cameron. The phone ringing interrupted her thoughts.

'Hey gorgeous, fancy going for a walk at lunchtime? If I don't get to lay my hands on you soon, I'm going to go insane.'

A sick feeling settled in the pit of her stomach. 'Hi, Cameron. That sounds like a good idea. I need to talk to you.'

'Oh, that sounds ominous. Should I be worried?' The cheekiness in his voice was gone.

'Shall we meet at the entrance to the woods at twelve?' Imogen didn't want to answer his question. She needed to stay strong and not break down on the phone.

'I think maybe we should meet now, Imogen.'

'I can't. Twelve o'clock, Cameron, please.'

'Fine, I'll see you at twelve.'

She spent the rest of the morning in a daze. She was on autopilot until noon, when she headed out to the woods. Cameron was waiting for her with his hands in his pockets.

'Hello, Imogen. I've been stressing out since I spoke to you. What's going on?' Cameron reached out to her but was sidestepped as Imogen walked into the woods.

'Imogen, I asked what the hell is going on?'

She stopped once she was away from any prying eyes. 'I've been thinking about us all weekend. It's too much for me right now—I think I need a break to clear my head. I can't do it. What we have is too much, Cam. I'm sorry.' Imogen's voice cracked.

Cameron was clenching his jaw.

'Bullshit. Tell me what's going on, Imogen. It's him, isn't it? He's got to you?'

'It's not bullshit, Cameron. Please don't make this harder than it is. I'm sorry—I'll understand if you never want to see me again, but I need time to think and sort my head out. I wasn't expecting to fall for you so fast, and I'm just not ready for what we have. Please trust me, Cameron.' Her pleading eyes were trying to get the message across.

'Whatever, Imogen, I don't believe you, but I won't force myself on you. I'm not like that, so if that's your wish, I'll have to accept it. Let me know when you've finished thinking and decide what you want.'

She watched as Cameron walked away, rooted to the spot and unable to chase after him. Imogen felt drained and weak as she sat on a nearby tree stump. The stress of the last few months came crashing down on her and flowed out through silent tears. Until this moment, she thought that leaving her life behind in London was the hardest thing she'd ever done. She was wrong. This was. She hoped it was worth it in the long run and prayed that she hadn't lost Cameron forever. Resolute in her determination to fix this mess, she got out her phone.

It's done, you sick fuck. Now show yourself or get out of my life.

There was only a split-second pause before she pressed send. One way or another, this was going to end. She wiped her eyes, took a few deep breaths, and walked back to the office. It was no longer a safe place for her—she'd have to watch her back, but the time for running was over. Now she was going to fight.

CHAPTER 21

Song Choice: The Last Time (The Script)

Cameron couldn't believe what he was hearing. He knew it was bullshit. How could Imogen say she needed a break? After Friday, he was sure they'd be in it for the long haul. He should've listened to his gut instincts at the start and not got mixed up with someone fresh out of a toxic relationship. He'd been such an idiot. Cameron Black didn't fall for women easily, so what was different about Imogen? He'd give her the space she wanted. It wouldn't be easy, but maybe that was best for both of them.

Something wasn't stacking up, though—how could she change her mind so quickly? He couldn't rule out that her ex had found her and got to her. His pride wouldn't let him think that she just wasn't ready to be with him. She'd asked him to trust her and give her time—but she didn't say he couldn't try to protect her from afar.

'James, what are you having?' Cameron met James at the pub for their Monday night get-together.

'I'll have a pint of Black Sheep, please chap—and a packet of pork scratchings.'

'Good plan. I'll join you.'

'What? You never eat that filth. What's the matter? Tell James all about it.'

'I don't want to talk about it. I'm too pissed off. I'm going to drown my sorrows, sleep at yours and then regret it in the morning.'

'That sounds very much like issues with a woman. Which woman?'

'It doesn't matter anymore apparently, so shut up about it and get drinking.'

'Well, being the best friend that I am, I'll be here for you and match you pint for pint. I'm sure Imogen will come to her senses soon enough.'

'Is it that obvious?' Cameron put his head in his hands.

'I'm afraid so, mate. Just don't make it awkward at work. She's doing an awesome job, and I don't want to lose her. Are you hearing me?'

'Yeah, I got it—I'm not an idiot, James. I think this is about her ex, and I need to know she's okay. I need you to keep an eye on her. Can you do me a favour? Let me know as soon as you notice anything suspicious or different around her.'

'No worries, I can do that. It's in my interest to make sure she's okay, too. This may have happened at the right time. The British Interior Design awards are coming up, and you know who'll visit us to sort out contracts, right?'

'Oh God, I could do without that, James.'

'I know it didn't end well with Fran, but I need you to do whatever it takes to keep the Divino contract with us, and if that means playing nice with her, then that's what you need to do. I know we only got the contract with her because you were blowing her mind in the bedroom—I'm no fool, Cam—but I need to keep hold of it.'

'James, not ending well is an understatement. I can't go back there. Imogen will get the wrong idea too—or are you not worried about her as long as it benefits you?'

'I'll look after her if you look after Fran Divino. I'm not asking you to marry her—just keep her sweet until she signs the contract extension documents. Then you can cool it off. Please, do this for our company. I don't ask for much, Cam.'

Cameron sighed, then downed his pint. 'Fuck it.'

'Now you're talking.'

CHAPTER 22

Imogen reverted to how she lived when she was with Mark. She turned off her feelings, made herself numb to the world and went through the motions. She made sure Cameron wasn't around every time she had to leave the safety of her desk. The rest of the day was hard.

The rest of the week was much the same. Working out in her lunch break meant that bumping into Cameron was less likely, and she could leave work while it was still light outside. Sam was there to walk her to her car, for which she was grateful. What had been a nuisance and unnecessary reminder of her past was a welcome comfort. She cancelled going to book club as she wasn't ready to go back to the pub. It was too soon for her to see Seth and the damage Mark had done.

Imogen played scenarios in her head. Should she tell Cameron what was going on? What would that achieve other than put him in danger? Should she call the police? And say what exactly? My weirdo ex-boyfriend sends me text messages, and there's no evidence that he's actually hurt, anyone? The more she thought about it, the more confused she got.

She hadn't received another message from Mark, but she didn't know what that meant either. Had he played with her enough? Perhaps her ending it with Cameron was his goal? Or was he planning his next move? And how the hell did he find her in the first place? The questions were going around, but she was no nearer any answers.

On Friday, as she was walking out of the office, Sarah stopped to talk to her.

'Hey, chick, what's going on with you and Cameron? Have you two had a fight? He's barely been in the office all week, and when he has been, he's had a face like thunder. You look like shit, too, by the way.'

'Thanks, Sarah—I needed to hear that. We split up, not much more to say other than that.'

'What? That's crazy. Why? I thought you two were made for each other. Oh, hang on a minute. This has got something to do with Twat-features, hasn't it?'

'No, it hasn't. I don't want to talk about it. I'm exhausted and just want to go home to sleep.'

'Okay, I don't believe you, but if you change your mind, you can call me. I can come over with a bottle of wine and a massive tub of ice cream. It always does the trick.'

'Cheers, hun. I'll let you know.'

Imogen had survived a week without Cameron. The pain hadn't lessened, but on the plus side, she hadn't heard from Mark.

'Morning, everyone. I hope you all had a good weekend. I want to kick off the meeting with an announcement. Fran Divino is coming to visit us tomorrow to start talks regarding our contract extension. I'm going to be stressed out this week, just to warn you. We then have the Design Awards at the end of next week. Imogen, I would like it if you came this year.'

Imogen looked startled. She'd only been half-listening. She pulled herself together.

'Oh right, yes, thank you—I would love to come.'

Usually, she'd feel great being invited and see it as a massive opportunity, but she didn't feel like celebrating anything. She was sure Cameron would be there, which meant she couldn't escape him. After the meeting, James called her into his office.

'Hey Imogen, how are you doing?'

'I'm okay, thanks, James. Thank you for inviting me to the awards. I promise to do a good job representing the company.'

'I don't doubt it, Imogen. I'll get Sarah to book you a room at the hotel. So, as you know, Fran is coming in tomorrow. I remember you saying that you're a fan, so I wondered if you wanted to sit in on the meeting?'

'Oh wow, that would be great, thank you.'

'No worries. Thanks, Imogen.'

She spent the rest of the day reading the terms of the current Divino contract to understand what they were talking about. Her mind drifted to the awards and what she was going to wear. Perhaps a shopping trip was in order. She could talk Sarah into joining her for some retail therapy. No further communication had come from Mark—his silence was worrying. Maybe he was watching and testing her to see if she had ended things with Cameron? She'd take her mind off things by speaking to Lucy about her new man. Even though she was hurting over Cameron, she was happy for Lucy.

'Lucy, tell me everything. How is Paul?'

'Oh, he's okay, thanks, Imogen. He's cool about things and

not one to message me loads. He's taking things slowly. I mentioned we were planning on coming to London soon, and he thought that was a good idea. I'm not sure if I'll be seeing him before then, though—he's pretty busy with things.' Lucy emphasised the last word, 'whatever that means. We had a lovely time last weekend. He even snuck out on Sunday morning to get me breakfast.'

'Ah, Lucy, that's lovely. I'm glad he's making you happy. It sounds like he's not rushing into anything, which is sensible, speaking from experience. I'm looking forward to letting my hair down with you guys. Shall we organise our night out for the week after the Design Awards? We could go straight after work on Friday.'

'That sounds like a plan. I can't wait.'

'I'll let Sarah know and convince her to come shopping with me. I have two evenings that require something fabulous.'

CHAPTER 23

Song Choice: Wicked Game (Grace Carter)

Cameron needed a coffee and a green juice. He'd had one too many pints with James the previous night and wasn't feeling great. His trip to the coffee machine was halted when he saw Imogen. It was inevitable that they'd bump into each other—it was a miracle they'd avoided it this long. She looked stunning and had made an effort for the Divino contract meetings. Her bottle-green paperboy trousers hit her curves in all the right places. She'd paired them with the cream silk blouse she wore on her first day. He was desperate to pop open another button and get the impact of her impressive cleavage. His mind wandered to how her breasts would brush up against his thighs while she went down on him. He felt a pair of eyes burning into him, snapping him out of his daydream and causing his heart to miss a beat. Imogen had seen him looking like a fool. Turning on his heel and abandoning the green juice, he returned to his office. Slamming the door closed, he sat with his head in his hands.

'Nice one. You made yourself look like a right tit there. For fuck's sake, I need to get a grip.'

'Oh dear, Cam. You know that talking to yourself is the first sign of madness?'

'Fran. I didn't hear you knocking.'

'Sorry, Cam, darling. I didn't realise I needed to knock on your door. Would you like me to leave?'

James' plea to keep her sweet ran through his mind. He regained his composure and planted a smile on his face. Cameron had been dreading seeing Fran again. He didn't need another complication in his life, particularly not one that could jeopardise anything happening with Imogen. He wasn't about to mess around with Fran, even if it meant losing the contract. It had taken a lot of long, painful conversations and a lot of tears on Fran's part before she agreed it was over. He didn't have the energy to go through that again.

'Fran, of course not—you know my door is always open for you. How've you been?'

'I think you know that I could have been better. But all things considered, I'm doing okay.'

'Fran, please, let's not open old wounds again. I'm glad you're doing well.'

'And how are you? Is there a new lady in your life I need to be jealous of?'

Cameron leant back in his chair and exhaled on a laugh, 'Let's not go there, Fran, it won't put either of us in a good mood.' He stood up to signal the conversation was over.

'Oh dear, is the sexy Cameron Black having trouble with a

woman?' Fran stepped towards him and put her hands on his chest, 'Joking aside, you look tired. I care for you. You can talk to me if you need to.'

'Excuse me. I'm sorry to interrupt. James has asked that I come and find you to let you know we're all set up and ready whenever you are. I'm Imogen Taylor, by the way, pleased to meet you.' Imogen's eyes weren't on Fran's face—they focussed on her hands and where they were currently resting. Cameron took a step back. Unable to make eye contact with Imogen, he focused on the floor.

'Oh, you're the infamous Imogen. I've heard so much about you. Apologies. I was just catching up with an old friend. Let's head over together. Bye Cam, darling, I'll see you later.'

CHAPTER 24

Imogen had seen photos of Fran Divino, but they hadn't prepared her for how strikingly beautiful she was in the flesh. Fran had the most incredible auburn hair that fell below her shoulders in perfect waves. She had piercing green eyes and a complexion you could only achieve with luxury beauty products and excellent genetics. Either way, Imogen felt inferior next to her. She wore a bodycon dress in deep crimson and had paired it with black patent heels that came with the all-important red sole. She matched Imogen in the height department but was slighter in the figure. Imogen held her head up high and breathed in. She had no idea what was going on with Fran and Cameron and felt like she had interrupted something more than a friendly hello. Perhaps Cameron wouldn't wait around for her after all. Until she knew more, she would do her best to continue as usual.

'Ms Divino, it's a pleasure to meet you. You've been an inspiration to me with how you run your business and show the world what you can achieve.' Imogen shook Fran's hand—thankfully, she didn't have sweaty palms.

'It's lovely to meet you, Imogen. Please, call me Fran, though.

They are very kind words—I appreciate them. Ah, and here he is. Hello James, darling, how have you been?'

'Hello Fran, I've been very much looking forward to seeing you again. I see Imogen found you.'

'She did indeed. I couldn't just walk past Cameron's office without giving him a quick hello, could I?'

'Of course not.' James cleared his throat.

'Here you go, everyone. I have your coffee, and I've added some extra pastries in case you get hungry.'

'Thank you, Sarah. You look after us well. We'll give you a shout if we need anything else. Right, shall we get down to business and discuss the contract extension?'

Marc, their lawyer, joined them, and the four of them sat around the meeting room table discussing the contract terms.

'I'm happy with what I see so far, James. You and Cam continue to do a great job. I'll take the paperwork away and let you know my decision. I don't like to rush anything, but it's looking good so far. Shall we go for lunch? Will you be joining us, Imogen?'

'It would be my pleasure—if that's okay with you, James?'

'Absolutely. I'll just give Cameron a shout as he'll be joining us—he's our ride there.'

Imogen tried not to react, but her heart rate increased, and she felt a flush rising. She should have known that he'd come—he was the co-owner after all—but having to sit in the car with him was going to be torture.

Imogen noticed Fran was very tactile with Cameron throughout the meal. Her hand was stroking him, almost continually. She missed his touch. Imogen had no right to feel jealous, but she did.

'So, Imogen, tell me—how are you enjoying your work at Spencer & Black Associates? I hope these two are making you welcome.' James' cough earned him a death stare from Cameron. It didn't go unnoticed.

'Yes, thank you. I feel at home here. I was thrilled to be offered the position, and everyone has made me feel very welcome.'

'James tells me you are doing a fantastic job. I look forward to working with you in the future.'

The rest of the meal was awkward, but Imogen tried to hide it. She couldn't stop glancing at Cameron—he looked tired but was still supremely hot. She hoped no one noticed she was sneaking looks at him.

'Cam, darling, try some of this. I think you'll love it.' Fran was feeding Cameron a piece of her roast duck breast. Her attention focussed on Imogen. 'He's such a talented cook, so very good with his meat, aren't you, Cam?'

Imogen noticed Cameron clenching his jaw again. Fran was riling him. She wasn't sure what was happening between them but played along. 'Yes, he's very talented.'

She noticed something flash behind Fran's eyes—Imogen suspected James saw it too.

'So, Fran, are you attending the Design Awards next week?' James tried to change the subject.

'I am, yes. I assume you'll all be there? It's always such fun. I had a brutal hangover last time, didn't I, Cam? This year, I'll eat dinner instead of sticking to a liquid diet.' Fran laughed, and the sound grated on Imogen.

After the meal, Fran demanded Cameron escort her to the car James had arranged for her. She took her time saying goodbye and continued her habit of stroking his bicep. When Fran leant in and gave him a kiss goodbye that lingered longer than it should, Imogen felt like someone had punched her in the gut. Unable to watch any longer, she got in the back of Cameron's car.

James' small talk on the drive back to the office wasn't enough to keep her mind from reeling. She was sure something was going on between Fran and Cameron and needed to get away, so he couldn't see what this was doing to her.

As they got out of the car, Cameron took hold of Imogen's elbow to hold her back.

'Imogen, I need to talk to you.'

'I'm going to leave you two alone. I'll see you guys back at the office.' When James was out of earshot, Imogen couldn't contain her anger.

'What is it, Cam darling? Are you going to have the balls to tell me you've moved on already?'

'What? No. Don't be ridiculous. I haven't moved anywhere. I wanted to check that you're doing okay and explain that it's not what it looks like.'

'I'm doing great, thanks—I enjoyed the show. Cameron, whatever's, going on with you two is none of my business. I'm exhausted and have enough to deal with without adding a love triangle into the mix. I'd best get inside. Enjoy impressing Fran with your meat.' Imogen walked away so he couldn't see her tears.

'It's not like that, Imogen. For fuck's sake, will you listen to me?'

But Imogen wasn't ready to listen. She had one ex to deal with, and she didn't need another.

CHAPTER 25

Imogen spent the week getting angry about the position she was in. She'd done as Mark had asked, and where had it got her? Nowhere. Was she supposed to sit around and wait for another text, or for Mark to show up at her door? How long should she suffer through the radio silence before she could move on with her life? She was done being Mark's plaything and was going to take matters into her own hands. Fuelled by anger, she picked up her phone and typed.

Mark, I've done as you asked, but I'm not playing your game anymore. It's over between us. I'll never come back to you. Give up. You can't hurt me anymore, but I can hurt you. I have a record of every message you've sent me and the card. I've written down everything you've inflicted on me. If you come after me or anyone close to me, I'll release the information to the police and your boss.

Imogen embellished a little to get her message across.

That stunt you pulled by attacking that man, well, you were caught on CCTV, and the police are already looking for you, so you'd better stay away.

She clicked send. This was going to scare Mark off or incite some action, and she'd be ready for him. She wasn't going to fear him. She'd phone the police as soon as she saw him—he'd get nowhere near her. The one thing she couldn't explain was how he got the card onto her desk. Her best guess was that he'd sent it to someone else in the building, and they'd put it there. She knew she was clutching at straws, but without an access card, he couldn't get in.

She threw her phone into her bag and met Sarah, who was taking her to a designer shopping village. It was her best bet to find the perfect dress for the awards night. They were going to make a day of it and then watch a movie at her place. She was looking forward to having a day that didn't revolve around the men in her life. She'd stocked her freezer with ice cream, and the fridge was full of wine.

'Right then, Jen, I think it's time we stopped for lunch. I'm starving, and I need fuel if we're going to find you the perfect dress.' They stopped at a restaurant based around the ethos of good food done well. The atmosphere was friendly, which was just what they needed to give them a break from the hustle and bustle of the shops. It was like the New Year's sales in every shop—Imogen had lost count of how much of her life had been wasted in queues just to get into a shop. They ordered a schnitzel with greens each and shared macaroni cheese. As they had a few hours before going home, they treated themselves to a glass of white wine.

'So, Sarah, are you going to update me on you and James? Is anything happening yet?'

'I'm not saying a word until you tell me what's up with you and Cameron. I'll accept none of your "We just split up" nonsense. I know there's more to it than that, and Cameron looks cut up about it, so I don't believe the decision was his. I know how much you like him, so I can't work out what made you end it.' Sarah took a swig of her wine.

Imogen wasn't sure how much she could tell Sarah, but maybe she could help her work out what to do.

'Do you promise not to tell anyone, especially Cameron?'

'Yes, I swear, Imogen—just tell me what's going on.'

Imogen watched as a bead of condensation trickled down the side of her wine glass while thinking about how to best explain everything. She let out a deep breath she hadn't realised she'd been holding.

'Mark got to me. I haven't seen him, but he sent me a card that accused me of cheating on him, and he threatened to hurt Cameron if I didn't end it. He asked if I liked the song he played for me in the pub, which makes me certain he attacked Seth. I don't know how he found me, but I can't risk anything happening to Cameron. Mark hasn't been in touch since, so I don't know where he is or what he's planning. I sent him a message earlier, though, because I'm done running scared of him. I've told him to leave me alone, or I'll go to the police and ruin his career.'

'Shit, Imogen, this is serious stuff. Why didn't you tell Cameron?'

'I don't think he'd want to hang around to get hurt. I don't know what Mark's capable of, but I decided it wasn't worth the risk. I'd never forgive myself if something happened to Cameron. I need time to sort this out with Mark once and for all. I was hoping I could get Cameron out of the picture long enough to find a solution or at least have enough evidence to take to the police. As it stands, I have some text messages telling me how much he loves me. That's not a crime, is it?'

'No, I suppose it's not.'

'Turns out it doesn't matter, anyway. Cameron has made no effort to get me back, and he's moved on. I'm sure something's going on between him and Fran Divino. You should have seen her over lunch. She was all over him, calling him "Cam darling". She even made an obvious comment to me about how good Cameron was with his meat.'

'Oh Jen, I don't know what to say. They used to be a couple about a year ago. I can try to find out what's happening, though.'

'I wouldn't worry. I shouldn't bring Cameron into the picture. Sorting out my own issues is my priority. When I'm ready to be in a relationship, I can take it from there.'

'What are we going to do about Mark, though? He knows where you are. Do you think he'll hurt you?'

'I don't know anymore. I'm going to see how he reacts to the message I've sent. It'll either draw him out, or hopefully—he'll give up. I suspect it'll draw him out, so I need to think about what I should do if I come face to face with him.'

After a moment of stunned silence, Sarah said, 'I think you should tell Cameron. He's tough—he could take Mark on if he shows his face and teach that arsehole a lesson. You shouldn't be dealing with this on your own.'

'Sarah, don't you dare say anything to him. I need to sort this out on my own, okay?'

'Only if you promise to keep me up to date with what's going on. Someone needs to be looking out for you.'

'Deal. Enough about my problems. Now tell me all about you and James.'

'There isn't much to say. I'm no closer to getting in his pants again.'

'Again? So, you've already been there?'

'Yeah, a few weeks ago, we finally acted on our desires. It was great, but he's been weird since. I'm not sure what's going on, but I intend to find out. Wish me luck.'

'Ha! I knew something had happened between you two. I hope it works out okay, Sarah. Good luck.'

Imogen felt better after talking to Sarah. It convinced her she needed to face Mark. Then she heard her phone ping.

See you soon, Imogen

CHAPTER 26

Imogen got an earlier train to London than James and Cameron. They had to finish some work before going to the hotel to prepare.

'You need longer to get ready anyway, Imogen—you ladies always take ages.' James had laughed.

As she found her seat, she felt anxious. The knot in her stomach had been there all day. Mark's last text message was brief, but it played on her mind all week, and she suspected that was what he wanted. She wouldn't risk running into him if she went straight to the hotel, the venue for the event.

James' conversation with her this morning replayed in her mind.

'Imogen, Cameron has asked that you get a taxi from the station to the hotel. He doesn't feel comfortable with you taking a tube on your own in London. Don't shoot the messenger. I'm not getting involved in your personal business, but I agree. Based on what I know, I'd feel better knowing you got there safely.'

Imogen had agreed. It brought her comfort to know that Cameron was still concerned about her. Maybe there was hope for them, or perhaps he was just a gentleman and would have done the same for anyone in her position.

The taxi pulled up under the impressive glass canopy of the Berkeley Hotel. The driver helped Imogen with her overnight bag and dress carrier.

'Let me take this for you, Madame. This way, please, and welcome to the Berkeley.' Imogen thanked the taxi driver and followed the doorman into the hotel. He hung her things on the luggage trolley and pointed her in the direction of the reception desk.

'Good afternoon. Are you checking in?'

'Yes, please. I have a room booked under Imogen Taylor with Spencer & Black Associates.'

'Ah yes, here we are. You've been upgraded to the Grand Terrace Suite.'

'Oh no, I should be in a normal room.'

'Let me check. A Cameron Black has requested the room upgrade for you. No mistake, ma'am. Well, I'd say someone is looking after you, Ms Taylor.'

'Wow. Well, that's marvellous, thank you.'

'Here's your key card. Please follow Spencer—he'll take you to your room and show you where everything is. If you need anything while you're here, please call down. Enjoy your stay and have a great evening.'

'Thank you.'

Spencer pointed out the minibar and showed her how everything worked, from the television to the air conditioning. She tipped him and closed the door.

She wondered what it meant that Cameron had upgraded her room. Did he expect anything in return, or was he feeling guilty about being with Fran? She was confused and stressed. She couldn't think but had three hours before meeting James, so she ran a hot bath.

The bathroom was luxurious. The roll-top bath was large enough for Imogen to be submerged. As she sank into the beautifully- fragranced water, she felt the tension melt away. She closed her eyes and let the gentle ripples of the water soothe her. Imogen washed her hair and wrapped herself up in the complimentary fluffy towelling robe. Feeling like a new woman, she walked barefoot across the solid wood floors, popped the cork on a bottle of chilled champagne and poured a glass.

She looked out of the glass doors that led to a terrace, and it was warm enough to go out. She admired the astounding view of St Paul's. The air was cool, but it felt cleansing to breathe it in so deep. When her lungs filled with the familiar scent of London, she had hope for the future. She'd put her feelings for Cameron to the back of her mind tonight. She'd earned a place at the table and was going to enjoy it. Mark and Cameron will still be there tomorrow. Tonight was for her.

The butterflies increased with every passing second that Imogen was in the elevator. She took a few steadying breaths as the doors opened, and when she stepped out, she locked eyes with Cameron. Her step faltered—he was magnificent in a tuxedo that looked like it came straight out of *Casino Royale*. She recognised the polished black dress shoes from the movie too. The tuxedo fitted him perfectly, showcasing his toned body, and she noticed his bow tie was the same navy-blue silk as her dress. He stood with one hand in his pocket, making him look straight out of a high-end fashion magazine. Imogen ambled over so that she could enjoy the moment—her plans to have a man-free evening were going to be hard to achieve.

CHAPTER 27

'Cameron, Imogen is on her way down. I've just sent her a text, and I said we'd meet here. I've checked out the seating plan, and we're not with Fran, so that's one awkward situation avoided. Please don't get weird tonight. We're here to network, not to sort out relationship issues. Got it?'

'Fuck off, James. Trust me—I'm already exercising more control than I'm capable of.'

His eyes were fixed on the elevator. He felt like he couldn't breathe. Everything had stopped around him, and he couldn't hear what James was saying.

He took her in, and his eyes swept from her head to her toes. She was breathtaking in her floor-length, navy-blue silk dress. The plunging cowl neck showcased the plump curves of her breasts. The dress was fitted to her waist where it then flowed out, and the back trailed along the floor. As she walked towards them, he caught sight of her heeled shoes decorated with diamante, which caught the light. He compared them to Cinderella's glass slippers.

Her hair sat in waves around her face, with one side tucked behind her ear so that he could see the understated diamond-drop earring. He noticed her necklace, which sat like a choker around her neck, with the same pear-shaped stone. It wasn't until she was standing with them that he realised the necklace was hanging down her back, where a larger pear-shaped stone weighed it down and held it in place at the base of her spine. Cameron took a sudden breath—the dress was backless, and it appeared to knot and flow into the fishtail at the bottom. He wanted to take her there and then. It would make him the proudest man in the room to have her on his arm and show her off as his. This was going to be a challenging evening.

'Cameron, are you there?' James was clicking his fingers in front of his face.

'Sorry, I was miles away.' Cameron pulled himself together. 'Hi Imogen, you're looking stunning.'

'Thank you.'

'You're welcome.' He locked eyes with her and felt he was staring into her soul.

'Shall we get this show on the road?' James' interruption provided relief to the awkward conversation.

'Yep, right, okay.' Cameron's brain was fried. He needed to get his shit together.

They exchanged pleasantries and made their way to their table, grabbing a glass of champagne from the passing waiter. James saw someone he knew, leaving Cameron and Imogen alone.

Imogen broke the silence. 'You look very handsome tonight. I'm getting strong Bond vibes.'

'Yes, well, I must confess the suit was inspired by our movie night. I bought it before you ended us. I figured I may as well still wear it.'

'Well, it's appreciated. And thank you for the room upgrade. I'm a bit confused as to why you did it, though.'

'You asked me to give you space, and you asked for time. I can give you those, but I can also show you what you'd get if you were with me. Also, I wanted you to be in the room next to me. Caveman instinct to protect you—can't do anything about that, I'm afraid.'

'I'm grateful for that, thank you. Why do all this for me, though, when you're with Fran?'

'I tried to explain that to you after lunch. We're not together. We dated a year ago, and it got too much. I ended it, and she went bat-shit crazy. We got it sorted, though, and moved on. James wants me to keep her sweet so we can extend the contract. He's pimping me out.' Cameron reached out and stroked his thumb across her cheek. She leant into his palm, desperate to deepen the touch.

'I haven't touched her, Imogen—please believe me. I'm waiting for you. Are you ever going to tell me what's going on with you?'

'I just want to get through tonight and have a great time. I don't want my issues to ruin everything.'

'Tell me. I can help you.'

Imogen was tempted to tell him everything. She felt like she had the weight of the world on her shoulders and was desperate to offload it.

'Right, guys—let's sit down. The awards are about to start.' James had great timing—he'd bought her more time.

Cameron whispered into Imogen's ear, 'This conversation isn't over. I will find out what's happening.'

Her skin crackled all over as he ran his hand down her exposed back.

CHAPTER 28

Spencer & Black Associates won the award for innovation in design. Imogen couldn't take her eyes off Cameron as he and James collected the award. His stride was confident, and he oozed power. She noticed he had another admirer. Fran was sitting at the table in the row in front of them, her eyes tracking Cameron. Imogen couldn't blame her but wondered if this woman, for whom she had the utmost respect and admiration, would be an issue. She hoped not but was wary of her.

After a short Thank You speech, James and Cameron returned to the table, stopping to shake the hands of well-wishers on their way. As they passed Fran, she seized the opportunity to embrace Cameron.

Imogen could see words being exchanged but couldn't make them out. She looked on, astonished, as Fran leaned in for a kiss. Her lips missed their mark as Cameron turned his head, forcing a platonic kiss on the cheek.

'Fuck this, I'm not playing games anymore, and I'm certainly not losing Cameron to his ex.'

'Did you see that?' Cameron sat down and turned to talk to

Imogen.

'Yes, I did. Don't worry—I also saw you turn your head, full-on snog averted.' She reached under the tablecloth and squeezed Cameron's thigh as she whispered in his ear, 'May the best woman win.'

'It won't be a fair fight, Imogen—you've already won.'

After the awards were announced, they worked the room and networked until the party got into full swing. As at a wedding, the tables were moved to the sides of the exquisite ballroom to reveal a dance floor. This was where everyone could let their hair down and celebrate a year of success.

'Cam, darling, will you join me for a dance?' Fran made a beeline for Cameron. She stood before them dressed in a beautiful green, floor-length dress covered in sequins. It was off-the-shoulder and showcased her porcelain skin while her auburn hair framed her face in waves. Around her neck was a stunning silver choker studded with emeralds.

Cameron looked at Imogen for reassurance and an answer. Imogen understood he needed to keep Fran sweet until she had signed the contract, and she took solace knowing that he hadn't forgotten she was there. Imogen gave him a smile and a slight nod.

Cameron turned back to Fran, 'Of course, Fran—it would be my pleasure.' Before he walked away, he squeezed Imogen's shoulder to reassure her.

Imogen watched them walk arm in arm to the dance floor. The way he moved impressed her—he had a natural rhythm, which she supposed she should've already known. She could tell he was careful where he placed his hands, his touch light.

'Hello, you're far too beautiful to be watching. Would you

care for a dance? I'm Simon, by the way.' Imogen was so distracted watching Cameron dance she hadn't seen the tall, handsome dark-haired man approach her.

'That would be lovely, thank you—I'm Imogen.' Simon took her hand and led her to the dance floor.

Simon was an interior designer for a company based in London. He was easy to talk to, and Imogen had a great time. He told her that if she ever wanted to move back to London, she should drop him a line and send her CV. Imogen could see from the corner of her eye that Cameron was watching her like a hawk. She smiled—she liked the idea of making him jealous.

'Excuse me, would you mind if I cut in, and may I introduce you to Fran? I'm sure she'd love to dance.'

Simon got the message. He reminded Imogen to look him up if she was in London and took Fran's hand.

'Nicely done there, Cameron.'

'I couldn't take it anymore, and Fran thought it was hilarious. We had a good chat while we danced. She knows I have something with you and is happy for me. I can't promise she won't try and have some fun with you, though. I just hope she signs the contract, or James will kill me.'

Cameron took Imogen in a close embrace—he ran his hands down her back, sending those familiar sparks flying. With one hand on her back and the other in a formal hold, he guided her around the dance floor with ease. He was adept at leading, and he rested his cheek against hers when the tempo of the next song slowed. Imogen closed her eyes—she wanted to commit every detail to memory. She felt the warmth of Cameron's hand on her back. His hard chest was pressed against hers, and she was sure she could feel his heartbeat. She put her arm under his jacket so she could stroke his back and run her fingers along the curves of his muscles. Everything in that moment was perfect, and she felt like she was in a fairytale dancing with her prince. The sound of Cameron's voice brought her attention back to the room.

'Shall we find somewhere quiet to have a chat? I think we need to work out what's going on, and you need to be honest with me and tell me what happened.'

'How about my room? Thanks to a very generous man, I have a beautiful room with a terrace.'

'Perfect.' Cameron led Imogen away.

By the time they reached her room, she was queasy with anxiety. She didn't know how Cameron would react, but he was right. She needed to tell him everything because keeping it to herself wasn't working out for anyone.

Imogen led Cameron through to the terrace. She noticed earlier that the table had a built-in fire pit and was looking forward to trying it out. As if reading her mind, Cameron lit the flame. Instant warmth radiated out and created a romantic glow.

'What would you like to drink? I think the minibar has got just about everything in it.'

'I could do with a brandy—I think I saw some earlier.'

'Good idea, I'll join you. Don't go anywhere.'

Cameron reappeared with two large glasses. He'd also undone his bow tie so that the loose ends hung around his neck—he looked stunning. He sat next to Imogen and turned to face her.

'Tell me everything, Imogen—what is going on?'

Imogen needed Dutch courage. The alcohol warmed her as she swallowed.

'Okay, but promise not to lose your shit or interrupt me? And don't tell me something I already know—I should have told you sooner—so let's move on from that.'

'Understood, now get on with it.'

'Do you remember I told you about the song Mark used to play to me?'

'Yeah, I looked it up—it's not one I plan to listen to again.'

'Well, it came on the jukebox when I was in the pub that Saturday with Sarah and Jess a few weeks ago when you were out with your mates. It scared me. It was the first time I'd heard it since I left him. I needed to get out and get home, but Sarah thought it was best if Seth, the barman, walked us back to my place. He was great and checked that the windows and doors were secure before he left us.'

Imogen had to stop Cameron from having an outburst, so she placed her finger on his lips.

'I know—before you say it—I should have phoned you, so park it. I brushed it off as an overreaction and got on with my weekend. On Monday, a red envelope was on my desk when I got to the office. It just had Imogen written on it, no address or anything, so I assumed you'd left me a love letter. It was a card from Mark. He asked if I liked the song. Then he said I'd been cheating on him, and he was going to make you lose your head—he was threatening to hurt you, or worse.'

Cameron clenched his jaw. 'Carry on.'

'He told me to end it with you. I was going to ignore him, but then I found out about Seth being beaten up, and I knew it was Mark because he told him to leave me alone. I couldn't risk you getting hurt. Part of me also thought it was too soon for us. I've fallen for you—big time, and I've never felt like this before. It scares the shit out of me. I can't get hurt again, especially while I'm trying to get away from Mark, and then there was the risk of you getting hurt.

'I decided the best thing to do for everyone was to end it with you while I sort my head out and somehow work out what to do about Dickhead. I may have made things worse, though.'

Cameron looked at her with a worried expression.

'What did you do, Imogen?'

She took another gulp of her brandy.

'I decided enough was enough. I sent him a message to say I wasn't playing his games anymore, it was over, and he was to leave me alone, or I'd go to the police and ruin his career. All I got in response was, see you soon.'

Cameron downed the rest of his brandy. He was silent for an eternity, his jaw clenching.

'Thank you for telling me the truth, Imogen. I appreciate it.' He pinched the bridge of his nose in frustration.

'I have some questions. How the fuck did he get a card hand-delivered to your desk in the office?' Cameron was trying to remain calm.

'I figured he sent it in another envelope addressed to a department like HR—you know, something generic.'

'Imogen, that makes no sense. Did you ask Sam to review the CCTV footage so that you could see if he got inside the building?'

'Oh, no. I didn't. I guess I didn't want to alert anyone.' Cameron stared at her.

'It sounds ridiculous now I'm saying it out loud to you.'

'Yeah, but at least you've told me. I'm going to message Sam and get him to review the tapes as soon as he can and try to work out how Mark got in.' Cameron tapped out a text message before putting his phone away.

'Imogen, you need to know that I don't care if some wanker

threatens me. It's about time he picked on someone his own size—I suspect I'm the bigger man. He can't hurt me, but I'll fucking kill him if he comes anywhere near you. Don't underestimate how I feel for you and the lengths I'll go to to protect you.' He paused and smiled at Imogen. 'Not everyone would bribe Sarah to find out the colour of your dress so that my bow tie would match.'

'Oh Cameron, that's adorable, you smooth bugger.'

'I know, I can't help it. Anyway, you say he beat up a barman? Is there any proof?'

'No, the CCTV footage didn't get an image of his face, and he attacked from behind, so Seth didn't see him either. This is the issue, Cameron. All I have are some text messages from him. They tell me he'll prove his love to me. There's no evidence that he attacked Seth, just a threatening card, but not enough to get the police to arrest him—he didn't even sign his name. I plan to draw him out and let him make a mistake by doing something in front of people, then at least we'd have witnesses.'

'Did you keep the card?'

'Yeah, it's in my desk drawer.'

'Well, you did one thing right. I'm not sure about you using yourself as bait, though, Imogen—it's not your wisest decision. I think you've been watching too many movies.'

'All right, don't be a dick about it. I feel stupid as it is. It's a lot for me to be going through, and you fried my brain with all the mind-blowing orgasms, so technically, this is your fault.'

'I thought it would end up being my fault, and I guess I need to make it up to you. We can't do anything about this tonight, so we may as well make up for the lost time.' He took Imogen's glass out of her hand and reached up to stroke her face. He fixed her with one of his breathtaking gazes.

'Imogen Taylor, will you do me the honour of being my girl-friend, officially and without hiding it?'

A tear ran down Imogen's cheek. The weight of the world had left her shoulders. If she'd known how liberating it would feel to tell Cameron everything, she would have done it sooner. For the first time, her mind was clear, and she knew the answer to his question without a second thought.

'Nothing would make me happier.'

He brushed her tear away and ran his hands along the delicate silk of her dress. 'This dress is sexy on you. How the hell are your boobs so pert in it—they are mesmerising.'

'Built-in support, almost as amazing as a dress with pockets.'

'However much I love this dress on you, the time has come for you to get out of it. We have some catching up to do.'

They'd barely made it into the bedroom before he'd unzipped her dress, and it fell into a pool around her feet. He paused, taking a moment to admire the view. 'You are gorgeous, perfect, and you're mine.'

Imogen reached up and removed her necklace. She was standing in nothing but her sexiest pair of Rigby & Peller Italian briefs in the same navy-blue silk as her dress—and her shoes.

'Do you mind if I make a request?'

'Anything you want.'

'Keep the shoes on.'

Imogen kicked her dress to the side and wrapped her arms around his neck. Their lips crashed together as they made quick work of removing Cameron's clothes. Within seconds, he was naked and highly aroused.

Imogen's legs hit the side of the bed, and they fell to the

mattress. His hands and mouth explored her body, desperate to be reacquainted. He hastily removed her underwear, discarding it in the pile of clothes on the floor. His touch was light as he skimmed his hands across her thighs. He settled between her legs, and when he spoke, his voice was full of lust. 'I need to taste you. It's been too long.' Her breath hitched as her body remembered his touch. Her hips bucked, urging him for more, as his tongue expertly dipped and sucked. Imogen's pent-up stress melted away, and she felt like she was floating. Her body was reacting with force to everything Cameron gave her. He slipped a finger inside, sending shockwaves across her body.

'I need you now, Cameron. I need to feel you inside me.'

Cameron gave her one last lick and crawled up the bed. Resting on his forearm and leaning over her, he entered her, and in one thrust, he was deep inside her. He stilled. 'I missed you so much. I shouldn't have let you walk away. I won't make that mistake again, Imogen.'

She responded with a deep and passionate kiss and grabbed his tight buttocks to encourage him to push deeper. He made love to her, their bodies moving in sync with each other. This wasn't about passion and fulfilling a carnal need—it was about reconnecting. Instead of the intense shockwaves of pleasure pulsing through her body, Imogen felt something else—warmth spread throughout her, and her heart swelled. At that moment, she felt safe and loved.

Cameron wrapped his arm around her with their bodies connected in every way and lifted her hips to meet him. Imogen rocked her pelvis, the climax building inside her. They came together, breathless, their bodies spent.

Holding her tight and still inside her, Cameron rolled on his side. He kissed Imogen and stroked her hair from her face.

'I'm not ready to let go yet. Can we lie like this for a minute?'

'Sounds good.' 'I have no intention of letting go either.' Imogen snuggled into his arms and breathed in his scent—it brought a sense of calm.

CHAPTER 29

Song choice: Feels like home (Hannah Grace)

'What have you got for me, Sam? Can you see anything?' There was a pause while he listened to Sam.

'Fuck. So, he accessed the building, and we need to work out how. Can you cancel all the access cards, reconfigure the system and issue new cards for Monday?' Another pause. 'Thanks, Sam—we need to sort this out. It can't happen again. You need to bring in extra staff—I want someone on-site twenty-four seven. You have my authorisation to do what you need to secure the site. Thanks, Sam. I'll speak to you tomorrow. Thanks for getting onto this so quickly.'

Imogen walked into the living room to find Cameron staring out of the glass doors, his hand running through his hair. He must have gone back to his room earlier because he was wearing jeans and a T-shirt. She took a moment to admire the view.

'Hey sexy, have you been up long? What did Sam say?'

Cameron took her into his arms. He knew she'd need to be held for what he had to say.

'Hey, you. It turns out that Mark got into the building. He hand-delivered the card.'

'Oh my God. If he can get into the office, where else can he get to me?'

'Don't worry—he won't get in again. I've had the access cards cancelled. No one can get into the building until Sam issues them with a new one. We'll have a guard on-site twenty-four hours a day, so you'll be safe whenever you're in the office.

'I asked myself the same question, Imogen—if he can get into the office, he's more dangerous and desperate than we gave him credit for. I need you to know that I'm not controlling like Mark, but I don't want you to go back to your house. How do you feel about moving in with me?'

Imogen didn't know what to say—this was moving so fast. Knowing that Mark had been in her office, touched her desk, her chair and probably looked through her things made her realise how vulnerable she was. He knew which pub she went to and where her house was. It hit her how stupid and reckless she'd been.

'I think that's best, but only until this is over, obviously.'

'We'll go to yours together and pack everything you need. I'll look after you and keep you safe—that'll be the only reason I may come across as controlling or neurotic. Please, understand that these are not normal circumstances and that I'm not like Mark at all.'

'It's okay, I understand. Thank you. I appreciate everything you're doing for me. I'm just so sorry that I've brought all this mess into your life.' Imogen looked at the floor with tears forming.

Cameron tilted her head to look her in the eyes.

'Never apologise to me for this. It's not your doing. This is all down to Mark, and I'll make sure he suffers for it. I'm just thankful that you're in my life, Imogen.' Cameron kissed her on the forehead and held her tight.

'Now, let's have breakfast, then we can go home. We can fill James in on everything on the train. I feel like we ought to go to my room and use that too.' Cameron winked at Imogen. 'What do you reckon, sexy—time for a quickie at my place?'

They pulled up outside Imogen's house. Cameron went in first to make sure Mark hadn't paid her a visit. He took her suitcase down while Imogen dashed around the house, grabbing everything she needed.

'I can't forget my Kindle. That's a thought, what am I going to do about book club? Do you think it's okay for me to go this week?'

'No, I don't. Mark's been to that pub at least once and didn't think twice about beating up the barman. What do you think about having it at our place? You can invite the girls over. I can pick them up so you can have a drink, and take them home, too. I'll be the chauffeur for the evening. I promise to disappear— you won't even know I'm there.'

Imogen had heard nothing after he said our house. She loved that he called it that. It was an innocent turn of phrase that made her realise how quickly they'd become so natural together. She decided not to bring attention to it.

'I can ask them and see if they're okay with it. Thanks, Cameron, you're awesome.'

'No worries, but you have to promise to keep trying out all the new sexy stuff you're reading—that is non-negotiable.'

'Deal.'

When they arrived at his house, Cameron dashed up the stairs to make room for Imogen's things.

'I've cleared out loads of stuff and made use of the furniture in the other rooms, so there's plenty of room for you. You have a bathroom cabinet to yourself in the en-suite, so you should feel right at home. How about you unpack and get settled, and I'll make us some lunch?'

'Sounds perfect, and Cameron, thanks again for this. I am so grateful to you. I don't know how I can ever repay you, and I'll be out of your hair as soon as this gets resolved.'

'Imogen, there's no rush. Consider this your home now for as long as you want it.' He kissed her to reassure her.

Thirty minutes later, she'd unpacked, changed into comfortable loungewear and slippers, and was snuggling up next to Cameron on the kitchen sofa. They were eating homemade tomato and basil soup. It all felt so natural.

'So, what's the plan, Cameron? What do we do about Mark? I never believed I was in danger until now, and I don't know what to do about it.'

'I think it's time to take it to the police. With the CCTV footage of him getting into the office, combined with the text messages and our suspicions over Seth, we've enough to get them involved. Even if they do nothing, it'll be good to have it registered with them. A chat from them might be enough to scare Mark away.'

'Okay, I guess it wouldn't hurt.'

'I'll call them and see if they can come to the office on Monday. I can get Sam to show them the CCTV footage. Until then, we've the rest of the weekend to enjoy. I need to work out later, but I'm all yours once I've done that. Is there anything you want to do?'

'Can I watch you work out? That sounds like all the entertainment I need.'

'Dirty perv—but I like it,' Cameron took their bowls and put them in the dishwasher.

'I was thinking about your book club. What do you think about turning it into a housewarming party for you? I could cook us a nice meal and have James and Julian over. The six of us could eat, then the men can go to my bar and play some pool while you ladies talk about kinky books. I have a feeling James might appreciate a chance to see Sarah too if you know what I mean.'

'Oh, do you know something about them? I think that's a great idea. Is Julian single, as Jess is on the market?'

'Wow, this is becoming a mass-matchmaking session, but yes, he is. And all I can say is that James is keen on Sarah. What do you know?'

'Sarah is keen on James but thinks he's weird about it, so she doesn't know what's going on.'

'That's sorted then. I feel the need to do some weights and punch a bag. Do you want to join me and build some strength in those arms? Let the matchmaking begin.'

'Will it involve me taking my slippers off? I'm comfy now.'

'All right, you can keep your slippers on, but you might regret that decision when you get hot and sweaty.'

Cameron took Imogen to his home gym. She hadn't seen all

of his house yet and was surprised that the space over his garage was a gym at one end and a bar with a pool table at the other. Cameron had changed into shorts and a T-shirt. Imogen didn't think she'd get a great deal done—she was enjoying the view too much. With every punch he threw, Imogen felt the temperature of the room increase. She could see the muscles flex and his thighs tense. She didn't doubt that she was in safe hands, and, oh, how she wished those hands were all over her. She lifted Cameron's weights as a distraction from her thoughts, but he sabotaged her plan when he did some bench presses. She couldn't contain herself any longer. Ever since she had seen his bench press in the gym at work, she had fantasised about straddling him.

'You're right. I regret staying in my loungewear. I'm getting too hot, Cameron.' Imogen took the hem of her baggy jumper and pulled it over her head. She took off her slippers and lowered her jogging bottoms to the floor, stepping out of them. Cameron watched her with great interest while she removed her bra.

'There's something that I have been fantasising about since the first time I saw you in the gym at work.'

'Oh, tell me about it?'

'I'd rather show you.' Imogen removed her underwear and straddled Cameron. She kissed and sucked on his bottom lip before working her way down to his nape. She could taste the salt from his sweat, and his scent was more potent than ever. It drove her crazy—the heat and need coming from her core was too much to bear. She ground her hips against his crotch. She lifted his top and kissed his chest, working her way down. Cameron's breathing quickened when she reached the top of his shorts. She took hold of the waistband and tugged it down, releasing his hard

173

cock. Kneeling between his legs, she licked along his shaft before taking as much as she could in her mouth. Her hand grasped the base and moved in time with her head, twisting her fist as she went down on him.

'Ah fuck, Imogen, that is amazing.'

Imogen had never felt the need to please someone so much before. She wasn't used to being in charge—it made her feel empowered, and it turned her on. She looked into his eyes and raised her body. With one hand wrapped around his length, she lowered herself onto him. She tipped her head back and groaned in pleasure as the position allowed him to penetrate deeper. Leaning back to place her hands on his knees, she ground against him. The combination of Cameron filling her and the friction on her clit was driving her to the edge. She leaned forward to enhance the pressure on her sex and took hold of the bar over Cameron's head. Cameron caressed her waist while her pace quickened, his hands guiding her. A sheen of perspiration covered her and mixed with his.

'Take what you need, Imogen, do what makes you feel good.' He understood that this was about Imogen taking control. He understood her so well.

She felt the pressure build, and within seconds she was climaxing. She rode every wave until they subsided and left her spent. Cameron sat up, wrapped her legs around his hips, and stood with ease. Imogen felt the wall at her back as Cameron took her in a passionate kiss. Now it was his turn. He rammed into her, fisting his hand in her hair and groaning with every thrust. The impact on Imogen's swollen clit sent her over the edge. She cried out as a second orgasm ripped through her. Cameron let out a groan as he came with force. As they tried to catch their breath,

Imogen released her legs. When Cameron pulled out of her, his come glistened on her upper thigh.

'Fucking hell, that is the horniest thing I've seen in a long time. It's enough to make me hard again.' He reached for his towel and wiped her clean. 'Feel free to join me for a workout whenever you like, although best keep that for the home gym.' Cameron kissed her before tucking his firm cock into his shorts. 'Shower time?'

CHAPTER 30

'So, do we drive to work in the same car, or are we going separately?'

'May as well go together. There's no sense in both of us driving. I feel overprotective and would rather take you.'

'Aren't you worried about people seeing me walk in with you?'

'Nope, I'm looking forward to showing you off as mine and not hiding anymore. Are you okay with walking in with the boss?'

'Oh, Mr Big Boss Man, I'm living every girl's fantasy. It's okay with me, but I worry people will think I'm sleeping with you to further my career.'

'Don't worry about that, you've made a great impression on everyone, even Fran liked you, so I don't think you've anything to worry about. It's cool, sweet cheeks. Who can blame you for sleeping with me? I'm hot property, baby.'

'You are so cheesy.' Imogen was laughing—she could get used to feeling this happy. She just hoped it would last.

Cameron kissed her in the car park. 'Don't worry, I'll be

professional in the office, no public displays of affection around colleagues. But I'm going to get what I can when I can.'

Sam met them as they walked to the office.

'Good morning, Mr Black, Miss Taylor. I have the CCTV footage on a memory stick, and here are your new access cards.'

'Thanks, Sam. We're going to see if the police will come in today, so I'll let you know when I need their copy of the footage.'

'I can sort that for your Mr Black. I have a friend on the Force, so I can make sure they come today. Leave it with me.'

'That's great, thank you.'

'Thanks, Sam. I appreciate what you're doing. See you later.'

'Goodbye, Miss Taylor. Don't worry—we'll keep you safe.'

'Hey Imogen, oh, and morning Cameron, how are you two this morning?'

'We're good, thank you, Sarah,' Cameron turned to Imogen with a big smile on his face.

'I'll make you a coffee and leave it on your desk as I need to speak to James. You fill Sarah in on what's going on.'

'Okay, I'll see you later.'

Sarah waited until Cameron was out of earshot.

'OMG, did you two come in together, as in together? And what's going on with the access cards? Tell me all, Jen.'

'Let's do lunch so I can fill you in on all the details.' Imogen gave Sarah an update and asked how she felt about having dinner at Cameron's on Tuesday.

'That sounds like fun. I'm sure as soon as I mention to Jess that there'll be another single man there, she'll be up for it. It'll be nice to spend time with James too. Are you sure Cameron doesn't mind driving us? We can get a taxi—it's not a problem.'

'I'll ask, but it was his idea, so I'm sure he'd rather drive than have you pay for a taxi. He's such a gentleman.'

'Okay, let me know, and I'll see you for the juicy details at lunchtime. And Jen, I'm glad you told Cameron. He'll sort this out for you.'

'Thanks, Sarah, a problem shared is a problem halved.'

As promised, Sam arranged for the police to speak to Imogen and Cameron that morning. They viewed the CCTV footage with Sam before Sarah took them up to see Imogen in Cameron's office.

'Good morning, I'm Detective Sergeant Abbott, and this is Detective Constable Miller. We understand that you're having some issues with an ex-boyfriend, is that right, Miss Taylor?'

Detective Sergeant Abbott was a tall, slender male with light brown hair cut short. In contrast, Detective Constable Miller was a shorter woman with wild blond curls in a ponytail.

'Yes, that's right. I moved here to get away from Mark, but he keeps sending me creepy text messages. He broke into the office to leave me a card—here, I have it for you.' Imogen handed it over.

'I understand that Mr Briggs, our security guard, has given you the CCTV footage of Mark getting into the building. For the record, he misappropriated the access card. We're trying to find out how he got hold of one. Imogen thinks he was responsible for the attack on a barman recently.'

The police asked further questions and gathered all the information on Mark that they could. Constable Miller took Imogen's phone to see the text messages and connected it to her laptop to download them.

'We'll look into this and compare images of your CCTV footage with what we have. You've made the right decision moving in with Mr Black. You shouldn't be alone until we get to the bottom of this. We'll get in touch with Mr Edwards for questioning, and we'll keep you updated. In the meantime, if you hear from him, please tell us straight away.' Detective Sergeant Abbott handed Imogen a card with his contact details on it.

Cameron showed them out and returned to his office to talk to Imogen. He sat down on the edge of his desk, exhaled, and pulled her into a hug between his legs.

'How're you doing?'

She sighed heavily into his shoulder. 'I just want this to be over so I can live my life. I'm not hiding away. All my hopes are on the police scaring him off. I'm done with letting him win.'

'Just don't do anything stupid—you don't want to get hurt.'

'I'm supposed to be going to London with the girls on Friday night. We've planned it for ages, and I need a night of fun. Do you know how long it's been since I did that?'

'I'm not sure it's a good idea.'

'Cameron, it's been years since I last went out, and he'd be crazy to come near me now the police are involved. He's stopped me from doing so much, and I won't miss out on any more of my life.'

Cameron pinched the bridge of his nose. Imogen knew he was trying to calm himself down.

'Okay, how about a compromise? I have a friend who owns a members-only club in London. I'll have a word with him, get you on the list, and make sure he knows not to let Mark in. Promise me you'll stick to that club. I'll pay the tab as a sweetener.'

'I think that's reasonable, Dom Pérignon all night, then?'

Cameron raised an eyebrow.

'I'm joking, Cam. I won't let you pay.'

'Drink all the champagne you like, as long as you stay in that club. This makes me nervous. I don't like it. I'm not promising that I won't make sure I'm close by. If you need anything, call, and I'll be there.

'I love that you're finding a workaround for us. I promise to be sensible.' She kissed him and walked out before he changed his mind.

Imogen got on with her morning. She went for lunch with Sarah and filled her in on the details before discussing their Friday night plans. Sarah was excited. She'd heard of the club they were going to and couldn't wait.

'I'd never get into that club. This is going to be fun, Imogen. Cameron is the best.'

'Ha, I guess he is. He's the best I've ever had.'

'Down, girl. We'd better get back to work. Tomorrow night will be good. I've never seen Cameron's house. I bet it's swanky.'

'Have you ever seen James' place Sarah, wink-wink?'

'OMG, Jen, that's enough. Tomorrow night might be the lucky night?'

'Fingers crossed. Do you think Jess will like Julian?'

'I don't know. I reckon he must be a top bloke if he's related to Cameron, so I see no reason why she wouldn't.'

'If I didn't know you better, I'd think you have a crush on Cameron.'

'Ha. There was a time when I'd willingly have tapped that, but not now. I've got my heart set on someone else.'

'Good to know.'

They parted ways in reception, and Imogen got back to work after grabbing a juice from the kitchen.

'Hey Imogen, how're you doing?'

'Hi, James. I'm okay, thanks. Are you looking forward to to-morrow night?'

'I get the feeling there's some matchmaking going on, but yes, I'm looking forward to it, especially as Cam's cancelled on me for tonight.'

'Oh, sorry, is that my fault?'

'Nah, don't worry about it. I think he's enjoying having some-one to go home to. I haven't seen him this happy since his rugby team came top of the league. Anyway, I came over to let you know Fran has signed the contract and is sending it over. I sus-pect she knows Cameron is off the market, so there was no point in going to the effort of coming here. Winners all round.'

'That's good to hear. I love her designs—I'd feel terrible if we lost the contract. So now you don't need to pimp Cameron out in the future?'

James burst out laughing.

'That's true. Although I'm not promising anything—he comes in handy.'

James walked back to his office, chuckling. He was in good spirits after hearing the news.

'Well done, Imogen. I hear you impressed Fran Divino. I hope you're going to celebrate tonight?'

'Thanks, Lucy. I'm not sure. I'll see if Cameron wants to do anything.'

'Oh, is there something you're not telling me?'

Imogen gave Lucy an overview of what had been going on and that she'd moved in with Cameron.

'He insisted. We've only just started seeing each other, but he's worried about what Mark might do. I'm sleeping better knowing I'm not on my own.'

181

'God, Imogen, that must be scary. I'd no idea it was so bad. Weirdly though, I guess it's flattering having someone go crazy over you. I wish someone would care about me enough to fight for me.'

'Be careful what you wish for, Lucy. Is it not going well with Paul?'

'I don't think so. He's gone distant, and he's preoccupied with something. He tells me work is crazy, but I don't know if I believe him. I'll see what he's like this weekend, but if things don't improve, I think I'll end it.'

'I'm sorry to hear that. I wouldn't wish what I'm going through on anyone. Although, the Cameron part I can recommend. Don't worry, we'll find you a great guy. Don't lose hope.'

Cameron was at Imogen's desk at five o'clock to take her home. As soon as they were out the door, he had his arm around her. They arrived home in no time—she could get used to being driven around.

'I forgot to mention yesterday that James is picking Sarah and Jess up on his way over in his taxi. You know what he's like. Julian's going to drive over from the restaurant as he's setting up for the evening.'

'That makes sense. Maybe James having a drink inside him will loosen him up around Sarah. Can I do anything to help with the food? It smells amazing, by the way.'

'No, don't worry, it's all ready. I'm doing my take on paella— it'll be easy, one big pan, and we can help ourselves.'

'Yummy, will it have a crusty bottom?'

'Is that how you like your bottoms? Interesting.'

'You know what I mean.' Imogen threw a tea towel at him. A rush of emotions hit her. She felt comfortable around him—and laughter came quickly.

'God, do you know I don't remember ever being this happy. Thank you for everything. I feel like you've saved me, Cameron.'

He stopped what he was doing and wrapped her in his arms.

'You came along at the right time for me, too. We've saved each other.' He gazed into her eyes, but the sound of the doorbell broke the moment.

CHAPTER 31

'Hey Jen, these are for you.' Sarah and Jess brought a bottle of white wine and a beautiful bunch of flowers. Imogen inhaled the scent of blush roses, chrysanthemums and eucalyptus.

'These are beautiful, thanks, ladies. Come on through.'

James was ahead of them and handed Cameron a crate of real ale.

'Here you go, chap. Is that your paella I can smell?'

'Cheers, James. Yep, it'll be another twenty minutes. Do you want to help yourself? There's beer in the fridge if you want it. Ladies, what can I get you to drink?'

Julian arrived as everyone had a drink in hand.

'Julian, I'd like to introduce you to Imogen.'

'Hi Imogen, it's nice to meet you. I've heard a lot about you.' Julian leant in and kissed Imogen on each cheek.

'Oh God, all good, I hope. It's a shame you weren't working when Cam brought me to your restaurant—it was fantastic, by the way.'

Imogen raked her eyes over Julian. She could tell he and

Cameron were related. He was as tall as Cameron and had the same strong bone structure. He had lighter hair, though—it was more dirty-blond, wavy, and longer on top. They had the same dark brown eyes. He looked after himself. His biceps were straining in his white shirt, and she could see the outline of some impressive pecs. Cameron's family had good genes. She was fortunate to be in a room with three men to rival any male model.

Imogen introduced Julian to Sarah and Jess. From the way he blushed when he kissed Jess, she figured he was interested. She looked over at Cameron and raised her eyebrows—he returned the gesture with a wink.

'Right then, you lot, dinner's ready. Do you want to go to the dining room, and I'll bring it through? Imogen, can you give me a hand?'

The centrepiece of the dining room was a chunky, reclaimed wood table surrounded by tan leather chairs. It was warm but masculine with natural wood furniture like Cameron's office. He and Imogen came in, and everyone took their seats with a large pan of paella, fried padrón peppers sprinkled with salt and a basket of warm crusty bread.

'Thank you for having us over. This smells amazing.' Jess was sitting next to Julian, who was serving her paella.

'You're very welcome. We're glad you could all make it.'

'What are the peppers? I haven't seen them before.'

'They are padrón peppers fried in oil with salt. They're a favourite of mine and come from northern Spain, and they're not all hot. They say that one in every ten will be hot, but I've found it's less than that, so consider yourself lucky if you get a spicy one.'

Julian reached for the bowl and picked one out.

'Here you go, Jess. Try this one.' He looked her in the eyes while she took the pepper in her mouth and bit it right up to the stalk.

'That is delicious—but not a hot one. I like this game. I'm going to pick one out for you.'

They passed the bowl around the table while they dished up mounds of paella.

'Sarah, try this one.' James picked a light green one. 'I have a good feeling about this.'

'Oh no, it's a hot one. Blimey, that is so hot.' Sarah downed her glass of white wine while James laughed.

'Looks like you've picked a hot one there, James.' Cameron was laughing, but everyone caught the double entendre. He raised his eyebrows at James.

James reached under the table and squeezed Sarah's leg. 'I picked a good one, didn't I?'

'I have to say, Cameron, you've got the perfect crusty bottom,' Imogen exclaimed, much to everyone's amusement.

'Cheers, Jen, that's not the most flattering compliment I've ever received, but I'll take it.' He reached over and kissed Imogen.

'All right, you two, get a room.'

The meal continued in high spirits—the wine and beer were flowing.

'Julian, can I get you anything else to drink? I think I've some more alcohol-free beer in the fridge.'

'Cheers, Cam. I'll get it, don't worry.' Julian went to grab a beer.

'So, girls, tell me about the book club. What are you reading?' James was intrigued—he'd heard about their book club from

Cameron, who was enjoying it by all accounts. He hoped Sarah might want to try out some scenes with him if he played his cards right.

'There isn't a great deal to say. We read trashy novels as an excuse to meet up in the pub once a week. Although, I could get used to meeting at Cameron's house for a lush meal.'

'That can be arranged, Sarah—you ladies are always welcome. I think on that note, we'll shoot some pool and talk shit while you girls do much the same, but without the pool. Hun, I've lit the fire in the living room if you want to sit in comfort.' Cameron kissed the top of Imogen's head as he left with James. They met up with Julian in the doorway.

Two squidgy sofas faced each other in the living room, with a wooden coffee table in the middle. A fire was roaring in an open fireplace made of stone at one end. Floor lamps ensured that the room was lit with a delicate glow.

'Cameron has done an excellent job with this place. Are you loving being here, Jen?'

'Yeah, I am, Sarah. I feel like I'm home—I settled in straight away. It's scary—I wonder what's going to happen when this shit with Mark is over. Will I want to move back to my place? Will Cam want me to move out? I'm worried that I won't want to leave, and I didn't move out here to depend on another man.'

'I wouldn't worry about it, Imogen. I've never met Cameron before tonight, but from what Sarah tells me, I'd say you've met The One for sure. You're perfect for each other, and it helps that he's bloody gorgeous. So, what's going on with your ex? Sarah mentioned you had to call the police?'

Imogen gave Jess an update on what was happening.

'I haven't heard from the police yet, but I guess they need a day or two to review the evidence before speaking to Mark. It's a waiting game. I won't let it get in the way of our night out. First, the chances of bumping into Mark are low. Second, Cameron has sorted us VIP entry into his mate's club. The doormen know Mark's name and know not to let him in. It's been years since I went out in London and had a good time. It'll be a good night.'

'What are we doing about getting home?'

'Cameron's offered to arrange for a driver to pick us up, so we won't need to worry about getting the last train. I think he knew not to offer to pick us up. That would be a step too far.'

'Maybe we could invite the boys? I wouldn't mind.' Jess looked sheepish.

Sarah turned to Jess. 'Oh really, does someone have a crush on Julian?'

'Do you blame me? He's gorgeous.'

'So, hang on, you and Cam are madly in love—I want to get into James' pants, and you want to get it on with Julian? So why the bloody hell are we sitting here under the pretence of talking about fictional sexy characters when we could be with real-life ones?'

'That's a good point. Shall we join them?' Jess was already standing up.

'Thank you for tonight. I've had a fantastic time. I'm glad I got to meet Julian—he's great.'

Cameron and Imogen tidied up after everyone had left. She snuggled in Cameron's arms. 'You and Julian are very close, aren't you?'

'Yeah, we're close. He's more like the brother I never had than a cousin. We went to school together and got drunk for the first time at the same party. We've got each other's back—that's why it was a no-brainer that I went into business with him at the restaurant.'

'I think it's safe to say Jess likes him. It's been a successful night for matchmaking.'

Cameron sang, *Love, is in the air,* and looked down into Imogen's eyes.

'I've had a great night. It feels good having you here. It's a shame it's not under better circumstances, but I want you to know I'm glad you're here.' Cupping her rear, he pulled her closer. He leisurely traced a finger along her collarbone until reaching the strap of her delicate lace nightdress. Easing the strap down her shoulder, he released her breast. He sucked her nipple, making Imogen release an encouraging groan of pleasure.

She pressed herself against his body, greedy for more. Taking her cue, he lifted the hem of her nightdress and moved over her, entering her. They gasped together.

'You were made for me.'

Cameron thrust his hips, his slow and deliberate movements driving her crazy.

'Cameron, I'm going to come. It feels too good.'

He grabbed her arse, lifting her hips to achieve the perfect angle. Within seconds Imogen was gasping his name and arching her back, the orgasm rippling through her with every thrust. Cameron kept up the pace and moved to his knees.

Imogen watched as he stretched out to reach the drawer in the bedside table. 'Time for round two.'

He thrust hard and circled Imogen's clit with the vibrator. She could see him in all his glory at this angle—strong, muscular, and virile. She thrust her hips to meet his, taking him deeper and increasing the pressure of the vibrator. The familiar sensation of warmth spreading from her core made her desperate, her hands clawing at the bedsheets. She was chasing another orgasm and could tell it would blow her mind. Cameron saw she was getting close—he increased his tempo and drove into her with precision. They came together, crying out each other's names, barely able to breathe. He collapsed onto her, trailing kisses along her collarbone.

'You're incredible. Do you know that?'

'Thank you. You're not too bad yourself.'

'Are you talking to me or BOB?'

'Lunatic. You, of course.'

Cameron pulled her close, her back pressed against his chest. She went to sleep with a smile on her face. She felt like she'd never have another nightmare while she was in his arms.

CHAPTER 32

'Are you serious? I don't know how to take this. Should I be worried that he's going to come for me?' Imogen received a call from Detective Sergeant Miller. She took it downstairs to be out of earshot of her colleagues. She had her head in her hands on one of the Divino sofas.

'I'm sorry we couldn't keep him in custody any longer, Miss Taylor. We had to release him after questioning since there wasn't enough hard evidence to charge him with anything. The CCTV from the attack doesn't show his face, and he has a strong alibi for his whereabouts. We've issued him with a harassment order, which he's signed. If he contacts you again or comes near you, you need to call us straight away to arrest him. If there are any further developments, we'll be in touch, but please call us if anything occurs going forward. I'm sorry there's nothing more we can do at this stage.'

Imogen hung up, her head still in her hands, wondering what she would do.

'Imogen, are you okay?' Cameron came downstairs, a look of concern on his face.

'That was the police. They've let Mark off with a harassment order. They said there isn't enough evidence to charge him. Hopefully, the order is enough to keep him away from me. I guess I just have to wait and see if he does anything. I don't know how much more of this I can take.'

'You're not alone. You have me now, and I'm strong enough for both of us.' Cameron crouched in front of her. 'A beautiful and intelligent lady told me I have sexy shoulders, so how about I carry all of this on them for you?'

That brought a smile to her face.

'Thank you, Cameron. I don't know what I'd do without you.'

'Well, you never need to find out, I promise.' Cameron took a seat next to her and put his arm around her. 'I think it's time you moved on, Imogen. I agree you need to live your life—we have to find a way that means you're safe. We'll have a chat tonight, okay?'

'Yeah, okay. I guess I'd better get back to work. James mentioned a new job coming in, and I need to grill Sarah about what happened after everyone left. That'll take my mind off things.'

'Tell me the gossip later. I don't want to hear anything about girl code.' Cameron made air quotes with his fingers.

'Only if you promise to do the same with the info you get out of James and Julian.'

'Deal. I'll see you later. If you need anything, shout.' Cameron gave her a quick kiss and squeezed her leg in a sign of reassurance.

The rest of the morning passed in a blur. Imogen didn't get the chance to see Sarah until she bumped into her, grabbing a juice from the fridge.

'Hey, Jen. Is there any update?'

Imogen brought Sarah up to speed on what the police said

before confiding in her. 'Cameron thinks it's time to move on. We haven't been together long. He wants to talk to me about it tonight. I'm worried he's going to make me move back home. I don't know if my feelings are so strong because he swooped in and rescued me, but I can't imagine not waking up to him every day.'

'I don't think he'll ask you to leave. You two were the perfect couple last night. I've never seen him this happy. James said the same, and he's known Cameron for ages. It won't be long before you're introducing each other to your parents.'

'Oh God, my parents. I haven't called them for ages because I didn't want to stress my mum out. If she knew what Mark was like, she'd have made me move back home, and that's the last thing I want to do. I won't phone her today. I'll wait until I've spoken to Cameron as I may be back at my place, and they won't need to know anything.'

Sarah hugged her.

'Don't stress about what you can't control, Jen—it'll work out in the end. You're meant to be—I can feel it. In the meantime, we've got Friday night. I've booked the train, first-class baby.'

'Oh, nice. I need this night out. I can't wait. We can start drinking on the way there.'

CHAPTER 33

Cameron couldn't stop worrying about Imogen. He understood she'd come from a controlling relationship, so he didn't want to come across that way. He knew he had to play it right, so she didn't feel the need to run. Unfortunately, he didn't know how to strike that balance. He'd have a chat with her that night—the office wasn't the place for this sort of conversation. Needing some advice from James, he rang him.

'James, any chance I can grab ten minutes with you before our meeting later? I need your advice, mate.'

'Yeah, of course, come over.'

When Cameron crossed the mezzanine to James' office, Sarah and Imogen were chatting in the kitchen. He gave them a wave on his way but didn't stop to talk.

'Hey, Cam, what's up?' He closed the door to James' office.

'Did Imogen tell you about the latest development with Dickhead?'

'Yeah. She seemed resigned to the fact that she's going to have to live with it.'

'That's what worries me. I hope he sees sense and leaves her alone, but how long do we have to live in fear of him coming for her? I'm stressing about Friday night, but I can't come across as controlling as that'll ring alarm bells for her. I've had an idea, and I need a partner in crime.'

'You know me, Cam, I'm in—unless you mean an actual crime—I'm not doing time for you, buddy. What's the plan, mastermind?'

'I need to be in London. I've spoken to Tom, and he said we can hang in his office, which gives me the benefit of watching the CCTV so I can make sure the girls are okay. How do you fancy sneaking out with me and camping out at the club?'

'Wow, you're freaking out about this, aren't you?'

'It'll be her first night on her own after the police issued him with a harassment order. He's either going to leave her alone or want retaliation. The chances of him seeing her are remote, but I want to be there if he turns up. He can't get in as his name isn't on the list at the door. And how would he know she's there? But he knows her phone number, where she works and which pub she goes to, so I'm not ruling anything out.'

'I'm up for that, but you'll be buying my drinks. I wouldn't mind spying on Sarah—I reckon that could be hot.'

'I'd say you shock me sometimes, but sadly, you don't. I plan to wait until they're leaving, then I show up and offer to take them home. Imogen will be happy to have a lift rather than be mad at me for watching her.'

'This guy is a proper psycho, so I can see where you're coming from. Hopefully, Imogen thinks the same—otherwise, you're in so much trouble.'

'Cheers, James, appreciate the support. Do you think it'd be too soon if I asked Jen to stay with me for good? I'm worried that she'll want to move back to her place and get on with her life now. I can't imagine her not being at home—she just fits there. Am I losing it, James? Do you think I'm too attached too soon?'

'I think when you know, you know. Life's too short to wait for when you think something is socially acceptable. Bollocks to it, ask her. What's the worst that can happen? She's coming this way for our meeting, but keep me posted on what she says.'

'Will do.'

'Hey, you two. Are you ready?'

'Hey, Imogen. Take a seat. So, a company called Walter and Holmes has been in touch and requested you by name.'

'Wow. That's amazing. The name sounds familiar. Are they a big company?'

'They're a financial services company based out of London, so maybe that's why you've heard of them? They're opening smaller offices around the country to reduce their dependency on high rental in London. Fran's been telling everyone how great you are, so that's pretty awesome.'

'That's nice of her. Okay, so what's the plan?'

'Cameron will handle the remodelling side. They need some structural work to take walls down as they prefer an open-plan layout. Like your previous project, they want you to design the reception and the client meeting rooms. They want to impress their current and potential clients, so they're looking for statement pieces. I suspect some Divino furniture would be welcome. They're finalising the lease on the office, and then they'll be in touch to set up a meeting and go through your preliminary designs. They think a month should be enough notice. Cameron, can you email the layout once your team has finished so that Imogen can start planning?'

He tore his eyes away from Imogen. 'Yep, no worries. I think they'll only need a few more days. We've hit a snag with one wall as it's load-bearing, but I think an RSJ will do the trick. Then we can work out the position of the pillars. I'll get it over to you as soon as possible.' He sat back and absentmindedly chewed the end of his pen, mulling over his earlier thoughts.

'Cheers, Cam. If you have any questions, Imogen, give me a shout. Thanks, guys.'

Cameron noticed that Imogen looked flushed as they were walking out. She gestured for him to lean in so could she say something.

'I don't think rolled steel joists are sexy, but when you talk all technical like that, it turns me on. I'll be imagining all the things you could do to me up against a pillar. Just wanted to leave you with that thought.'

She sauntered back to her desk without waiting for a response, with a faint smile on her lips. Cameron felt a familiar rush of blood—he needed to get back to his office or take a cold shower. His mind was made up—she was a keeper.

CHAPTER 34

'Do you fancy eating out tonight? You haven't been to my local yet. I think you'd like it.'

'Sounds good. Do I need to get changed?'

'You're perfect as you are. I'd change into some flat shoes, though. We'll walk there.'

Imogen wondered if he wanted to eat out to discuss her moving out without making a scene. She took some deep breaths and changed her shoes.

They found a table close to the open fire. It was the perfect country pub with flagstone floors, neutral walls, and no jukebox or pool table. It was softly lit but didn't feel dark and dingy like some old country pubs. This was the sort of place that you went to for a civilised pint and excellent food.

'I'm not going to lie, part of the reason I moved into this village is that I like the pub. The food is amazing, and the cask ale is well kept.'

Cameron ordered their drinks while she looked at the menu. She didn't feel hungry—a feeling of nausea washed over her. She was convinced he was going to ask her to leave.

'Do you fancy sharing the baked camembert with me and then getting some fries on the side?'

'That sounds perfect. I don't feel very hungry tonight.'

Cameron went to the bar and ordered while Imogen calmed her nerves. When he sat down, she saw he was fiddling with the menu, and his pint was going down fast. He was nervous about something.

'So, how was your afternoon? Did you look at the new project?'

'I did. It's a nice one to get my teeth into. I can't believe they requested me by name. Don't you think it's weird that Fran would recommend me to someone? I know I wouldn't be so nice if you had a new girlfriend.' Imogen felt foolish for saying it out loud. She sounded like a lesser woman.

'I think you caught her on a good day, but you're doing a great job. You fit in and are impressing James. He speaks highly of you, and not just because I'd punch him if he didn't.'

'Thanks, Cam. It means a lot.'

'Here you go, guys. Enjoy your meal.' They thanked the waitress, and conversation stopped while they dipped triple-cooked chunky chips into the molten cheese. It was so rich and creamy that Imogen couldn't help but close her eyes in appreciation. This was the sort of comfort food she needed. It took her mind off her worries. She absentmindedly sucked some errant cheese from her finger.

'I love to watch you eat. I don't know anyone that can make melted cheese and chips sexy.'

Imogen couldn't take it any longer. She needed to know what Cameron wanted to do. He hadn't been himself, but when he was flirting with her, it was messing with her mind. She tested the water.

'I've been thinking about what you said earlier, about me moving on with my life.'

'What've you been thinking?' Cameron downed the last of his pint.

'I think maybe I should move back to my place and get out from under your feet. I figure that's the best way to get on with things.'

'Is that what you want, Imogen?'

She'd make it easier for Cameron. He'd helped her so much that it was the least she could do.

'I think so, don't you?'

He clenched his jaw.

'I think I need another pint. Do you want another drink?'

'Yes, please.'

Cameron took the empties to the bar and ordered. He tapped his foot impatiently while he waited. Imogen picked up on his change in mood—had she read him wrong? A piece of warm bread took the brunt of her frustration as she dunked it into the cheese. She dolloped the sweet and sticky onion marmalade on top. As she filled her mouth, Cameron came back to the table. Her mouth was so full that she couldn't say thank you, so she gave him a thumbs up. She wondered if she could be any lamer.

'Right, as you have your mouth full, you can't spout any more crap at me. I want you to listen.'

Imogen's eyes bulged at his gruff tone, but she was silent.

Cameron took a box out of his jacket pocket and put it on the table.

'I will not go along with your nonsense for fear of hurting my pride. We are not in a TV drama, so I'm going to break from tradition and tell you how I feel. I want you to have this.' He pushed the box towards Imogen.

She nearly choked on her bread but managed to swallow it. Before taking the box, she took a drink of her gin and tonic. Her heart rate increased with anticipation.

She opened the box and saw a beautiful Cartier heart-shaped keyring. Attached to it was a door key.

To answer your question on if I think you moving out is the right thing to do—no, I do not.' Cameron put his finger up to tell her not to interrupt him. 'I've been stressing out all day about asking you, as I don't want to come across as controlling. But I would like it if you would move in with me. Properly. For the foreseeable. If you want to move out, I guess I'll have to get over it, but I don't want you to think that's what I want. I can't imagine waking up every morning without you there. So, Imogen, will you move in with me?'

'I can't believe I've been such an idiot, Cameron. I'm sorry. I thought you wanted me to move out. The thought of going back to my place makes me feel empty.'

'Just to be clear. Is that a yes?'

'Yes. I'd love to move in with you. If you're sure you want me?'

Cameron let out a sigh of relief. 'Yes, I'm sure. Bloody hell, Jen—don't do things like that in the future, please.'

'I promise not to guess at what's going on in your head again.'

'I think that's sensible.' Cameron dipped two chips into the cheese to scrape up the last of it and fed one to Imogen before eating the other.

Imogen smiled. She wondered how she'd got so lucky meeting someone like Cameron.

'I can phone my parents now and brush over everything with

this news.'

'What do you mean, brush over everything? Haven't you told them what's been going on?'

'No, my mum would worry too much, and my dad would have gone to Mark's house and killed him, and trust me, that wouldn't have been pretty. Mark wouldn't stand a chance, and my dad would end up in prison. He grew up with a hard man for a dad. He knows how to take care of himself.'

'Wow, can't wait to meet him. He sounds brilliant. We could go and kneecap Mark together, father-son bonding.'

'Now you're jumping the gun. I'll call them when we get home later. I could do with another G&T, though—I need the courage to confess to them.'

'No need to look at the dessert menu. I have champagne on ice and a can of whipped cream at the house.' Cameron raised his eyebrows at Imogen. She couldn't wait to get home.

'Hey Mum, it's me.'

'Imogen, it's lovely to hear from you. I thought you'd forgotten about us.'

'Yeah, sorry about that. I've been busy at work. I settled in quickly, and I joined a book club too.'

'That sounds lovely, darling. I'm glad you're doing okay. So, tell me everything. How are you managing your little garden? Are you looking after it?'

'That's what I want to talk to you about.'

'Your Garden?'

'No, silly. It's just that I've not been home much.'

'Really? This sounds ominous—is there a man friend involved?'

Imogen smiled. Her mum was so cute sometimes.

'Yes, Mum, there's a man involved.' Imogen explained how she met Cameron and that he made her happy.

'I have to say, I think it's a shame that you and Mark didn't stay together. He was always so caring, and he looked after you. He popped round just after you moved out since he didn't have your new phone number. Did you get the rest of your things from him, by the way?'

'What? Did you give him my number?'

'Well, yes, dear. Did I do the wrong thing? He said he needed to drop off some stuff you'd left behind.'

'It's not your fault, Mum. I should have been honest with you all along. I need to tell you why I haven't been home much. Are you sitting down?'

Imogen explained everything and then heard it being relayed to her dad. She heard him getting angry in the background— just what she was afraid of.

'Please tell Dad he must not get involved. The police are handling it, and I think it's over now. Cameron's been the most amazing man ever, and he's arranged extra security at work. He wanted me to move in with him when it got serious so he could make sure I was safe. I'm okay, Mum, I'm better than okay. I have the most amazing job, fantastic friends, and I've fallen madly in love with the most gorgeous gentleman you'll ever meet.'

'Well, I want to meet this Cameron, and your father wants a word with him now, if he may?'

'Right, I'll just get him. He won't embarrass me, will he?'

'You know your father—I can't make any promises.'

Imogen went to the kitchen, where she found Cameron watching TV. She whispered.

'Cam, I'm sorry, but my dad wants to talk to you.'

'Oh shit, I'm not sure I'm ready for a dad chat.' 'Okay, give me the phone. He crooked his neck—and looked like he was getting ready to go into the ring.'

'Hello, Mr Taylor, this is Cameron.' There was a moment of silence while he listened.

'I agree. Yes. I will. No, I won't. That I can promise. A lot. X5—no points. Oh really, chocolates, well, that's good to know.'

Cameron looked over at Imogen and smiled. The look in his eyes was full of good humour and something that Imogen couldn't put her finger on.

'No worries, Mr Taylor, I'll hand you over.' Cameron passed the phone to Imogen and mouthed the words "Smashed it" to her with a double thumbs-up.

'Hi Dad, did he pass the test?'

'So far, yes, but I'll reserve judgement until we've met. Although, I'm not an excellent judge of character. I'm sorry, Imogen, I let you down by not seeing Mark for what he is.'

'Dad, don't be like that—you would never have known. How could you? You only knew what I wanted you to. There was no sense in worrying you over it. Anyway, it's over now. I can change my phone number, and he'll never get to me again. It's all good.' Imogen wasn't convinced it was true, but she wanted to make her dad feel less guilty.

'Does Cameron make you happy, sweetheart?'

She looked at him, and her heart skipped a beat. She cleared the lump in her throat before answering.

'He does. You're going to love him. He means the world to me, and he makes me feel safe.'

After promising to have them over soon, she hung up and went in for a hug.

'Thank you for handling my dad so well. I think you impressed him. What on earth was he asking you?'

'You know, the usual. Will l look after you? Will I kill Mark if I ever see him? How much money do I have?'

'Oh God, did he really ask you that? I'm so sorry, Cam.'

'Don't worry about it. He just wants to make sure I can provide for you. I don't mind. My choice of car went down well. It's a nice safe one, apparently. He also told me that if I ever piss you off, I should buy you fancy chocolates.'

'That's true. I'd rather you didn't, though—just lavish me with chocolates anyway. Paul A. Young are my favourites.'

'Consider it done. Now, let's crack open the champagne and the whipped cream and take this party upstairs.'

CHAPTER 35

'Are you ready for an awesome night out, ladies?' Sarah was ready and raring to go, dressed in tight black leather trousers, a black silk camisole top, and patent silver stilettos. She looked stunning. Cameron had given them a lift to the station. He anxiously tapped on his steering wheel for the entire journey.

'It's going to be fine, Cameron. Stop worrying.'

'Call me the minute you need me for anything. I'm okay with you having a good time, but I'm nervous about not being there to protect you. I promised your dad, after all.'

'We'll be okay.'

Cameron was cautious about commenting on Imogen's outfit because he didn't want to sound like Mark. She looked beautiful in a black knee-length halter neck dress and some patent green stilettos that matched her jacket. She was wearing her one-piece underwear set but had changed the configuration of the straps so that it was a halter neck.

'You look amazing. I'm looking forward to getting you home and doing all sorts of naughty things.'

'Well, in that case, I may be home earlier than planned.'

'I'm okay with that. Have a good time, ladies. Keep an eye on my girl, won't you? Any problems, just shout. I won't drink tonight, just in case you need me. I'm only a phone call away.'

'Cam, you're the best.' Sarah kissed him on the cheek before hopping out of the car. Jess and Lucy slid along the backseat after her. Jess had dressed up for the evening in a deep purple fitted dress with a Bardot neckline that stopped above the knee. In contrast to Jess's skin-tight dress, Lucy had opted for a silk tunic in a gunmetal grey colour that was loose and didn't show off her figure. A single slash from shoulder to shoulder formed the neckline, and the kimono style sleeves went to her elbows. She'd paired it with opaque black tights and black boots.

As Imogen closed the car door, Cameron hopped out and ran round to meet her, taking her into his arms. 'I want you to have the best time tonight, gorgeous. You should be safe in Tom's club, so let your hair down. You deserve to have some carefree fun.' He lowered his head, so he was at eye level. 'I'll keep you safe, I promise.'

'Thank you. I'm grateful for everything you're doing for me.'

He pressed his lips hard against hers and held them there for a few seconds before Sarah's catcalls interrupted them.

'Come on, Jen, we're going to miss the train.'

As the four of them boarded the first-class carriage, they turned a few heads. Imogen opened a paper bag she was carrying and produced four miniature bottles of Prosecco.

'Here you go, ladies, something to get the party started. I've some good news that I've kept from you so we can celebrate in style.'

'Well, you're not pregnant—otherwise, you wouldn't be

popping a cork, and you can't be engaged. That would be way too soon.'

'Sarah, why don't you let her tell us instead of trying to guess?' Jess rolled her eyes at Sarah across the table.

'Okay, so on Wednesday night, Cameron took me out for dinner and asked me to move in with him permanently. I said yes.'

'Wow, Jen, that's amazing, and just think—that day you were worried he was going to ask you to move out. You numpty.'

'I know, right—I nearly ruined it by telling him I wanted to move out first.'

'Oh, you didn't? I hope you realise how much he likes you now.' Sarah sang, 'Imogen and Cameron sitting in a tree, K. I. S. S. I. N. G.'

'A toast. To you and Cameron and lots of naughty sex.' Jess lowered her voice for the last part of the toast as other passengers were staring.

'Cheers.'

'That's my news. Jess, what's the deal with you and Julian?'

'He's so dishy, and he's a good kisser. When he dropped me off at home, we kissed for ages in his car.'

'You didn't invite him in?' Lucy looked shocked.

'No, I like him, so I want to take it slow. He's boyfriend material.' Jess smiled and blushed.

'Well, I think that's very sweet. I couldn't get hold of Paul the other day, and he's gone quiet. I think work is stressing him out. Paul and I are taking it slow, too, although I feel like he's slowed down too much.'

'That's right. You mentioned you weren't sure what was going on. Are you still planning to see how this weekend goes and then knock it on the head if things don't improve? I'm sure Cameron must have another cousin somewhere we can call on for you. In the meantime, you'll have a great night.'

'Yeah, that's true. He'd better appreciate the effort I've gone to for him. I had my heart set on a sexy little number. He's asked me to text him when I'm ready, and he'll come and pick me up.'

Alarm bells went off in Imogen's mind.

'You need to keep an eye on that sort of behaviour, Lucy. I'm not saying that every time a man makes a request, it's because he's a psycho, but just be careful. That's how it started with Mark.'

'Yeah, I know. I have a feeling it won't be an issue after this weekend, but let's see.' Wanting to change the subject, she turned to Sarah, 'Sarah, what's James up to tonight?'

'I think he's going to keep Cameron company. Make sure he doesn't go crazy worrying about Imogen.'

'Cameron is lovely. I'm missing him already.'

Sarah downed her Prosecco and made an announcement.

'Right, when we get to the club, I have a rule for Imogen. Every time she says Cameron, she has to do a shot of tequila.'

They all cheered—although Imogen felt nervous since she'd promised Cameron that she wouldn't do anything silly. Still, she figured she was in good hands. They got out of the taxi and looked at the queue of people waiting to get in.

'Oh bloody hell, that queue is ridiculous. We're going to waste most of the evening standing outside.' Sarah wasn't amused.

'Miss Taylor—Imogen.' A tall man dressed in a smart black suit called her from the doorway. They turned to look, and all enjoyed what they saw.

'Yes, hello, that's me.'

'Imogen, if you and your friends would like to come straight through, I'll show you to your VIP area. I'm Tom, Cam's mate.' He held his hand out and shook Imogen's, kissing her on the cheek.

'Hi Tom, pleased to meet you. Thanks for having us this evening.'

'No worries, it's my pleasure.'

Lucy whispered in Sarah's ear as they walked in, 'If it doesn't work with Paul, I'm asking about Tom. He's lush.'

'Too bloody right you are.'

'Wow, Tom, this building's amazing. It's not what I expected.' Imogen was looking around.

'Thanks, Imogen. Tom was proud of his club and for a good reason. The architecture made me want to have my club here when I bought it five years ago. It's a Grade II listed building from 1827, so we had to be careful when converting it and work with the original layout. I called on Cam to help me out. He was amazing—I wouldn't have got this place ready for its opening night if it wasn't for him.'

Spread over three floors, the building comprised multiple rooms, each a distinct part of the club. Two rooms made up the ground floor, separated by the reception area and cloakroom. The first was a typical gentlemen's bar. It had dark wood floors, tables, and a bar with cut crystal glasses hanging from a rack overhead, catching the light and adding a sparkle to the room. The rich and famous, dressed in their best, laughing and drinking expensive cocktails, filled the room. Music played in the background, but it didn't drown out the conversation and laughter.

The other room was a casino. This was a more subdued room, with just the sound of chips clinking against each other on tables of rich green felt. Waiters walked around, delivering glasses of amber liquid to the gamblers, while they quietly prayed they'd be lucky tonight.

'We're going downstairs. You're in for a good night, ladies. Cameron asked that I reserve you a table in the fun part of the club as he thinks you'll love the dance floor there, and I agree.'

With each step they took down the broad wooden staircase, the sounds of the club grew louder, and the lighting became softer. They walked along a short corridor before reaching the entrance to the club. As soon as the door opened, a wall of sound hit them, base beats, talking, laughing, and glasses clinking. They looked at each other and smiled—they were in for a good time.

'Your table is over here, ladies.' He turned to Imogen. 'You'll be safe in here. No one can enter the club without signing in, and I've stationed a bouncer near your table. Cam has made it very clear that your safety is my top priority. You must be an exceptional lady. I've never seen him like this over anyone.'

'Thank you, I'm very grateful for the trouble you've gone to. And, yes, Cameron's an exceptional man.'

'He is.' Tom turned back to everyone. 'You'll find a rather nice bottle of Dom Pérignon waiting for you on the table—compliments of Cam, smooth bugger. Oh, excuse me, my phone's ringing. Have a good evening, ladies.'

'Yes, let's get that cork popped.' Sarah was ready with her glass.

'Girls, have you seen the dance floor?' Lucy was staring across the room with a look of glee on her face.

'Wow! Let's have a drink and then get on there.' Jess shared Lucy's excitement.

The dance floor was straight out of the seventies and made of floor tiles, each lit with a different luminous pink, yellow, green or blue. Moments later, it was black and white chequered, and the floor lights pulsed with the beat of the music.

Imogen felt alive and excited. She was going to let her hair down tonight and forget her troubles.

'Ladies, let's do this. Cheers to Cameron and his awesomeness.'

'Cheers.'

'Hold that thought.' Sarah raised her hand to the lady behind the bar and whispered in her ear.

'What was that about?'

'You'll see.' She had a mischievous glint in her eye.

Moments later, a tray filled with tequila shots, lime wedges, and a salt shaker was delivered to the table.

'Take a shot. You said his name.'

'Shit, I'm going to be ruined, aren't I?'

The tequila burned Imogen's throat before filling her with a warmth that spread as soon as it hit her stomach. It reminded her of how she used to party before Mark came along, and she realised she was getting back to her old self.

'Right, you lot—you're all doing a shot with me and then we're hitting that dance floor.'

CHAPTER 36

'Tom, I'm driving in now. Can you open the gates?' Cameron and James arrived at the club and drove into the underground car park.

'Yeah, no worries, I've just left Imogen—she's in high spirits. The champagne was a nice touch, by the way.'

'Glad to hear it. See you in a minute, mate.'

They parked up and walked through the back door that led to Tom's office on the top floor. Tom was waiting for them.

'Hey, can I get you a drink? He shook Cameron and James' hands and slapped them on the back.

'I'd love a brandy, please, mate. It's great to see you. It's been a while.' James was going straight for the hard stuff.

'I'll just have a beer, cheers, and then I'll be on soft drinks. It's been too long. It's a shame we're not meeting up under better circumstances. Next time we'll be down here having a great time together, I promise.'

'From the way Imogen looked whenever she mentioned your name, I don't doubt you'll be wanting this place for an engagement party.'

'All right, mate, calm down. It's still early days.' The smile on Cameron's face said otherwise, though.

'You can watch the CCTV cameras from here. I don't think there'll be any trouble tonight, though, so you can relax.'

'I won't relax until she's safe at home. I've got a bad feeling in my gut about this. I don't see Mark being the sort to leave her alone. I think he's just waiting for the right time. I know how quickly I've fallen for Imogen. How I feel about her after a short while is ridiculous, so I can only imagine how someone unstable like Mark can feel about her after four years. Trust me, this isn't over yet.'

'Fucking hell, Cam, you have got it bad, haven't you?'

'Yeah, I have.'

Cameron settled in a leather armchair. James was in the chair next to him, facing the wall of screens. He saw her on the dance floor having a great time. She was dancing and singing, arms in the air. She looked sexy as hell.

'Oh, look, there they are. Wow, Sarah looks hot. I feel quite voyeuristic watching them dancing with each other. If she's not pissed off with me for spying on her all night, I'm screwing her brains out tonight.'

'Bloody hell, James, you're like a dog in heat. Although I can see what you mean, this isn't a bad way to spend an evening.'

CHAPTER 37

Song choice: Tequila (Jax Jones, Martin Solveig, RAYE and Europa)

'A nother shot, Jen.'

'What, did I talk about him again?'

'We're out of shots,' Lucy called from the table.

'Right. To the bar, Miss Taylor.'

Sarah spoke to the same lady behind the bar, and seconds later, she was handed a bottle of tequila. She turned to Imogen with a wide grin—she was up to no good, and Imogen could feel it.

'Turn around and lean back on the bar.'

Imogen was too drunk to argue, so she went with it. Before she knew it, Sarah was kneeling on a barstool and leaning over her.

'Open wide, Jen—get ready to swallow.'

Imogen opened her mouth just in time as the amber liquid hit the back of her throat. She fought the urge to gag and spit it out, swallowing it down triumphantly.

'You're a legend,' Jess shouted.

'I want to have a go at that—it looks like fun.' Lucy was letting her hair down. The others hadn't seen this side of her before. She leant back over the bar as Sarah poured the drink in. After she'd had her share, Lucy wiped her mouth.

'And do you know what else? I'm fucking hot in these tights—they're coming off. Back in a minute, ladies.'

Lucy danced across the floor and went to the ladies' room, returning moments later without the thick tights. She'd pulled down her dress on one side to be off the shoulder and asymmetrical. She looked transformed—she'd been hiding beautiful slender tanned legs.

'Yes, now the party has started.'

They went back to the floor. Imogen closed her eyes and felt the tequila taking hold. She swayed to the beat of the music, a feeling of euphoria spreading through her. She raised her arms in the air as her hips swayed in time to the music. Her euphoric moment was interrupted when she felt two unfamiliar hands on her hips. The unpleasant scent of alcohol-fuelled breath bombarded her nostrils. She turned to see a tall, stubbly man giving her a smarmy grin. She took hold of his hands and moved them off her hips, but he didn't take the hint. He tried to dance with her again, but Sarah was there by her side.

'Back off dickhead, she's not interested.' Sarah stepped in between Imogen and the sleaze.

'And who are you? Her girlfriend? I can take you both if you like?' Before Sarah had a chance to slap him, the bouncer was at their side.

'Excuse me, sir, I need to ask you to leave.'

'What the fuck? I've done nothing wrong.'

'These ladies don't want your attention. Now please walk away, sir.'

'Fine, whatever. They're not worth my time, anyway.'

'What a twat. Why do men have to be such douchbags? Things like that make me wish we had our men with us.'

'I know what you mean. I miss Cam, but I'm having the best time. I haven't danced this much for years. Time for another bottle of fizz too. I'll get one.' That lifted Sarah's spirits.

Imogen ordered another bottle of champagne. She went to hand her card to the bar staff, but he gave it straight back.

'Don't worry about paying, Miss Taylor. We're under strict orders to add all your drinks to a bill in the name of Mr Black.'

'Oh, okay. Thank you.' Imogen was stunned. She hadn't expected Cameron to pick up the tab.

They sat back at the table to top up their glasses.

'Oh my God, that was so sexy.'

'What was?' Lucy looked baffled.

'I was just told the tab is being settled by Mr Black. I felt like I was in a Bond movie or something. God, Cameron is so sexy—I'm totally in love with him.'

'That is awesome. Now, take another shot.'

They all sang in chorus, 'Shot. Shot. Shot. Shot.'

'You girls are going to be the death of me.' Imogen took the shot. She felt dizzy and sat down.

'Miss Taylor, I have a bottle of water for you. Mr Black requested that I bring one over.'

'Right, thanks.' Imogen looked at the others, a confused expression on her face.

'Cameron's asked that I drink some water. Do you think he's

watching me?'

'That is weird. Maybe it's because I just texted James and told him we were making you do shots?'

'You didn't? He's going to be stressing out about me now. Text James and tell him I've had the water, and I'm okay.' Imogen poured a glass and passed the bottle around the others.

'Done. I've informed James that it's all okay. Now we're rehydrated—it's time for more dancing.'

'I'm tempted to text Paul to tell him not to bother picking me up. I've decided he's not right for me. Can I come home with you guys?'

'That's okay with us, no worries.' Jess put her arm around Lucy.

'Jen could find out from Cameron if Tom's single. He looks like he'd be a good rebound.' Sarah wiggled her eyebrows suggestively.

Imogen couldn't believe what she was hearing. 'Bloody hell, woman. She's just dumped one guy. She's hardly ready to move on to the next.'

'Even if I was interested, it doesn't matter. He's way out of my league. Let's forget about the men in my life and get on with our evening, shall we, ladies?'

CHAPTER 38

'Bloody hell. Why do they keep doing shots? Look, what they're up to now?'

James laughed. 'I've just had a text from Sarah. She said that every time Imogen mentions your name, she has to do one. Technically, it's your fault. That's hilarious.'

'It's bloody not. She'll be sick. I'm getting some water for her. Oh, Christ, she's bending over the bloody bar now, and they're pouring it into her from the bottle. This is driving me insane.'

'It's all right, mate. The others will make sure she's okay. She needs to let off steam. Remember, she hasn't had this kind of night out for years.'

'Yeah, okay, I get it—I do. I just wish it was me down there with her having a great time instead of being up here wondering if Dickhead is going to show up. This woman is going to be the death of me.' Cameron was pacing the wall of screens.

'Look, Lucy has taken her tights off. She looks hot. I haven't noticed that before.'

'James, stop looking at Lucy's legs and look at what's happening now. Who is that sleaze bag with his hands on Jen?'

James got up to get a closer look.

'Looks like a right wanker. Don't worry, Sarah's onto him. My God, she looks so hot when she's in fight mode. Don't judge me, but I've got a semi.'

'No judgement here—I'm used to your level of depravity.' They stood in silence and watched as the girls sat down.

'Oh, hang on, I've got a message. Sarah says Imogen has her water and is okay. You can stop worrying about her. We'll be in so much trouble when they realise we've been watching all night. Hopefully, the make-up sex will be worth it.'

'You all right, chaps?' Tom came into the office to see how they were.

'Yeah, good, thanks. These girls are killing us. Although I think Cam is about to have a heart attack with a hard-on.'

'Ha, I know. I sent the bouncer over to move that guy on. I haven't seen him in here before.'

Cameron's phone pinged.

Hey sexy gorgeous Mr Black, I miss you and can't wait to see you later. I'm having the best time. Lucy's ditched Paul, so she's coming home with us. She reckons Tom is out of her league. That's crazy. I think he'd love her. Xxx PS: thank you for the drinks xxx

'It sounds like Jen's having the best time. I get the impression the girls are trying to set you up with Lucy, Tom. Jen mentioned that Lucy has ditched Paul.

'Oh really, she's the hot brunette that's taken her tights off, right? I might have to say hi later.'

'Cool. I shall respond to my drunk girlfriend.'

Good evening, Miss Taylor. I miss you too and can't
wait to have you naked. Tom likes Lucy—he will come
and chat with her later. Please take it easy on the
tequila. PS: enjoy the champagne. Xxx

Cameron looked at the screens to watch over Imogen. Within
seconds, the smile in his eyes was gone and replaced with
darkness.

'He's here. I'm sure it's the same guy as on the security cam-
era at work.' Cameron growled the words out, but before the
others could see the screen, he was on his way out of the door.

'Tom, get security in there now.' James was quick to follow.

Cameron felt a red mist descend. He needed to get to Imogen
before Mark could hurt her. Conscious that there were multiple
flights of stairs between him and Mark, he took them four at a
time, adrenaline pumping through his veins. He could feel himself losing any shred of self-control. His body went into autopilot
and was getting ready for a fight.

He reached the lower ground floor and crashed through the
door into the club. He couldn't see Imogen through the crowd of
people but forced his way through.

It was time to end this.

CHAPTER 39

Song Choice: Courtesy Call (Thousand Foot Krutch)

The girls were sitting around their table, having a break from dancing and taking the opportunity to have another drink.

'Crap, I think my text to Paul has pissed him off.'

Jess turned to her. 'Why's that? Did you get a response?'

'No, he's headed this way.' She looked across the crowd of people. Imogen followed her gaze, the colour draining from her face. The drink in her hand slipped to the floor, and the glass smashed.

'That's not Paul. It's Mark.' Imogen backed away. She looked around to see if she could attract the bouncer's attention, but the smarmy man from earlier, and his friends, were distracting him. She locked eyes with Mark across the dance floor. His lips curled into a smile that sent an icy chill spreading down her spine, freezing her to the spot.

'Shit. Imogen, stay behind us. He can't hurt you in here.' Sarah stepped in front of her, and the others followed. Lucy looked horrified. She turned to Imogen.

'That's Mark? I'm confused. What the hell is going on? I'm going to talk to him.'

'Lucy, no. He's not someone you want to mess with.' But it was too late—Lucy was striding towards Mark.

She didn't have to go far as Mark had increased his pace once he had got through the dance floor crowds and was only yards away from them.

'What are you doing here, Paul? Or should I call you Mark?'

'Fuck off, Lucy. Get out of my way, you stupid little girl.'

'I want answers, Mark. And I'm not letting you get anywhere near Imogen.' The tequila coursing through her system gave Lucy the confidence to stand up for herself.

'Oh, little Lucy wants answers.' He looked at the others and laughed. 'Did you think I was with you for your good looks and your charm? Or maybe you thought it was your skills in the bedroom that kept me coming back? I assure you it wasn't either of those, little Lucy. You were a means to an end, my dear. You've already let me get near Imogen. Now get the fuck out of my way.'

Lucy pulled her shoulders back and tried to hide her broken pride. 'If you want to get to Imogen, you'll have to go through me. I'm not moving.'

'You're even more foolish than I realised, you stupid tart. You can't stop me.' Before Lucy had time to react, Mark's right hand swung through the air, contacting her cheek. The impact's force was so great that Lucy fell backwards, the sofa breaking her fall. The blow left her disorientated, and the alcohol hindered her recovery. Jess ran over to her while Sarah widened her stance in front of Imogen and prepared to fight.

'It's okay, Imogen. He won't hurt you, I promise.' Sarah could see that the bouncer had dispatched the sleazy guy and was only a few yards away—she was sure he would reach them before Mark could do any more damage. She just needed to distract him for a bit longer.

'Brave words, I'm guessing you're Sarah. I didn't have you pegged for an idiot. I think you know it would be a lot easier for everyone if you stepped aside and let me have a chat with my Imogen.' Mark reached out to Sarah, but before he could grab her, he was pushed to the ground. Cameron was standing over him, breathing hard. He looked pumped and ready to do whatever it took.

'Get the fuck away from Imogen, you coward. Come and fight with someone your own size.' He had taken Mark by the scruff of his neck and pulled him to his feet.

'Cameron, what are you doing?' Imogen was frantic. This was all happening so fast she couldn't make sense of it in her tequila-dulled head.

Mark threw a punch that connected with Cameron's shoulder. It was all he needed to give him the green light to release the rage that had built up inside him.

Running on a heady mix of endorphins and adrenaline, Cameron pulled his free arm back and threw a punch that hit Mark's nose. The sound could be heard over the music and caused Mark to slump. He would have hit the floor if it wasn't for Cameron holding him up in readiness for another shot. Before Mark had a chance to retaliate, he pounded his face again.

The bouncer intervened and grabbed Cameron's arm,

stopping him from pummelling Mark any further. James and Tom reached the scene. It took the combined force of all three of them to separate Cameron from Mark. Imogen heard Tom shouting orders to his security team as they arrived.

'Get them out the back door now. James, take care of the girls.'

Three additional bouncers took hold of Cameron and Mark, ushering them out of a back door behind Imogen. She ignored Tom's pleas to stay where she was and followed Cameron. The loud chatter and music reduced to a faint bass beat in the background as the door closed behind them. It was eerily quiet.

Imogen took a moment to look at Mark. Blood was gushing out of his nose and mouth. Cameron had done a lot of damage.

'What the hell are you doing, Mark?' Imogen was trying to make sense of it.

'Did you think I was going to let you get away with having me arrested? You cheating bitch.' Mark sprayed blood as he spat the words at Imogen with venom. Cameron turned and threw another punch. This time, Mark went down, crashing to the concrete floor of the underground car park.

'No one talks to Imogen like that, do you hear me? You're lucky I don't snap your fucking neck right now.' Cameron was breathing hard, his hands held in tight fists. He was struggling to keep it together while he paced. He grabbed Mark by the collar and pulled him to his feet. The veins on his temples bulged. The look in his eyes said he was ready to kill him.

Tom held his hand up to the bouncers to stop them from intervening.

'This dickhead mistreats women. He's getting what he deserves. Cam knows when to stop.'

In silence, they nodded and took a step backwards. Their crossed arms showed they would stay out of this fight. Cameron had the height advantage over Mark, so he dominated when he squared up to him.

'You're going to leave, and you're going to stay away from Imogen. We could call the police right now and have you arrested for breaking the harassment order, and you'd end up doing time. There's also the matter of your assault on Lucy. Take this chance while I'm feeling generous. Walk away and pretend you never met her, or I swear to God I'll rip your heart out with my bare hands. Understand?'

'You two deserve each other. She's a shit lay, by the way. To be honest, I don't know why I fucked her as much as I did. Next time you fuck her, remember my cock was in the slut first.'

Something in Cameron snapped. His assault left Mark hunched over, spitting blood and unable to stand. Cameron followed with an uppercut that landed on Mark's chin. He collapsed to the ground, the air in his lungs escaping with a groan. But Cameron wasn't finished. He stepped in and kicked Mark in the stomach with a force that lifted him from the ground. Cameron's years of playing rugby were evident with the power of his kick.

'Cameron, stop.' Imogen hadn't seen this side of Cameron, and it scared her.

'Get him out of here, lads,' Tom nodded to the bloodied heap on the floor. Imogen was watching from the sidelines, so shocked she couldn't process what was happening.

'Cameron, what are you doing here? What's going on, and what's wrong with you bloody men?' She took a deep breath before throwing her hands up in exasperation.

'Tom, I need some time alone with Imogen. Can you give us a

minute? Make sure the others are okay, and I'll meet you soon.' Cameron was breathing heavily and trying to calm down.

'No worries, mate. I'm going to find out how the bloody hell he got in here in the first place.'

Tom walked off, the sound of his footsteps growing quieter until there was only the sound of Cameron trying to slow his breath.

'What are you doing here, Cameron?' Imogen raised her voice—she was confused, scared and frustrated, and the alcohol coursing through her veins wasn't helping.

'Seriously, that is what you're mad about? It's a good job I was here. I hate to think what might have happened if Mark had got close to you.'

'I've put my life on hold so I could escape a man who wouldn't let me out without him, and I find out you're in the club after telling me you were staying home. What the fuck, Cam?'

'I know. Listen, I came because I need to protect you, not control you. Please know that I'm nothing like Mark.' Cameron ran his fingers through his hair in frustration. 'I wanted you to have a great night with your friends—you deserve it. I just couldn't shake the feeling that something bad would happen. It didn't feel right. How did he know where you live? Where you work? And how did he get access to the office? I figured he must be getting his info from the inside, so he might know you'd be here tonight. I don't know how he got into the club—I'm going to speak to Tom.'

'I think I know the answer to some of the questions. In fact, I know the answer to all of it now.'

'Go on. I'm listening.'

'Mark is Paul.'

'What? As in Lucy's Paul?' Cameron looked stunned.

Imogen nodded her head.

'He found out where I was working—probably from my over-ly-trusting mother—and used Lucy to get the info he needed to work his way into my life again. He must have taken her card when he stayed at her place. I remember her saying he popped out one morning to get breakfast, which must've been when he put the card on my desk.'

'Shit. I should've punched him harder for Lucy, too.'

'I think you've done enough. I don't think he'll be back to bother me now, do you?'

'I hope not, for his sake.'

'Have you been here all night? How did you know he was here before the bouncer knew?'

'James and I have been watching the CCTV in Tom's office.'

'Oh my God, you've been spying on me all night?' Imogen raised her voice.

'For fuck's sake, Jen, are you seriously pissed at me? I needed to protect you. Can't you see it was a good job? I trusted my gut?'

'By never letting me out of your sight? It's not normal, Cameron.'

'This isn't a normal situation, though, is it? I've had to watch someone I love suffer because no one was around to protect them, and I vowed I'd never let that happen again. I understand how you feel, but you need to hear me out.'

'What are you talking about, Cameron?'

'When I was young, my mum was pregnant with my brother. One evening, she worked late on one of their building sites. She was walking back to her car when a man attacked her. He beat her up badly, but she fought back with everything she had. His movements activated the security lights, which was enough to scare him off, so he left her for dead on the floor. Mum lost the baby.' Cameron paused.

'I'm so sorry.' Imogen reached up and stroked Cameron's face.

'They never caught the man that did it, so my mum lived in fear for years. She didn't go anywhere on her own. She lost her spark for a long time. To this day, my dad hasn't forgiven himself for not protecting his wife. I decided I'd always do everything I could to protect her and anyone else in my life. You need to understand that my behaviour is because I want you to be safe. It has nothing to do with controlling you. Please believe me.'

'I'm all over the place, Cameron. I don't know what to think.'

'Don't listen to what your head says, Imogen. What does your heart say?'

Cameron grabbed her in a tight embrace and kissed her with a need like nothing he'd felt before. His body was crying out for a release, and only Imogen could give him what he needed.

She kissed him back with just as much force.

'I'm on the edge, Imogen. I don't think I've much self-control left.'

'I'm okay with that.'

Cameron wasted no time as he picked Imogen up and sat her on his bonnet. He kissed her so hard she was sure he would bruise her lips. He ran his hand up her thigh and touched her underwear, ripping the pop studs open. Imogen undid the zip on his trousers as quickly as she could, but it wasn't quick enough. Cameron reached down and released his erection. He looked into Imogen's eyes—he wanted to make sure she was okay with this.

'Do it.'

229

Cameron entered her deep and hard, releasing a groan that echoed around them. She gasped with the intense sensation as he filled her completely. She wrapped her legs around him while he bombarded her with hard thrusts. Her back ached from being pushed against the hard metal, but Cameron's intense need was turning her on.

He was reaching climax, his groans loud and animalistic. This spurred Imogen on, and she could feel herself go. She cried out his name and begged for more. Cameron's need for release was painful. He drove into her and came with force. With satisfaction, he collapsed over her, his breathing ragged.

'I needed that. Sorry if that was too rough—I was running on adrenaline.'

'It's okay, Cameron. I'm not going to break.'

Cameron stood and did up the poppers on her underwear. He helped her down from the car.

'Steady there.' Imogen's legs wobbled.

'I think I had too much tequila and excitement tonight. I feel shit-faced.'

'Shit-faced? You sound like Sarah.' Cameron smiled at Imogen and put his arm around her as they walked to the entrance.

'I need to go to the ladies' room and clean myself up.'

Cameron went with her and waited outside the door. He wasn't going to leave her side any time soon.

They rejoined the others in Tom's office. Lucy looked pale, and Tom had his arm around her.

'Oh, thank God. Imogen, are you okay?' Lucy got up and went in for a hug as soon as Imogen entered the office.

'I'm okay—really, I'm okay—everyone.'

'How are you doing, Cameron? Do you need some ice for that

fist?' Tom went for the ice bucket with a napkin.

'Cameron, your fist is bleeding.'

He hadn't noticed, but now they'd pointed it out to him, he felt the pain setting in. 'Yeah, some ice would be good. Cheers, mate.'

'I'm so sorry, Imogen. He should never have got to you in my club.'

'It's okay. By now, you'll know that he was going by another name, so you wouldn't have known he was here. I think Cameron's scared him off. Are you okay, Lucy?'

'I think so. It's all a shock. I feel stupid.' Imogen recognised the look—Mark had broken her, something that she knew all about. Imogen crouched down next to her so that she could whisper.

'Hey, Lucy. You're not stupid, okay? Mark is a nasty piece of work. He manipulates every one around him—he did it to me for years. Please don't pay any attention to the things he said.'

Lucy nodded, but her slumped shoulders and downcast eyes told Imogen she wasn't okay.

Tom brought them a glass of brandy while Lucy talked through everything that Mark had asked her while they were seeing each other. It was clear he'd pumped her for information.

'I'm sorry you got dragged into this, Lucy.'

'I guess I'm just naive. I'm sorry I told him so much.'

'It's not something you'd think of, though, would you? It could have been any of us.' Jess put her hand on Lucy's shoulder to comfort her.

'Cheers, Jess.'

Tom handed Lucy some ice wrapped in a towel. 'Here you go. Your cheek looks a little red. Is it sore?' He knelt to take a closer look.

'It's okay. It stings, but nothing a shot of tequila won't fix.'

'That can be arranged, although I think some painkillers might be a better option.' Tom gave her a reassuring smile.

'Now our cover's blown. Can we go downstairs and have a dance? I feel like I've been missing out all evening. Oh, and you two,' James pointed to Sarah and Imogen, 'if you want to grind with each other, I'm okay with that.'

Sarah smacked him on the arm.

'Come on then, you dirty perv, come and dance with me.'

Imogen looked over at Lucy. 'Do you want to go back downstairs, or do you want to head straight home?'

'I'm okay. Let's go downstairs for a bit. It'd be a shame for the boys to miss out.'

The others followed James and Sarah, but Tom hung back. He gave Cameron a look that said to stay with him.

'Hold on, Imogen, I'll just be a sec. Thanks for your help with the Mark situation, Tom. And thanks for letting me teach him a lesson and not calling the police.'

'Don't mention it. The shit deserved more. I wanted to let you know that I've deleted the CCTV footage from the car park— including the good bits.' Tom winked at Cameron.

'Oh shit. Yeah, thanks, mate.'

'No worries. Glad you made it up already. Now, let's have a bit of fun to end the night on a high.' It was good to put it behind them and enjoy each other. After an hour on the dancefloor, they were exhausted.

'Right, you lot, we need to think about heading home. I need my bed now that the adrenaline's worn off.'

'Good idea, Cam. Are you sure you're okay to drive?'

'Yep. As long as you're happy to go in the extra seat in my boot, James.'

James gave Cameron a thumbs up.

Before they left, Tom took Lucy to one side. 'Can I have your number? I'd like to call you and meet up soon. Would that be okay?'

Lucy nodded but didn't believe him. Any confidence she had earlier was gone. She gave him her number with no expectation that she'd hear from him again.

The drive back was subdued. Everyone processed the events of the evening, and Cameron didn't take his hand off Imogen's thigh for the entire journey.

The familiar sound of crunching gravel under the tyres woke her up. She was home and safe at last.

CHAPTER 40

'I've something to show you.' Cameron was in bed, smiling at his phone. Imogen had woken up after a fitful sleep, no doubt the result of the events of the evening and the excessive alcohol consumption.

'What is it?' Cameron handed over his phone. He was watching a video recording, 'Oh my God, is that your dash-cam recording?'

'Yep, it appears that what we did on the bonnet was forceful enough to trigger the car's security system to record. It flagged it under the heading, *Potential front-end collision*. I didn't look at my phone until this morning. I think I'll save that video.'

'Thankfully, you can only see the top of my head. You look hot—I feel horny watching it, which is saying something, as I feel pretty rough this morning.'

'I'm not surprised with the amount of tequila you put away. I've put some painkillers and a pint of water on your bedside for you. How are you feeling about what happened?' Cameron lay on his side, propping himself up on his elbow.

'I feel numb. I was too drunk to comprehend what was

happening, and I'm not sure I thanked you for what you did.'

'Did you see the video I just showed you? That was thanks enough.'

'No, seriously. Most men would have walked away from me at the start. You went out of your way to make sure I could have a great night, and then you watched over me to keep me safe. You got to me before the bouncer who was only yards away. I hate to think what Mark would've done if you hadn't been there. I've never seen him look so twisted.'

'Jen, I'm not like most men. I protect the people around me, and I stop at nothing for the people I love.'

Imogen wasn't sure if he intended to imply that he loved her, so she ignored the comment, but on the inside, she was beaming.

'You're the perfect gentleman. Thank you for opening up to me. I feel awful about what your mum went through, and I understand why you behave the way you do. I get it, Cameron. When I feel less like I'm going to throw up, I'll show you how much I appreciate what you did for me.'

'That's so romantic. In the meantime, I want to take you shopping, so take your painkillers and get in the shower—you stink of booze.' Cameron jumped out of bed and went into the en-suite.

'What are we shopping for?' Imogen called out but regretted it—it was too loud for her head to cope with.

'You'll see.'

Thirty minutes later, they were in the car. Imogen's damp hair was tied in a messy bun. She'd dressed for comfort in jeans and a sweatshirt. Before she knew it, they were pulling into a parking space, and Cameron ushered her out of the car. He took her by the hand and led her through the High Street.

'Here we are.'

'Why are we at a phone shop? I don't need a new phone.'

'Yes, you do. I want to buy you a phone that's never had a message from your ex on it. I want it to be a fresh start for you, and I want to be the one to give it to you.'

'You don't have to, Cameron. That's way too much.'

'Do I look like someone that'll take no for an answer? New phone number, new phone, fresh start. Deal?'

'Okay, deal. On one condition.'

'What?'

'In the future, if you get a gut feeling about something, discuss it with me instead of turning into a secret agent. I think you may've watched too many Bond movies.'

'All right, agreed. And you have to promise to let me know if anyone's bothering you.'

'Agreed.'

It didn't take long to choose a new phone. The saleswoman almost pounced on Cameron as they walked in, and his instruction was simple.

'My girlfriend will have the newest model, please.' All Imogen had to do was choose the colour and the case.

'I want my number to be the first one stored in there. You can give your mother the new number on the strict instruction she's not to pass it on to anyone else, no matter how much they beg for it.'

'Don't worry, I don't think she'll make that mistake again. Thank you for this. I love it.'

'You're very welcome.'

'Do you mind if we go clothes shopping? I need to buy a whole new wardrobe, continuing with the fresh start theme.'

'Sounds like a plan. Will it include more of that sexy underwear that I can rip open?'

'Maybe, if you're lucky. I need to grab an energy drink first—I'm having a relapse.'

'Have you had any thoughts about what you want to do with your house?' They were back home and unpacking Imogen's new things.

'I haven't given it much thought. I should get it on the market and sell it.'

'I think it'd make a great investment to keep and rent out. You were lucky to get that property. It'd be mad to sell it.'

'I guess I could do that. I'll look into it.' Imogen wondered if it was a good idea to keep the property as a backup in case things didn't work out with Cameron. It crossed her mind that he might be thinking the same.

'Just in case you're trying to second guess me again. No, I'm not suggesting that, so you have somewhere to live if we don't work out. Us not working out is not an option.'

'Okay,' Imogen held her hands up in mock surrender. 'Message received and understood.'

'So, I've been thinking about how it would be nice to meet your family. Shall we see if your mum and dad are free tomorrow? I could cook a Sunday roast.'

'Okay, I was going to ring Mum soon anyway to give her my number, so I'll ask her. Your garden will impress her. Get ready to discuss the names of plants—in Latin.'

'I've no idea. I refer to them as the spiky one, the bushy one and the one with flowers. I'll stick with your dad and discuss cars.'

'Sounds like a plan.' Imogen called her mother and invited them over. She didn't discuss the previous night's events—it could wait until they were there in person. To her delight, her parents were free and looking forward to meeting Cameron. Imogen felt nervous. She couldn't believe it was Cameron's suggestion—this felt like a big move in their relationship. Meeting the parents was a big step. She hoped they all got on.

'I'd like to meet your parents too.'

'Don't worry, you will. My mum keeps nagging me to introduce you, so I won't get away with keeping you to myself for much longer. They're at their place in Italy, but they'll be back in a couple of weeks.'

'Wow, I love Italy. Where is their villa?'

'It's in a town called Monteriggioni. It's near Sienna, and it's amazing. I'll take you there soon. You can escape the world. There are fields and cypress trees as far as the eyes can see. There's barely any internet or phone access, and that's the way we like it. We'd have to find our own entertainment while we're there.' Cameron gave Imogen's rear a squeeze.

'Sounds amazing. I think we could do with some downtime.'

'You chill out—I'm going to pop to the shops to get everything in for tomorrow. What shall I do for dessert?'

'I'll sort dessert. I make a great apple and blackberry crumble.'

'Okay. I'll be back soon.'

Imogen used the time to sort her old clothes for the charity shop and send her phone number to her friends and her parents.

Hey Sarah, this is Imogen from her new phone! Cameron took me out this morning and treated me to it so I could have a fresh start. How are you today?

Hey, Jen, that is so sweet of him. You two are the best couple. I'm good thanks, just at James' place at the moment. Had a great night. How are you feeling about what happened with Tosspot?

Oh, still at James'? I won't ask what you've been up to all day! I'm okay. I'm hoping Mark will leave me alone now. The state of his face after Cameron finished with him was awful. I don't think he'll be in a rush to have another beating. My parents are coming for lunch tomorrow—Cam's idea. I'm feeling nervous. I'm sure they'll love him, though.

Oh wow, big step. Let's do lunch on Monday so you can tell me about it. I'm glad Mark got the beating he deserves. He'd be a total nut job to bother you again. James is distracting me in ways you don't want to know, and he says hi. I'll see you on Monday. Have a great day tomorrow, xxx

Have a great weekend, too, if you ever get out of bed. X

'You look nervous. Are you okay?' Imogen laughed as Cameron flitted about the kitchen. His usually calm demeanour was out the window.

'I am, yeah. What if they don't like me?'

'Not going to happen, so chill out.' Imogen kissed Cameron as the doorbell rang. They went to answer the door together.

'Hello, Mum and Dad, come in. This is Cameron. Cameron,

this is Mum and Dad, also known as Claire and Paul.'

'It's great to meet you.' Cameron kissed Imogen's mum on the cheek. Imogen's dad went to shake his hand.

'Do you mind switching hands? I'm carrying an injury on this one.' Cameron shook Paul's hand and welcomed them into the house.

'May I ask how you injured your hand in what looks like a spectacular fashion?'

'I finally met the ex, and if you think my fist looks bad, you should see his face.'

'Oh my goodness. Are you okay, dear?' Claire looked at Cameron's hand with concern.

'Stop fussing, Claire. Look at the man—he's fine. I'd say I feel sorry for Mark, but I dare say he got less than he deserved. Well done, Cameron. Thank you for doing what I'm not allowed to.'

'You're welcome. He's lucky he's still breathing, but hopefully, he won't be back to bother us. Anyway, come in, and I'll get you a drink. Did you have a good journey?'

'It was good, thanks. The traffic wasn't bad, which is a bonus when you're trying to drive out of London.'

'You have a lovely home, Cameron.' Claire was looking around as they walked through to the kitchen.

Claire was the same height as Imogen and had chin-length, chestnut-brown hair tucked behind her ears. She wore glasses and looked very stylish in well-fitting jeans, red patent pumps, and a matching red jumper. Paul was a tall man with broad shoulders and short grey hair on his crown. He looked like he could handle himself.

While Cameron put the finishing touches to dinner, they chatted in the kitchen, the conversation flowing easily. Before they knew it, the smell of roast beef and gravy filled the air.

'I must say, Cameron, this meat is cooked to perfection, and your Yorkshire pudding has risen beautifully. Do you have an interest in cooking?'

Cameron explained how he loved to cook and was a partner in a restaurant.

'You'll have to visit for a weekend next time, and I'll take you to the restaurant. I think you'd enjoy it.'

'That'd be lovely. We'll look forward to that, won't we, Paul?'

'Sounds good—I'd like that. Imogen, did your mother tell you about Izzy?'

'No, what about her?'

'She's having a baby. Isn't that lovely? She said she'd love to make up with you, that she misses you something terrible. Imogen. I don't understand why you two fell out so badly.'

'She didn't like Mark. That's all it was, really.'

'I like the sound of her. She sounds like a sensible woman.'

'Cheers, Cameron. Turns out she's a better judge of character than I was.'

'Well, I'd say you've got over that now.' Claire gave Cameron a big smile. 'She's coming to visit in a few weeks with Miles. Why don't you see her then and bury the hatchet? It would mean the world to me if you two were friends again.'

'I'd like that. I could have done with her the last few months.'

'Well, Imogen, I'm sure if you'd bothered to tell us what was going on, she would have been there for you. We all could have been.'

'Yeah, sorry, Dad, I was just in a weird place. Everything's perfect now, though.' Imogen squeezed Cameron's thigh under the table.

'So, you two, tell me everything about Friday night.'

'I'll sort the kitchen and bring dessert in. I'll let Cameron fill you in. He probably remembers it better than I do.' Imogen cleared the table and went to get dessert.

After they finished their meal, Imogen offered to take her mum around the garden while Cameron talked cars with her dad.

'Let me see your car then, Cameron. Imogen tells me the engine sounds amazing.'

'I've something else that will interest you. I haven't even shown it to Imogen yet. Come this way.'

Cameron led Paul to his garage and opened one of the doors. Inside was a car under a tarpaulin.

'After Imogen, this is my pride and joy.' Cameron lifted the cover to reveal a beautiful British racing green sports car.

'Oh my goodness, is that an E-type Jaguar?'

'It is indeed, 5.3-litre V12 engine. It's a mark one.'

'It's a thing of beauty. Do you drive it much?'

'No, not a lot. I save it for summer weekends as it's best when the top's down. I can't wait to take Imogen out for a drive in it.'

'She'll love it. You're serious about her, aren't you?'

'Yes, I am, and I promise to never hurt her.'

'You've already proved yourself to me, young man. I officially approve.'

'Thank you, that means a lot.'

'He is such a handsome man, isn't he?'

'Yes, he is, Mum. I fell for him the second I saw him in the office.'

'How old is he?'

'He's thirty-one. Why?'

'Oh, you know, just wondering how long it will be before he wants to marry and have children.'

'Don't jump the gun, Mum, crikey. We've only been together a short while.'

'And look how much you've been through. You've already moved in with him—I think he's in it for the long haul, Imogen, and I couldn't be happier. When it's the right one, it can happen very quickly. Just look at your father and me. Within six months of meeting, we were married and had Izzy a year later.'

'All right, Mum, don't scare Cameron off by talking like that around him, will you?'

'I think nothing will scare that man off. He's proved that already, hasn't he?'

'I guess so.' Imogen tried not to get too excited about her future with Cameron. She was going to take each day as it came.

CHAPTER 41

Song Choice: I'm Yours (Jason Mraz)

'You didn't tell me you were hiding a classic car in the garage. What other secrets do you have, Mr Black?' Imogen and Cameron snuggled in front of the fire, her parents having left an hour before.

'It's not a secret. I just hadn't got around to showing it to you yet. I'm looking forward to taking you for a drive in her. Maybe I could risk getting her dirty and take you out next weekend.'

'I'd like that, but maybe keep the top up.'

'No way. To get the full experience, you should have the top down. I'll buy you a woolly hat, don't worry. Your dad loved the car. I think I won him over.'

'My mum loved you. You won them both over. I think my mum's already planning which hat to buy for the wedding.'

'Your dad gave me his blessing. Do you think they're trying to marry you off?' Cameron laughed—it was a sound that brought warmth into Imogen's heart. She snuggled down, and he kissed her on the top of her head.

'Cameron?'

'Mmm.'

'I love you.' Imogen couldn't look at Cameron when she said it. She feared what she'd see. He lifted her chin, so she was looking into his eyes.

'I love you too.' He sealed his words with a tender kiss. The touch of his lips against hers sent shivers down her spine, and her nerve endings came alive. At that moment, she felt truly loved, and the feeling was mutual.

'I think it's time I thanked you for what you've done for me. Wait here.' A minute later, Imogen returned with a can of whipped cream. 'Time for dessert.'

Cameron raised an eyebrow. 'I hope you're thinking what I'm thinking.'

Her eyes were full of excitement as she popped the lid off. Kneeling, she settled on the floor between his legs. She undid his belt and the buttons of his jeans. Cameron reached down to stroke her hair but remained silent—the look in his eyes said it all—he knew what was coming.

Imogen took hold of Cameron's length, and it came to life. She gave the can a shake and dispensed the whipped cream along his shaft before looking up into his eyes. 'I seem to remember you like to watch me eat.' Keeping eye contact, she slowly licked away all traces of the cream. He flexed his hips in encouragement, a moan escaping from his lips.

'I don't want to come like this. I need to be inside you.'

She didn't respond to Cameron's pleas. She wanted to drive

him crazy and didn't intend to stop until he was close to reaching his pinnacle. Confident that he wouldn't be able to hold out for much longer, she removed her underwear. She was only wearing the oversized T-shirt she'd changed into earlier. Cameron lifted his hips to help her pull his jeans and boxers down.

'The anticipation is killing me. I don't know how much longer I can last.'

She brought her lips to his as she straddled him, just barely touching her opening to the tip of his erection—she felt it twitch beneath her.

She lowered herself slowly, inch by inch. His hips rose in encouragement, desperate for more, but Imogen hovered, teasing him. She bit her lower lip as she lowered, taking him all in.

'You're perfect, Imogen. I can't get enough of you.' Cameron lifted her T-shirt to suck her nipples, drawing them into his mouth before biting them with enough force to elicit a gasp. Imogen fought against her desires and kept the pace slow. She rose to his very tip and then slid down an inch before repeating the sinful torture. As she sank onto him, taking his full length, they both released groans of pleasure. The sensation was too much to bear.

Cameron couldn't take any more—he needed to control the pace, or he wouldn't last much longer. He grabbed her rear and flipped her onto her back. He wrapped her right leg around his waist, and her left leg hung off the edge of the sofa, with her foot resting on the floor. She was open to him. He took one of the cushions and put it under her hips. As he drove into her, his pelvis rubbed across her clit, the friction bringing her close to climax.

She held his arse and encouraged him to push harder, the

sensation driving her wild. Seconds later, they both cried out as they came together.

'I love you so much, Imogen.' He was panting, almost unable to speak the words.

'I love you too, so much it scares me.'

He cradled her in his arms and peppered her with kisses.

'Let's go to bed so I can show you how much I love you all over again.'

'Oh, Mr Black, you're spoiling me.'

'I don't want to get out of bed this morning. As you're the boss, can't you order me to stay in bed with you all day?'

'I'd love to, but I've a feeling that James would get pretty pissed with me. I have a lot on today, so that's not possible.'

'Well, that's just rubbish. I guess I'll have to get my arse into gear. Are you seeing James tonight for your Monday night drinks?'

'I was planning to. I'd prefer to be here with you, but I'd feel bad for dumping him.'

'That's cool. I thought I could be your taxi so you can drink then come home to me, rather than sleep at his. How does that sound?'

'I think it sounds like I get the best of both worlds. You're awesome.'

'Thanks. I know, though.' Cameron slapped her playfully on the arse as she walked past.

'Good morning, you two,' Sarah spoke in a singsong voice.

'Good morning Sarah, good weekend?'

'Yes, thank you, Cameron. Jen, are you up for lunch?'

'Totally, can't wait. Have you seen Lucy today?'

'No, not yet. We should invite her to lunch to make sure she's okay?'

'Good idea—I'll ask her when she comes in.'

Lucy arrived later that morning, just in time for the Monday morning team meeting. She entered the meeting room with her arms full of muffins and cookies.

'I've been baking all weekend, so I hope you're all hungry.' Lucy put on a big smile as she dumped the boxes of baked goods on the table. James looked at Imogen with concern. He could see the smile was fake. Imogen turned to Lucy.

'Hey Lucy, are you doing okay?'

'Hey, Imogen. I'm good—just keeping busy. Shall we catch up later?'

'Yeah, sure, come to lunch with Sarah and me.'

'Okay.'

Lucy had force-fed everyone so many muffins and cookies that Imogen wasn't hungry at lunchtime. Still, as soon as the clock said twelve, she prompted Lucy to get ready for going out. The three of them were outside and clear of the office when Sarah turned to Lucy.

'So, how are you doing, Lucy?'

'Oh, I'm fine—it's Imogen that's been through the most. How are you doing, Imogen?' She was babbling and not herself.

'I'm okay, but I'm worried about you. You don't need to put a brave face on for us. We're here for you. Be honest—how are you, really?'

Lucy sighed in resignation. 'Not great. I feel violated and like an idiot. I don't know why I thought Paul—' She shook her head.

'I mean, Mark would be attracted to me. Nobody ever approaches me in a bar, and no one's ever been attentive to me. My last and only boyfriend showed little interest in the years we were together. I felt good about myself, and now I'm back to being a loser. How can I ever trust anyone again?'

'Oh God, Lucy, please don't feel like that. You're one of the most beautiful people I've ever had the pleasure of knowing. When you started at work, you won us all over with your charm, although the muffins helped too.' Sarah gave Lucy a big smile.

'I agree. I think you're beautiful and so loving and kind. I saw how Tom couldn't take his eyes off you the whole time he was near you in the club. Cameron told me he was interested in you the minute he saw you.'

'Really?'

'Yes, Lucy. Please don't let Mark beat you. What happened is because of him, not a reflection of you. And your ex-boyfriend was an arse. Have you heard from Tom?'

They reached the coffee shop and waited for their order to arrive.

'He called me on Saturday morning to make sure I was okay. He said he was worried about me.'

'See, you've pulled a right hottie there, Lucy. Tell us more.' Sarah leaned closer to show her interest.

'He wants to see me again and asked if I'd visit him this weekend. I'm not sure, though. I don't know if I'm ready.'

'I can understand that, but I think you should go for it. Tom seems like a gentleman. I think it would do you good to get back on the horse, as they say.' Imogen wanted Lucy to be happy. She felt responsible for what happened to her.

'Text him and take him up on his offer.' Sarah handed Lucy

her handbag.

'Okay, I'll do it. You two are going to have to give me a pep talk, though, and maybe some tips. I'm a total novice at all this.'

'Just be yourself, Lucy—that's all you need to do.' Imogen put her hand on Lucy's, reassuring her.

'Yeah, totally be yourself. But I can also teach you plenty of tricks.' Between mouthfuls, Sarah divulged the sordid details from her past exploits.

'Oh, Sarah, TMI. I'm not sure I can look at you in the same way now.' Imogen covered her ears in mock shock. Lucy couldn't stop blushing at the things she heard but paid close attention so she could pick up some tips.

'Well, this feels like nothing compared to what you two have been up to, but I have some news.'

'Oh my God, you're not pregnant, are you?'

'Bloody hell, Sarah, give it a rest with the pregnancy talk. No, I'm not. I told Cameron I love him, and he said it back.'

Sarah and Lucy squealed with delight.

Imogen felt free—her life was back on track.

'Have a great time tonight. Call me when you want picking up.' Imogen leant over to kiss Cameron goodbye before he got out of her car.

'Will do, sweet cheeks. Thanks for the lift. Have a lovely evening and try not to miss me too much.'

'I'll do my best, but it's going to be tricky. I'll have my book to distract me and a nice cup of tea.'

'Sounds good—I'm jealous. Right, see you later, sexy. Love you.' Imogen would never tire of hearing those words or how he said them with such ease. She drove home and settled in for a quiet night with a big smile. She'd reached the end of her book, where Melissa and Johnny tied the knot. Her phone rang, so she absent-mindedly picked it up, not taking her eyes off the last page.

'Hey sexy, you ready to be picked up?'

'Oh, hi, Imogen—it's Izzy.'

'God, Izzy, sorry—I assumed it was Cameron.'

'Ah yes, the perfect boyfriend I've heard so much about.'

'I assume you've spoken to Mum then, and she broke the rules and dished my number out.'

'Yeah, she figured you wouldn't mind me having it, what with me being your sister and not a bat-shit crazy ex. Sorry if that's not the case.'

'Ah, Iz, don't get pissy with me. You know I didn't mean it like that. I'm glad you called. I've missed you.'

'I've missed you too, Jen. I'm sorry I walked away when I should've stuck to my guns. I can't help but feel I could have protected you from what you've been through. Mum told me everything—well, everything you told her—which I suspect isn't the whole story. I just want you to know you can tell me. I won't talk to anyone else about it, but I'll be here for you. From now on, I'll never walk away again.'

'Thanks, sis. I'm sorry for not listening to you when you tried to warn me. I promise to in the future. So, I hear congratulations are in order?'

'Yes, Miles and I are very excited. We're only eight weeks into the pregnancy, so we haven't officially told everyone yet.'

'How are you feeling? Have you had much sickness?'

'I feel great. It's the weirdest feeling, though. An actual person is growing inside me—it's scary.'

'I'm so excited to be an aunty. I wish you didn't live so far away.'

'Well, we're thinking of selling the farm down here and moving back to be nearer to you guys. I don't want to have a baby and be so far away from my family. Miles doesn't have any family here, so he doesn't mind moving. Mum told me you live in a gorgeous village in the countryside, so that got me thinking, maybe we could move to your neck of the woods. What do you think? Can you cope with having me in your life full time?'

'Oh my goodness, Iz, that would be amazing. I'd love that—really, I would.'

'That's good to hear. We're coming up in a few weeks to look at places. We didn't tell Mum because I didn't want her to get excited in case we didn't find somewhere suitable. It's not easy finding land or farms for sale.'

'I'll keep it to myself, no worries. Oh, Iz, I can't wait to see you, and I can't wait to introduce you to Cameron. He's the best. He's an architect that likes to get his hands dirty—it's so sexy when he's in his gear for the building sites. I'm sure he could help you find somewhere and even build your house for you. It'd be amazing.'

'He sounds perfect—intelligent and sexy. I assume he has no overly-controlling tendencies?'

'Nope, he's a perfect gentleman. He protects me and looks out for me, but not in a psycho way. I feel safe with him and loved. It's amazing, Iz. I'm so happy.'

'I'm pleased for you. I might even be crying a little bit. Jen, I'm so happy we've sorted this out. I can't wait to see you.'

'Same here. Let's not be dickheads again, shall we?'

'Sounds like a plan. I'd better go—it's past my bedtime, and

I'm exhausted. Call me soon, or just text me a lot. I don't want to miss any part of your life now, okay?'

'Okay, Iz. I'll keep you updated. You'll have to stay here and see how you like the surrounding area.'

'Good idea. Goodnight, Jen—I love you, sis.'

'Love you too. Sleep well, mummy-to-be.'

As Imogen hung up, she felt complete. When she left Mark, she could not have imagined how far, and how quickly, her life would change for the better. Her thoughts were interrupted by her phone ringing. This time Cameron's face came up.

'Hello, is that Taylor's taxis?'

'It is indeed. Do you need my services?'

'Always.'

'Okay, I'll head out now.'

'Imogen, bring my car this time.'

'Okay, I'll see you soon.'

Imogen grabbed Cameron's car keys. She was looking forward to hearing the engine come to life. When she pulled up outside James' house, Cameron was waiting outside.

'How did you know I was here?'

'I tracked you on my phone, but not in a stalker way, just in an "I want to make sure you get here okay" kind of way.'

'You're sweet. It's a good job. I didn't take it on a joy ride then.'

'You can take it on a joy ride now if you want.' Cameron gave her a look that was pure sex. She knew what he meant by a joy ride, and he'd had a few to drink.

'Come on, you sex pest—let's get you home.'

'Did you have a nice evening?'

'I did, thank you. Izzy phoned me, and we cleared the air.

253

They're looking to moving back this way, that's why they're visiting. It'll be nice to have her back. If you hear of any land or farms available, can you let me know?'

'Yeah, sure, my friend owns an estate agency. I can ask him to tell me if anything comes up. He'll give us first dibs.'

'That'd be great. Thank you, Cam.'

'No worries, sexy', he ran his hand up Imogen's thigh. 'Fancy pulling over? Something has come up.'

Imogen laughed. 'You're insatiable, but I like it. Let's get you home.'

CHAPTER 42

'Imogen—Walter and Holmes have brought the deadline forward to see the initial drawings. Do you have them ready?' James called Imogen into his office as soon as she arrived.

'Yes, thankfully, I do. I got them ready the other day.' Imogen had spent the week working hard to get ahead on her designs. The last few weeks had distracted her, and she wanted to get her old self back—she prided herself on her work ethic.

'Great job. I knew I could count on you. They want to see the designs next Tuesday, and I'd like you to take Lucy with you. I think she could do with getting out of the office and seeing how you handle the clients. I won't come along—I want to hand this over to you. Are you okay with that?'

'Wow, yeah. That's great, thank you. I'll speak to Lucy, and we can start on the presentation. Thank you, James. It's great to have the opportunity.'

'Don't thank me—you earned it.'

Imogen went to her desk and took Lucy through her designs. Lucy had some excellent input for the presentation. It was good to see her thinking about something other than the weekend's events.

'How're you doing, Lucy? Have you heard much from Tom?'

'I'm okay, thanks. Tom calls me almost every night after he closes. I'm knackered, to be honest, as it's always late, but I love going to sleep after hearing his voice. He has such a sexy voice, Imogen. I'm not going to get ahead of myself this time. Just take it slowly, one day at a time.'

'That sounds great, Lucy, and you don't need to be nervous. Just be yourself. At least you know he's a normal guy. Cameron wouldn't be friends with him if he wasn't.'

'That's true. I meant to ask, would you guys mind if I joined your book club? I think it's time I stopped being such a prude, and I had a good time with you all before twat-features turned up.'

'I think the other two would love that. We're about to start a new book, so your timing's perfect. We'll meet in the pub in Oundle. I'll be driving this time, though, as I'm not within walking distance, so I can pick you up on the way. Are you close by?'

'Yeah, I am. I'm looking for somewhere to live, so maybe I should look in Oundle.'

'Oh, what's happening to your place?'

'The owners want to sell it, but it's out of my price range. I could only just manage the rental on it.'

'I've just had an amazing idea. You can rent my old place if you like. I'm putting it on the market. If I rent it to you, it'd save me a load of money on fees, and I'd much rather it went to someone I know and trust—you'd be doing me a favour.'

'Oh my God, that would be great. Are you sure? It would be

perfect.'

They discussed the details and agreed that Lucy could move in at the weekend as her landlord hadn't given her much notice. Imogen could clear out her belongings on Saturday, and Lucy could move her stuff in when she got back on Sunday.

They worked on the presentation for the rest of the afternoon until they only had a few more points to cover. They'd be ready to have a run through with James on Monday. Imogen was looking forward to leading on it. She told Cameron about it over dinner when they got home.

'I think that's great. You've earned it, Jen. You work so hard, and with everything that's been going on, you should be proud of yourself—I know I am. Take my car to the presentation—the boot is more practical than your Mini. You'll fit all the drawings in without a problem.'

'Thanks, Cameron. I'm proud of myself, and I'll gladly take your car. It's nicer to drive than mine, although parking yours may prove interesting, I'm used to getting into small spaces.'

'Don't worry, there's a button for parking—it'll do it all by itself.'

'Fancy pants.' Imogen laughed and wondered what other buttons the car had.

'I spoke to my mum today, and they're back from Italy next week. I asked if they were free next weekend. Mum can't wait to meet you. Are you okay to go to theirs for dinner on Saturday?'

'Yeah, that sounds good. I'm looking forward to meeting your parents. I hope they approve, especially your mum—mums of sons are always a nightmare, you know.'

'Don't worry, my mum'll be fine. She's easygoing. What do you fancy doing this weekend? I need to work out in the morning.'

Imogen raised her eyebrows and gave Cameron a cheeky smile. 'Not that kind of workout, Jen—I need to do some exercise. I'm sure I'm putting on weight since you moved in—I must be content.'

'I think you look hot, but I'll leave you alone long enough to get a workout done. I have to move the rest of my stuff out of my house as Lucy's moving in.'

'Right, that's handy. I'll help. I can meet you there so we can load both cars.'

'That'd be great, thanks. Get your workout done first so I can get everything bagged up, then you can turn up in time for the heavy lifting. I'm leaving it furnished because Lucy needs it, so that saves me the job of working out what to do with all that stuff.'

'It's working out perfectly, isn't it? Do you get the feeling that this is meant to be, or am I just being soppy?'

'No, I agree. I feel like I'm right where I'm meant to be.'

'I know where I want you, and that's underneath me and naked.'

Imogen pulled up outside her old house and took a moment before getting out of her car. This cosy home had made her happy for the few months she lived there. It was her stepping-stone to getting away from one life and starting a new one. She loved it and was glad she could keep hold of it. She was very happy with Cameron, but she wasn't ready to cut all ties to her independence, so Lucy renting the house was perfect.

Imogen let herself in and grabbed some bin bags from the kitchen. Looking through her cupboards and drawers, she realised that everything she owned was a reminder of a past she'd

rather forget. The clothes left here were the ones that Mark fa-
voured, and she never intended to wear them again. She put the
lot in a bag for the charity shop.

Home. It felt so natural to call Cameron's house her home.
She couldn't put her finger on it, but something about the place
felt so right. Or maybe it was just that Cameron lived there.
Imogen went to the shelf at the top of her built-in wardrobe.
There were a few pairs of shoes and a box. Her hand hovered
over the box for a few minutes before opening the lid.

She stared at the photos and other memorabilia from her years
with Mark, unsure why she'd kept them. She'd thrown her belongings together in a rush when she left London and hadn't giv-
en it much thought. Now was the time to let it go. She'd wasted
so much of her life with Mark. Instead of partying with friends
and having a good time, she was stuck by his side, following his
rules. As she sifted through the photos, she saw how sad she
looked. She wondered why she couldn't see the issues sooner.
Why didn't she leave him? She'd lost all her close friends to him,
but it happened gradually and went unnoticed.

Imogen stuffed the box into the bag destined for the bin
just as she heard the familiar engine roar outside. Her stomach
filled with butterflies, and her skin was hot to the touch. She
grabbed her filing box from the bottom of the wardrobe and met
Cameron at the front door.

'Hello beautiful, how's it going?' Cameron hugged and kissed
her.

'Good, I think I'm done. I just need to dump this bag in the
bin outside, then we can go.' Imogen filled a laundry basket with
her books and other possessions that were too heavy for the bin
bags as Cameron filled up his car.

He loaded the last bag into the car while she took a moment standing in the hallway.

'Are you okay with this, Jen?' Cameron had come back to see what was keeping her.

'Everything in my life has changed so quickly, but I'm ready to move on. Thank you, Cameron, for setting me free of my past.'

'Hey, you got yourself to this point. I'm lucky enough to have found you on the way. It took a lot of strength to come this far.'

Imogen took a shaky breath and sighed. 'Right, let's go.' She locked the door for the last time and walked down the path. She started her engine filled with hope for her future. She had let go.

CHAPTER 43

'Hey, Imogen.' Lucy stopped by to pick up the keys to the house.

'Hi Lucy, do you have time to come in for a cuppa or are you eager to get the moving started?'

'I'd best head off. My parents are helping me move, which is handy, but they're eager to get started. Thanks for this. You've saved my bacon. Let's hope your old place is as lucky for me as it was for you.'

'I hope so, Hun. You deserve some happiness. You never know, Tom could end up being your knight in shining armour.'

'Let's see about that, shall we? Anyway, I must dash. Thanks again.' Imogen noticed that Lucy's cheeks had turned a light shade of pink.

She closed the door and smiled. Her old house had saved her too. She figured it was a lucky house for ladies in need.

Lucy and Imogen sat in the kitchen with a coffee and pastry the following day while they ran through their presentation and made a few tweaks. They were presenting it to James that morning and wanted to make sure it was polished.

'So, now that the presentation's done, you can tell me how the move went and then about your weekend.'

'The move went well. It's easy moving when all you need to do is pack your clothes. There was no heavy lifting, and I think my dad was pleased about that. I have to keep the cat in until she knows where home is, but other than that, it's perfect. Thanks again, Imogen.'

'Hey, no worries. Like I said before, you were doing me a favour. So how was your first weekend in the new house?'

'It was great, thanks. I felt right at home. I feel like I've had a fresh start and can put things, or rather, people, behind me.'

'I know exactly what you mean.'

'Yeah, I guess we have a similar experience on that front.' Lucy looked at Imogen with some awkwardness.

'We do. I think we're part of a special sisterhood now, Lucy— we can look out for each other.' Imogen put her arm around her shoulder and gave her a reassuring squeeze.

'Plus, joining the book club will open your eyes to a whole new world. You'll be a new woman in no time at all.'

'I'm looking forward to book club—it'll be fun.'

'It will.' Imogen checked her watch. 'We'd better get a move on, let's go and impress the pants off, James.'

'Oh God, no. I'd rather he kept his pants on.' Lucy giggled. The mood lightened.

Twenty minutes later, they finished and were waiting for James' verdict.

'Amazing, ladies. You've done a fab job. I'm suitably impressed, and more importantly, Walter and Holmes will love it.'

'Oi, bitches! Where are you going without me?' Sarah was sitting behind her desk. It looked like she was on hold on the phone when Imogen and Lucy were leaving to grab some food.

'We're just going to the sandwich van—you want anything?'

'Nah, I'm all right, thanks. James is taking me out soon. Lucy, Jen says you're joining us for book club tomorrow. We're picking the next book, so do some research tonight to see if there are any you want us to consider.'

'Will do. Although, I have no idea what I'm looking for, so I'm happy to just get told what to read.'

They went to the sandwich van and grabbed lunch. Imogen bought Cameron his favourite chicken baguette as she knew he was busy in his office.

'Sarah is perfect for James, don't you think, Jen? They have very similar characters.'

'If by that you mean they're both loud and crass, then yes, they're perfect together.' Imogen laughed. 'They're good together. I enjoy being around them both, so I hope whatever is going on doesn't end badly. I can't imagine having to work with them if they fall out.'

'I know, awkward.' Lucy exaggerated the word awkward. 'You could say the same for you and Cameron. Although, I reckon you two'll be married soon with babies on the way—I've never met such a perfect couple.'

'Oh God, you'll make me blush. Before Cameron, I'd have said that I'd been in love before, but now I realise that what I felt wasn't love. What I have with Cameron is off the charts. Clichéd romance movies have got something right when they harp on about soul mates. I've found mine.'

'I'm so happy for you, Imogen, and insanely jealous. I hope I find that kind of love soon.'

'I think you will. I feel it in my bones. Well, I'd better make sure that my relationship continues and give Cam his lunch—otherwise, he'll be hungry.'

The rest of the afternoon was relaxed. Imogen spent most of it chatting with Lucy and going through the presentation. At five o'clock, Cameron was at her desk.

'You ready to go home? I'm shattered.'

'Yep, I'm good to go. See you tomorrow, Lucy,' Imogen turned her laptop off and left with Cameron.

'Has it been a tough day? I haven't seen you come out of your office.'

'Yeah, it's been brutal. I had to redesign the Walter and Holmes job as the MD didn't like the new layout. He sounds like a dick. I reworked the designs and sent them to his secretary, and low and behold, he preferred the original drawings. I instructed the team to carry on as planned after putting them on hold all day. Don't look so worried—it won't impact your work.'

'Thank goodness, I thought you were going to tell me I had to do some last-minute tweaks. Let's get home. I'll cook comfort food for dinner, then we can have an early night. I want to be on top form tomorrow. Oh, unless you're with James tonight?'

'Nope, we cancelled it. I'm too tired, and he wants to take Sarah out. Can you believe that? So much for dicks before chicks.' Cameron rolled his eyes, but he meant it with good humour.

'I think that's sweet. Lucy and I were talking about them to-day. Do you think it's going to work out?'

'Yeah, I do. He's a bit of a tart, but he's been nowhere near another woman for the last few months. It's like he's turned over a new leaf, a Sarah-shaped one.' He wrapped his arm around

Imogen on their walk to the car.

'Cheese toasties?' Cameron looked up from his favourite spot on the kitchen sofa.

'Yep, tuck in. Be careful—they're hot.'

'How did you make these? I don't own a sandwich maker—I disagree with them.'

'Well, we come as a package deal. It's the toasty maker and me, or you're on your own.'

'You drive a hard bargain, but I'll make an exception, just this once. If you unpack an electric blanket, then you're out.'

'Oh blimey, I hate those. I heard you can die if you wet yourself.' They laughed, and Cameron burnt his tongue on the molten cheese.

'You know what? I like how the bread crusts go hard and chewy. I think you've converted me.'

'The crusts are great dipped in ketchup.'

'That's a step too far, Jen, even for you. I consider myself more of a brown-sauce-with-cheese kind of guy.'

Imogen tidied up after dinner, and they sat on the sofa watching cooking shows. Cameron had his arm over her shoulder, holding her hand.

'You know, I could go to sleep like this. Can we watch TV in bed?'

'Yeah, come on, you look shattered.' Neither of them made it to the end of the episode they were watching. They fell asleep in each other's arms within minutes of getting into bed.

'What time is your meeting?' Cameron handed her his car keys as they walked to the office.

'Eleven. We're going to leave at ten-thirty—that should get us there in plenty of time.' Imogen had dressed to impress in a navy-blue dress with a round neckline. The sleeves were three-quarter length, and it finished just below her knees at the front but was cut longer at the back. It had a bottle green contrast trim, so she wore it with her green patent shoes. She was glad she'd bought the matching green cardigan, as the weather had got a lot colder over the last few days.

'Okay, cool. Come and see me when you get back. I want to know how it goes. Although, I'd love anything you have for me looking like that. We might have to frost the glass in my office when you get back. I have plans for you and that dress, and it won't wait until we get home.'

'Saucy. I'll try not to think about that while I'm presenting. They might mistake my red flush for anxiety.'

'I'll be thinking of nothing but you.' Before they went in, Cameron kissed Imogen. While it was slow and gentle, it was no less passionate than any of his other kisses. 'See you later, beautiful.'

CHAPTER 44

Mark looked around the room with a self-satisfied grin on his face. It was perfect. Imogen would love it. She could die happy in a room like this. He'd paid close attention to detail, even down to the thread count of the cotton sheets on the bed. Nothing less than six hundred would be good enough for his Imogen. He took a moment to imagine how beautiful the contrast of her crimson blood would look against the white sheets.

He'd placed her favourite scented candle, peony and blush suede, on the bedside table. Next to the candle stood a vase filled with peonies. Their once beautifully-scented, pink petals were now discoloured and dried, which he decided poetically represented their love.

Mark filled the wardrobe with all the clothes he loved to see Imogen wear. Arranged neatly on the dressing table were her cosmetics and jewellery. It wasn't his original intention to turn this room into her final resting place. He hoped he could keep her here long enough for her to see the error of her ways and give her heart to him.

'It's a shame it will be too late, though, my love. You had your chance to come back to me, and you blew it.' He spoke out loud to the empty room. Turning to leave, he took his phone from his back pocket.

'Hi Juliet, it's Mark. I'm okay, thank you, healing nicely, but still looking too ghastly to meet with people, I'm afraid. Can you handle the Spencer and Black meeting without me? Good. Call me as soon as the meeting finishes and tell me how it went.' Closing the door to Imogen's room, he paused to check the lock was secure. Satisfied that everything was ready, he walked to his car and checked that he had what he needed. The rope and knife were in the boot. It was time.

CHAPTER 45

'Good morning. You must be from Spencer and Black. I'm Juliet Swanson, pleased to meet you.' Juliet shook Imogen and Lucy's hands. She was tall, blonde and glamourous, dressed in a close-fitting black dress paired with black patent stilettos. Imogen thought she looked like a classic beauty from a time gone by.

'Thank you for meeting me here. As you can see, we aren't set up yet. I don't even have a receptionist. Apologies for bringing the meeting forward. Our MD wanted to move fast on the relocation. He was hoping to meet you today and see the plans himself, but unfortunately, he's off sick at the moment.'

'That's a shame. We hope he feels better soon. I'm Imogen Taylor, and this is my colleague, Lucy Steele. I shall be managing this part of the project, so James thought it best that we come today.'

'Fantastic. Shall we get started? I've cobbled together a table and chairs and ordered some coffee. We thought it best to hold the meeting here to get a feel for the space and envisage your designs. I hope this is workable.'

'Yes, don't worry. Cameron, our architect, has taken me through all the drawings and some 3D imagery, so I have a good feel for the place already.'

'Ah yes, Cameron Black, he's been great. He did a fantastic job on the layout and found solutions to all the problems. He's been a pleasure to work with.' Juliet had a look on her face that Imogen didn't like.

'Yes, Cameron's the best in the business. Shall we take you through our presentation?'

'Yes, right this way, ladies.'

As Lucy and Imogen fell in behind Juliet, they exchanged glances. The moment wasn't lost on Lucy either.

'You can't blame her. He is damn fine.' Lucy whispered under her breath.

'All right, Lucy, I've got to stay professional and not think about Cameron—otherwise, I'll go red.'

Lucy let out an inaudible giggle.

'Here we go. Again, apologies for the lack of formal meeting space. Do you have everything you need?'

'Yes, we're all set, thank you.'

Imogen and Lucy worked well together, and Juliet seemed impressed with what she'd seen. She was particularly impressed with the Divino furniture.

'I haven't heard of Divino before. I must say, I'm already a fan.'

'Really? We must have been misinformed—we were told you came to us on Fran Divino's recommendation.'

'Perhaps that was before they put me on the project. I transferred from one of our other companies at short notice, so I'm not fully up to speed. I'm glad I know about her now—her designs are beautiful. Okay, ladies, thank you so much for coming in today. I like your ideas and can't wait to see them come to life. I don't have any suggestions for changes so consider this the green light. Here's my business card. Apologies, it's my old one as I haven't got new ones printed, but the number is the same so if you have any questions, just call me.'

As Juliet handed over her business card, Imogen felt she'd been winded. She recognised the company logo as one of Mark's subsidiary companies. She felt a nudge in her side and turned to see Lucy staring at her. She realised she must have been gaping.

'Okay. Great, thank you so much. I'll get the finer details and send the finished design for your approval. If you think of any changes in the meantime, please let me know. Our numbers are in the pack we gave you.'

Imogen was desperate to get out of the building and into the safety of Cameron's car. She walked at a brisk pace.

'Hey, Imogen, wait up—I can't keep up in these heels.'

'Sorry, I just need to get to the car.'

Imogen had the keys out and opened the boot as they reached the car. She threw the design boards in before scrambling into the front seat. She took a few moments to take calming breaths while Lucy loaded the boot and got in.

'Imogen, what's the matter? You look like you've seen a ghost.'

'Did you recognise the company name or logo on her business card, Lucy?'

'No. Why?'

'It's a subsidiary company of Mark's office. What if he's behind this job?'

'Oh my God, do you think he'd do that?' Lucy brought her hand up to her mouth in shock. 'What am I saying? Of course, he would. The guy is a total nut job. How would he arrange all this? And why?'

'I don't know. Weirdly, the project manager hadn't heard of Divino when we were told they came to us because Fran recommended me by name. Did you ever talk to Mark about Fran?'

'Let me think. I may have done, it's hard to say. I might've mentioned that you did a great job and impressed her so that we got a contract extension, so yeah, I guess he knows. But why would he get a subsidiary company to relocate just to give you some work? It doesn't make sense.'

'I don't know, but I have a bad feeling about this. I'm going to talk to Cameron and James as soon as we get back.'

'Okay. That's a good idea—let's see what they think.'

Imogen drove around the car park, impatiently trying to find an ample-enough parking space for Cameron's car. The tyres squealed on the concrete. Her sigh of relief was audible as they reached the third floor, and a space appeared directly in front of them. She reversed in, thankful for the parking assist the car offered.

Fully laden with imageboards, Imogen struggled to press the button to lock the car.

'More haste, less speed, Imogen. Come on, you can do this.' Her pep talk helped her calm down long enough to lock the door. The distraction, however, meant that she didn't see the person standing in front of them.

'Hello, Imogen, did you miss me? I bet you hoped you'd seen the last of me? Oh, and here's little Lucy.'

Imogen froze. Her heart was in her throat. 'Mark, what are you doing here? I'll call the police.'

'Don't worry, Imogen, I'm already on it.' Lucy was reaching into her handbag to retrieve her phone.

'I don't think so, you little bitch.' Mark was on Lucy and snatched her phone, throwing it to the ground. It smashed on contact.

'I've gone to great lengths to set this up today, and you're not going to get in the way this time.' Before either of them knew what was happening, Mark had taken a swing at Lucy. His fist made contact with the side of her face. She blacked out as she fell to the floor.

'Lucy.' Imogen dropped everything in her arms and went to her friend's side. She looked up at Mark with tears forming in her eyes. 'What are you doing? Why can't you just let me go?'

'I think I made it clear, Imogen. I'd rather see you dead. I've been patient with you, and I've given you plenty of chances to do the sensible thing and come back to me. You, however, brought Cameron Black into the picture. How could you cheat on me, Imogen? How could you? After everything I've done for you. I warned you repeatedly. I'd rather see you dead than with another man. I warned you.' Mark was spitting the words at Imogen. He was losing control.

'Just walk away, Mark. You don't want to do this.' Imogen raised her hand, trying to calm him down.

'You've left me no choice, you whore. I have to teach you a lesson.'

'No, you don't. Mark, please, let us go. Lucy needs help. Let me help her.'

'Oh, now you care about others. Where were you when I was getting beaten? I came to take you back, and the thanks I got was a kicking from your neanderthal boyfriend. Where were you

273

when I was dragged into the streets and left for dead? Did you think that was going to be the end? Did you think I was going to stay away? If I can't have you, no one can, Imogen.'

She was frantic. She scanned her surroundings, trying to find anything to help her get out of this situation.

'Lucy.' Imogen tried shaking Lucy to get her to come round. 'Lucy, please, you have to wake up. We have to get out of here.'

'You're coming with me. Haven't you listened to a word I said? I suppose you couldn't change the habit of a lifetime. You're beyond help. Get up.' Mark snarled as he reached down and grabbed her arm.

'No!' Imogen tried to back away, but he had too firm a grip on her. She mustered all her strength and pulled away from him.

'Where do you think you're going?' He lunged for her, but this time Imogen kicked out at him. Her pointed shoe hit his shin. The pain was enough to distract him. She saw her opportunity to get away, but Mark pulled her back. He grabbed her and swung her around. She lost balance and fell into his arms.

'You'll pay for that.' As he said the words, he threw Imogen hard onto the car's bonnet. He grabbed her wrists and had her pinned. He pressed her face into the warm metal. She could feel his breath on her neck. The sensation made bile rise in her throat.

'I'm going to take you home where you belong and make you see what you've been missing out on, and then I'll teach you a lesson for the way you've treated me. Maybe I should show you what you've been missing out on, right here, on this bonnet. Would you like that, you slut?' He covered her mouth with his free hand to stop her from screaming. He kicked her legs to widen her stance, settling himself on top of her.

Lucy regained consciousness. From where she lay, she could

see two sets of feet against the front of the car. She heard a muf-fled scream and Mark laughing maniacally.

CHAPTER 46

Song choice: Bleeding Out (Imagine Dragons)

'Have you heard from Imogen yet, James? I thought she would've been back by now, and a notification on my phone told me the car's been parked in the car park for ten minutes.'

'Nope, not heard a thing. I bet they're sitting in the car, talking boys.'

'They're not twelve, James—but they do like to talk.' He felt his phone vibrate in his pocket. 'Oh, hang on, maybe this is her now.' he pulled his phone out and looked at the screen. 'Apparently, she's had an impact. What's going on?' He watched the video footage that opened on his phone.

'Fuck. Call the police, James. Now! Mark's got her.' Cameron ran out of the office. The red mist took over again as he hurtled down the stairs.

'What's the rush, Cameron?' Sarah called as he ran past. He didn't reply—he had to get to Imogen.

Cameron had never run so fast in his life. His polished leather shoes slipped on the wet tarmac. He reached the car park but had the impossible task of determining which floor Imogen was on. He prayed it was one of the lower floors. And then he heard it, a scream. Adrenaline pounding through his veins, he picked up his pace and was soon on the third floor.

As he ran up the ramp, he saw Imogen pinned to the bonnet of his car with Mark leaning over her while she struggled.

'Get off her, Mark.' The anger in Cameron's voice echoed and ricocheted off the cement walls.

Mark grabbed Imogen's throat and pulled her upright. He'd tied her hands behind her back with the rope from his car.

'Oh, it's you, again. Why do you insist on showing up and ruining my plans? Never mind, I'll take great delight in dealing with you, too.'

'Fuck off, Mark. You won't get away with this. I'm warning you. Let Imogen go.'

'Really? You don't scare me, Black. You're not surrounded by a team of thugs this time.' Mark spat his name out with venom. 'I've come prepared. Let's see how tough you are now.' As Mark said the words, he pulled a knife out of his pocket. From what Cameron could see, it looked like a hunting knife. His thoughts went to protecting Imogen. He could feel his heart beating out of his chest. And then Mark did what he was dreading—he turned the knife on Imogen and held it against her throat. Her eyes were full of fear and panic.

'Cameron, please stay back,' Imogen begged, tears streaming down her face. She couldn't let Mark harm him. She'd rather die than see Cameron hurt at his hands.

'Shut up, Imogen, let the men do the talking.' Mark let go of her bound wrists and covered her mouth with his hand. The feel of the blade pressing against her throat stopped her from struggling as Mark's hold forced her into his chest.

'I came here to take Imogen home where she belongs, but in her usual style, she won't co-operate, so I'll have to take her by force. If you want to stay alive, I suggest you step out of the way.'

'Are you insane? I'm not going to let you take her anywhere. She's staying here with me. Now let her go.'

'Now, here's the thing, Cameron—no one can love Imogen as much as I do, but she's made it very clear over the last few weeks that she's deluded and not willing to see sense and come back to me. I've warned her over the years that if I can't have her, no one can.'

The muffled voices grew louder, becoming more apparent. Lucy tentatively opened her eyes. The light blinded her, making her aware of the throbbing in her skull. She needed to focus. She must remember why she was on the floor. The sound of Imogen's whimper pulled her back and focussed her mind. She looked up, trying not to alert anyone to her state of consciousness. Seeing the metal of the knife at Imogen's throat and hearing the desperation in Cameron's voice, she knew she needed to think fast. Reasoning with Mark was not an option. Lucy remembered Tom had given her a can of pepper spray at the club. Her handbag was by her side, close enough for her to touch it.

Engrossed in his maniacal exchange with Cameron, Mark didn't notice her sliding her arm out. She welcomed the feel of the small canister in the palm of her hand. Before Mark spotted her, she returned her arm to her side and remained still. She just needed to wait for the right time to use it.

'You don't know what love is, you sick bastard. I won't ask again—let Imogen go.' He forced the words out between gritted teeth. Clenching his hands into fists, Cameron was ready to do whatever was necessary to keep Imogen safe.

'Very well, I'll deal with you first. Perhaps Imogen will learn her lesson quicker if she sees me dispose of her latest fuck.'

Mark threw Imogen to the floor. With her hands still bound behind her back, she couldn't break her fall. Her head hit the ground. She was disorientated, her vision blurry.

'Imogen.' Cameron ran to her, but Lucy had lunged forward with the can of pepper spray before he could reach her.

'Take that, you wanker.' Mark dropped the knife as his hands flew up to wipe frantically at his face before laughing out loud.

'Oh Lucy, you poor pathetic individual, you can't even spray me properly. You missed most of my face.' His laugh was evil. 'You were an unfortunate but necessary part of my plan, one I'd rather not be reminded of.' Mark shuddered. 'Now, do us all a favour and fuck off.' Lucy saw Cameron inching closer to Mark—she kept him talking.

'Our meeting was unfortunate for both of us. I can't believe I carried on seeing you after we slept together that first night. It makes me feel sick.' Lucy had hit a sore spot and could see that she'd raised Mark's hackles.

'Well, it's hardly my fault—you're like a sack of potatoes. Trust me, Lucy, it's all on you.'

While his attention was elsewhere, Cameron ran at Mark, rugby-tackling him to the ground. He didn't hold back and got the first punch in. His fist landed on Mark's injured nose. Mark cried out but fought back by taking hold of Cameron by the throat. Cameron grabbed Mark's face and pushed his thumbs into his eye sockets, causing enough pain for Mark to release his grip.

Lucy ran to Imogen to check that she was okay. She was on the floor in a daze and was barely conscious. Lucy untied her hands, fumbling with the knots so that they could run and get help.

Cameron and Mark were fighting. Mark threw a punch, strong enough to rival Cameron's, the rage giving him strength. Cameron went down and hit the hard concrete. Mark seized his opportunity to retrieve the knife.

Lucy had managed to untie the rope and was helping Imogen to her feet. They saw the glint of metal.

'Cameron.' She called out, but it was too late.

Cameron threw another punch. Mark sidestepped him and plunged the blade into Cameron's abdomen.

He doubled over, his hand reaching to his stomach. In shock and confusion, he looked at Imogen—his gaze travelled to where his hand was concealing the wound. His shirt changed from white to red as the torrent of blood seeped through his fingertips.

'Imogen.' Her name passed his lips as a whisper before he collapsed to his knees. He tried to steady himself on all fours but was too weak. The blood loss was too much. Imogen ran to his side.

'Not so tough now, are you? And where do you think you're going, little lady?' Mark stepped in front of Imogen, dropping the knife and grabbing her. Before getting a firm hold, James threw him to the floor. The impact was so strong that Mark lay winded and dazed.

Imogen ran over to Cameron and skidded onto the concrete. She cradled his head in her lap—it felt heavy in her hands—a dead weight.

'Stay with me, please stay with me. Keep your eyes open for me, Cam. Please, keep your eyes open.' She took off her cardigan and tried to stem the bleeding.

'Call an ambulance. Call one now.' Imogen was screaming with all that was in her. She looked into Cameron's eyes—she could see the pain in them. She watched helplessly as they closed.

'Cameron, please stay awake. Open your eyes, Cameron.' She looked at Mark. 'You bastard, what have you done?'

James was by her side and hadn't seen Mark stand up.

'I warned you, Imogen.' Mark didn't get to say anymore. He froze, eyes wide in shock, and dropped to his knees.

Lucy had grabbed the knife and drove it into his back. Tears were streaming down her face, her words a whisper as she looked at Imogen. 'I'm sorry. He was going to kill you. I had to do it. I'm sorry. I didn't mean to.'

Mark tried to get up and steadied himself on one knee before James was over him.

'No, you don't.' Without hesitation, James kicked Mark square in the face, knocking him out cold. He fell backwards, driving the knife in deeper. Mark exhaled with a sudden rush as blood spurted from his mouth.

Imogen heard sirens in the distance while she rocked Cameron in her arms and prayed they didn't get there too late. Everything after that was a blur.

CHAPTER 47

Song Choice: Control (Zoe Wees)

'Imogen, you need to move out of the way so they can help him.' Imogen didn't understand what was happening. She felt James put his arms around her shoulders and encourage her to let go of Cameron and stand up. She felt as if she was underwater. All the sounds around her were muffled, and the world was moving in slow motion.

'You have to go in the ambulance. I'll speak to the police. Imogen, can you hear me?'

James guided her towards an ambulance. She could hear the paramedics attending to Cameron, trying to stop the bleeding and putting a drip in his arm.

'Okay, everyone, on my count. 1. 2. 3.' Cameron was moved onto a stretcher. The team wheeled him to the ambulance, their progress halted by organised chaos erupting.

'He's crashing. I need the defib now.' Imogen lost sight of Cameron as the paramedics surrounded him.

'What? No, Cameron, please stay strong. I can't live without you.' She tried to hold his hand, but James was holding her back. He needed her—why couldn't she go to him? Imogen looked around, desperate to find someone to help her reach Cameron. Sarah was hugging Lucy while they both sobbed and consoled each other. Imogen struggled to process what was happening. There were so many pockets of people busying themselves around her. She felt like she was spinning, and she wanted to scream. Her attention returned to Cameron, her sights only set on him.

'Clear.' The paramedics were doing all they could. Imogen looked over and saw Cameron's body lift off the stretcher with each shock he was given.

'Okay, I have a pulse, but it's very weak. His CO2 is dangerously low. We need to get him moving now.' The paramedics worked fast and loaded Cameron into the back of the ambulance. One of them came over to Imogen.

'You have to go in the other ambulance, sweetheart. We need to look at that head injury. Is there someone who can come with you?' Imogen wasn't aware of an injury—she touched her forehead and felt something sticky. She looked blankly at the paramedic.

'I will.' Sarah was at her side. She took Imogen and guided her to the ambulance. The sirens coming from Cameron's ambulance snapped her out of her daze.

'Mark! Someone needs to get Mark.' Imogen was frantic. She tried to run back to the car. Sarah grabbed her shoulders, looking at her with sympathetic eyes.

'Jen, Mark is dead.' She spoke softly to make sure Imogen understood what she was saying. Sarah turned to look where Mark lay, a black plastic sheet covering the body. Imogen followed her gaze, and then all she saw was black.

'James, help.' Sarah tried to hold Imogen up, but she was a dead weight in her arms. She was out cold. James ran over, scooping her into his arms and running her over to the waiting ambulance. He lay her on the stretcher and let the paramedics take over.

'Go with Imogen and call me with an update on them as soon as you can. Sam and I will deal with the police, and I'll call Julian and Cam's parents.' Sarah nodded and got in the ambulance.

The journey to the hospital was short, and Imogen was soon pushed through the doors. Sarah ran alongside her. The ceiling lights hurt her eyes, and she turned her head to avoid them. Then she saw him. Cameron was lying on a bed, surrounded by masses of medical staff, all in different coloured scrubs. Blood-soaked dressings were strewn over the floor. She could see a nurse trying to intubate him. Another one was cutting off his clothes. Imogen cried out to him but was pushed past him.

'Cameron, what's happening to Cameron?'

'Jen, they're doing everything they can to save him. He's going to need you to stay strong for him.'

A nurse cleaned up Imogen's head injury with a few stitches. She took the sedatives under protest. They only dented the surface of what she was feeling, but she wanted to stay alert for Cameron. Sarah held her hand. The physical contact kept her grounded.

'Do you want me to try and find out where Cameron is?'

Imogen nodded, unable to speak. If she spoke, she'd break

down—or puke—or both. Sarah ran into the corridor. The few minutes she was gone felt like hours.

'He's in surgery. They're still trying to stop the bleeding. The nurse couldn't tell me any more than that.'

'Okay, thanks, Sarah. Do you want to phone James?'

'Yeah, I'll do that now.' Imogen wasn't left alone for long as the nurse came back in.

'You're well enough to be discharged, but I understand you came in with the patient with the stab wound, is that right?'

'Yes, it is. Do you know how Cameron is?'

'I'm afraid I don't, but you can sit in the family room in area D. The surgeons are working on him and will update you as soon as they come out.'

'Thank you.'

'No worries, now try to take it easy. If you feel weak, dizzy or nauseous, please come straight back here.'

'Will do.' Imogen got off the bed and put her shoes on as Sarah came back in.

'Hey chick, any news while I was outside?'

'They've discharged me, but I can go to the family room to wait for news about Cameron.' Imogen shivered. Without her cardigan, the delayed clinical shock hit her. Sarah took her coat off and wrapped it around Imogen's shoulders.

'Come on, I'll come with you, and we can grab a cup of tea on the way.'

They found area D and took a seat. The room smelt like hospitals, a mix of disinfectant and sorrow. The plastic chairs were cold and hard against Imogen's skin, but she couldn't sit still anyway, so she paced around the room. The sound of footsteps pulled her attention to the corridor. She hoped to see the surgeon but was equally relieved to see Julian striding towards her. Saying nothing, he wrapped his arms around her and held her tightly. She broke down in tears, sobbing into his chest, leaving tear stains down his shirt.

'It's okay now, Imogen, you're safe, and Cameron will pull through this. He loves you too much to leave you now.'

'But what if he doesn't? I can't live without him, Julian, he's saved me and look where it's got him.'

'You can't think like that. Stay strong. He needs you now.' Julian looked over to Sarah, 'Hi Sarah, how're you doing?' He kept stroking Imogen's hair.

'Hey, Julian. I'm okay, thanks—pretty shocked, to be honest. Everything happened so quickly.'

'Has James given you an update on what's going on with the police?'

'Yeah, they've taken Lucy to the station for questioning, as she was the one who stabbed Mark. They'd better not charge her with murder. It was self-defence. James said he'll get her the best criminal lawyer. He won't let them charge her without a fight. Fucking Mark, he got off lightly if you ask me. Death is too good for someone like that.'

'I agree. At least we don't have to worry about him anymore. Once Cameron gets home, you guys can live happily ever after.' He looked at Imogen, who was staring into space. She offered Julian a weak smile.

'James found Cameron's phone on the floor in the car park and realised that his dash-cam had recorded everything. The police have taken it as evidence. Hopefully, that will prove that Mark caused this, and they'll close the case.'

'Let's hope so. It looks like Cameron's OCD with security has paid off.'

They sat in silence for a while, waiting for any kind of news. Nurses came and went. The minutes felt like hours. The sound of rushed footsteps broke the silence.

'Julian, is there any news on Cameron?' Imogen didn't recognise the couple running towards them. She assumed they must be Cameron's parents.

'We haven't had any updates since he went into surgery. He's been in there for a couple of hours now.'

'We got the call from James as we were driving back from the airport. Thank goodness we were in the country—I don't know what I'd have done if we were still in Italy.' Julian guided his aunt to the seats. His uncle followed.

'Let me introduce you to Imogen. Imogen, this is Liz, Cameron's mum, and this is David, his dad.'

'I'm so sorry we're meeting like this. I'm just so sorry.' Imogen sobbed.

Cameron's mother took hold of Imogen's face. Imogen noticed how warm her hands felt against her chilled skin.

'Now you hear me, never apologise to me for this. This is not your fault, understand?'

Imogen nodded, unable to say anything out loud. She felt she didn't deserve this level of understanding from Cameron's parents.

'Can someone tell us exactly what happened? James only said that Cameron was in the hospital after being stabbed by a lunatic.' His voice was strained, the stress clear on his face.

'I'll tell you everything.' Imogen motioned for them to sit down. She explained the events leading up to the stabbing. Cameron's parents had a look of disbelief on their faces. Imogen realised she'd been blanking the most recent events out of her mind. Or maybe that was the sedatives at work—she didn't know. The details came back to her, bit by bit. A heavier feeling crept into her stomach with each part of the story she told. By the time she finished, she was drained and exhausted.

'Well, it sounds like this Lucy girl did the best thing for Mark. They don't always get the justice they deserve, do they, Liz?' David looked over at Liz and held her hand.

'No. No, they don't.'

'I'm so sorry for putting your son in harm's way. This is all my fault.'

'Nonsense, the fault lies with that poor excuse for a man and no one else.' David's anger at Mark was evident. 'What's done is done. We need to focus on Cameron now.'

Their attention was drawn to the sound of the doors swinging open and a man coming in wearing green theatre scrubs. His rubber-soled shoes squeaked on the linoleum.

'Are you Mrs Black?'

Imogen stuttered, 'Um, no, we're not married, but I'm his girlfriend, and we live together. These are his parents.'

'Okay, that's fine. The good news is that Cameron has made it through surgery. Thankfully, the knife wound didn't hit any vital organs. He was incredibly fortunate. One centimetre to the left, and it would be a different story. He lost a lot of blood and went into cardiac arrest on three occasions.' Liz and Imogen both sobbed at hearing this.

'It's okay. He's out of surgery and stable. He's still unconscious, and he'll need to stay in for observation for a few days. We don't anticipate any lasting damage. He'll need to take it easy for six weeks or so, but other than that, he will be right as rain in no time. He's been very lucky.'

Imogen sighed with relief. 'When can we see him?'

'I'm afraid he can't have any visitors this evening, but you can come in tomorrow morning when he should be out of intensive care.'

'Thank you, thank you so much.'

David took the surgeon's hand and shook it vigorously. 'Thank you so much for saving our son. We're forever in your debt.'

'Not at all—it's what we do. I suggest you all get some rest while Cameron is asleep. Now, if you'll excuse me, I have another patient waiting.'

'I'll call James to let him know the news, and I'll stay with Imogen tonight. I don't think she should be alone.' Julian, would you be able to give us a lift to get my car?

'Of course, anything you need.'

'Well, David, I guess there's nothing more we can do. We may as well go home and come back tomorrow. Imogen, will you be okay?'

'Yes, I think so. Sarah will stay with me, and they've given me some strong sleeping pills for tonight.'

'I'll sedate myself with a stiff drink when I get home. I'm not happy about you driving here tomorrow, so I suggest we come and pick you up in the morning. Does that sound okay?'

'Only if you're sure. I'd be okay driving.'

'We're sure. Cameron would kill us if he found out we let you drive after everything you've been through. We'll see you in the morning.' Liz hugged Imogen. 'Don't worry, we raised a strong boy, Imogen.'

Julian led Imogen and Sarah to his car and drove back to their office.

CHAPTER 48

Sarah and Imogen said their goodbyes to Julian as Sarah started her car.

'Your handbag is on the back seat, Imogen. I found it on the floor with Cameron's car keys, so I've put those in your bag, too.'

'Oh, Christ—I forgot about those. It's a good job you found them—otherwise, we'd be sleeping in the car.'

The drive home was quiet, something that Imogen was grateful for. She wasn't up to talking—her mind was on Cameron.

When they got home, Imogen had to shower and change. Her dress was covered in blood, and she felt filthy. She looked in the mirror, shocked at what she saw. The attack had left her forehead bloodied and bruised, and blood matted her hair. The remnants of her makeup were smudged on her face. She felt embarrassed that she'd met Cameron's parents in such a state. Pushing her thoughts aside, she got changed, tied her clean hair into a bun, and headed downstairs to Sarah, who was waiting in the kitchen.

'Thanks for everything today, Sarah. I couldn't have got through it if you weren't there holding my hand.'

'Hey, that's what friends are for. Do you feel better after having a shower? You certainly look better.'

'Yeah, I do. I think I'll be sore in the morning, though. I hit the ground hard.' Imogen looked at her hands and picked her nails. 'Fucking Mark, why did he have to turn out to be a psycho?'

'I don't know the answer to that, Jen. How do you feel about what happened to him?'

'I don't know. I'm numb—like it's a bad dream. All I can think about is Cameron and how close I came to losing him. I was so scared, Sarah.' Imogen stopped the tears from flowing.

'Well, if you ask me, Mark got what he deserved, and we can sleep better knowing that he can't hurt anyone again. Cameron is tough, he's going to be okay, and you two can get on with your lives like any other couple. Plus, you've now got a great story to tell people at dinner parties.' Sarah smiled at Imogen.

'Thanks, Sarah. I appreciate the humour.' Imogen looked exhausted.

'You look like you need a glass of something strong. Shall we get a drink and chill out?'

'That's a good idea. My mum swears by a nice drop of brandy at times like these. Oh, bloody hell, I should call my family, but I just don't have the energy. Maybe I'll call them tomorrow.'

The doorbell interrupted Imogen's thoughts.

'Who is that?' Imogen went to the CCTV to see who it was before buzzing them in.

'It's the police. I recognise them. It's the same people that spoke to me about Mark.' Imogen pressed the button to open the gates.

'I'll get the door. You need to sit down. You don't look too well, Jen.' Sarah put the brandy down and went to the front door.

'Good evening, I'm Detective Sergeant Abbott—this is Detective Constable Miller. We were hoping to speak to Miss Taylor. Is she in?'

'Hello, yes, she's here. Please come in. Imogen's exhausted. I'm not sure she's got much left in her tonight.' Sarah closed the door and directed them to the kitchen. 'We've just got back from the hospital. It's safe to say that today's been a rough day.'

'I can imagine. Don't worry, we won't stay long. We just need to get some details, then we'll be on our way.'

'Good evening, Miss Taylor. How are you feeling? No, don't get up.'

'I'm a bit shaky, but on the whole, okay—considering.'

'We didn't have time to speak to you at the scene today, but we've seen the footage from Mr Black's car. Isn't modern technology great? It does a lot of the work for us. We understand that he's out of surgery and stable?' DS Abbott was poised with his notebook and pencil.

'Yes, I haven't seen him, but I'm going to the hospital in the morning. Hopefully, he'll be conscious by then.'

'I'm sure he will. Now I just need a few details from you, Imogen, are you up to telling me your side of events?'

'Yes, I'll do my best. It gets a bit hazy partway through.'

'Okay, so tell me, where was your meeting this morning, and how did that come about?'

'A contact from Walter and Holmes got in touch with James and requested me by name. Then they moved the meeting forward to today, which was cutting it fine. It was a good job, and we had the material ready.'

'I see, and would you say it was normal for a company to

request a designer by name?'

'It can be, but that only happens when the designer is a lot more established than I am, so it took me by surprise.'

The room was silent apart from the sound of a pencil scratching across paper. 'And why do you think they moved the meeting forward?'

'I think it has something to do with London.'

'London?'

'Yes, can I say something off the record?'

'Not strictly, Miss Taylor. This is a murder investigation, so we have to keep everything on the record.'

'Okay, I understand. I was in London last Friday, and Mark found me there and came after me. Cameron had a feeling he'd show up, so he was watching the CCTV footage in the club and saw him. He intervened. They fought, and the bouncers removed Mark. I don't think he took it well.'

'I see. Would you be able to tell me the name of the club?'

'I'd rather not if that's okay? I've dragged enough people into this already.' Imogen explained what Mark had done to Lucy. 'I don't understand how he was involved in the project I was working on and how he got me onto it. He worked for a different company in the Group.'

'We've been speaking to Miss Steele. She told us everything that happened in the run-up, and your stories match. Interestingly, she also wouldn't confirm the name of the club.

'What I can tell you is that Mark was recently promoted to Managing Director of Walter and Holmes. He's put a lot of work into his plan to come for you, and we believe his intentions were sinister. To secure the role, he pulled in many favours and threatened to dish the dirt on some of his senior colleagues. During a search of his address, colleagues discovered a locked bedroom. We believe the bedroom was somewhat of a shrine to you, Miss Taylor. More disturbingly, it contained a number of restraints and knives. We believe his ultimate intention was to end your life in that room.'

Imogen gasped, the colour draining from her face. Sarah put her arm around her in comfort.

'We don't doubt that Mark was a dangerous man, Miss Taylor. You made the right decision to leave him.'

'I can't help but think that if I hadn't left him, none of this would have happened. Cameron wouldn't be in the hospital fighting for his life.'

DC Miller stepped forward with a look of determination on her face.

'You can't think like that, Imogen. Men like him are unstable. Even if you'd stayed with Mark, you would have ended up hurt or worse. His mental state would have deteriorated to a point where the smallest thing would trigger him. He was a walking time bomb, and thankfully he won't get the chance to go off.'

Imogen nodded. She understood what DC Miller was talking about. She got the impression she was speaking from experience.

'What about Lucy? Can you tell me what's happening to her?'

'It will please you to know we have released Miss Steele without charge. We conclude that her actions were in self-defence and necessary to prevent Mr Edwards from harming anyone else. To echo DC Miller's opinion, we think he got what he deserved, and we won't be wasting time investigating his death. But that is not common knowledge.'

'Oh, thank goodness.' Imogen realised she'd been holding her breath.

'We're sorry that we couldn't do more to protect you from the start, Miss Taylor. It's awful that Mr Black has sustained injuries because of this, but we hope you can find peace now and move on with your life.' DC Miller smiled at Imogen.

'Now, if you'll excuse us, we have a mountain of paperwork to get through. We'll need to take a statement from Mr Black and then await the autopsy results on what killed Mr Edwards. Preliminary findings are that the initial knife wound wasn't the fatal one. When he fell onto the knife, he sealed his fate. So I hope that Miss Steele doesn't feel like she has blood on her hands.

'Now I suggest you drink that brandy and get some rest. In the best way possible, I hope not to see you again.'

Imogen showed the detectives out, sank into the sofa next to Sarah, and downed her brandy. It burned but then warmed her.

'He was a nice man, wasn't he? Not what you'd imagine a Detective Sergeant to be like.'

'I know, I think they feel bad that they couldn't do more earlier. I think DC Miller has personal experience with it, too. She gave me a look that said she understood what I was going through.'

'I'm pleased that Lucy hasn't got into trouble. That's a relief. We need to focus on Cameron now and make sure he heals, and then we can move on from this. You two should get married and have lots of gorgeous babies.'

'Can I concentrate on getting him home alive for now?'

'Yeah, all right. Come on, let's get to bed and see what tomorrow brings. Can I borrow something to sleep in?'

'Of course, I'll get you some PJs.'

Sarah heard her phone vibrate in her bag.

'I've got a message from James. He says he hopes you're okay and asks if we've heard the good news about Lucy. He said the office is closed tomorrow as we all need some downtime to process what happened. There you go, chick—every cloud has a silver lining.'

Imogen rolled her eyes at Sarah but with a smile. She took her sleeping pills and went to bed. Sarah slept by her side to make sure she was all right, but Imogen thought Sarah didn't want to be alone either. She was okay with that.

Imogen spent the morning fussing with her hair and trying to cover the bruising on her forehead. She wanted to make a better impression on Cameron's parents. She tried to look as normal as possible for Cameron. Liz and David were quiet in the car—it seemed inappropriate to fill the space with small talk.

'How do you feel about seeing Cameron?' Liz was glancing at Imogen in the rearview mirror.

'I feel a bit anxious. I've no idea what to expect, and I'm nervous that I'm going to fall apart as soon as I see him.'

Liz gave Imogen a kind smile. 'He'll look worse for wear, but you'll see past that, don't you worry.'

They stopped outside the door to Cameron's room. 'Now, please remember that he is still under heavy sedation. He's awake, but he's very drowsy, so please don't expect too much from him.'

Imogen stole a glance through the glass in the door. She gasped before she could gain control of her reactions.

'We need to stay strong, remember? He looks weak now, but he'll soon be right as rain.' Imogen wondered who Liz was trying to convince.

As they entered the room, Cameron stirred and opened his

eyes.

'Hi, it's great to see you three.' His voice was weak and rasping.

Liz ran to his side and hugged him.

'Not so hard, Mum—I'm still sore.' Imogen hung back—she felt like an imposter encroaching on family time. She needed a few minutes to compose herself.

'Imogen, you'd better come and kiss me. I've missed you.'

'I think that's our cue to grab a coffee, my love. Let's leave these two lovebirds alone.'

'I saw a nice little coffee place over the road. I'm not drinking that hospital rubbish. I've had my fill of that for a lifetime. See you in a bit, son.' Liz gave Imogen's shoulder a reassuring squeeze on her way out.

'I see where you get your love of good coffee from.'

Cameron smiled and held his hand up for Imogen. She entwined her fingers with his, eager to feel his skin. She sat down next to the bed and rested her cheek on the back of his hand.

'Thank you so much for everything you've done for me. I'm sorry you got mixed up with me and ended up in hospital.'

'Don't mention it. I don't regret it, and I'd do it again a thousand times to keep you safe. But can you give me a kiss now? They always make me feel alive, and I could do with some of that.'

Imogen leaned over Cameron and pressed her lips gently to his. He let out a soft moan.

'Thank you. That did the job.' He stroked her forehead. 'Are you okay? That looks sore.'

'I'm good. It looks worse than it is, with only a few stitches and a mild concussion. More importantly, how're you doing?'

'I'll live. The nurse told me I could go home in a few days. I can't wait, although they're very attentive here.'

'I bet they are. You're insanely hot even when you're recovering from being stabbed. That reminds me, I've brought you some clothes, so you don't need to lie here semi-naked—not that I'm complaining about it.'

'Thank you, I'll have to get the nurse to help me put them on later. I have tubes coming out of all sorts of places.'

'Is it wrong that it makes me jealous?'

'I wouldn't be. I'm not looking too great, but I'm going to have an awesome scar.'

Imogen was quiet. She appreciated his attempt at humour, but her emotions were threatening to break through, and she was trying not to cry. 'He's dead, Cam. He's dead.'

'Yeah, I know. The police were here this morning. He can't hurt you anymore, Jen—you're free.'

Cameron reached up and wiped away the tear making its way down Imogen's cheek.

'I guess that means you don't need me anymore?'

'What? You must've hit your head when you fell yesterday. I need you more than I needed you before. Seriously, Cam, I don't know what I'd do if I lost you. You have to promise not to die on me.'

'I was kidding, Jen, but that's good to hear. I've every intention of spending the rest of my long life with you.'

'Well, by the way, you two are staring at each other. I'd say we're interrupting something, wouldn't you, Liz?'

'Thanks, Dad, impeccable timing.'

'Here you go, love, a nice cup of coffee. I realised I didn't ask how you take it, so I assumed you'd like it the same as Cameron.

Hopefully, I was right?'

'Perfect, thank you.'

They chatted while they drank their coffee. Liz did most of the talking and regaled Imogen with stories of Cameron when he was a child.

'I think it's time we let you get some rest. We'll come again tomorrow if you want us to?' Liz could see that Cameron was struggling to keep his eyes open.

'That would be great. Thanks, Mum. And thank you for bringing Imogen. I don't want her driving around with that head injury.'

'Cameron, I'm okay.' Imogen hung back so she could be alone with him before he fell asleep.

'I love you, Cameron. Make sure you get lots of rest, okay?'

Cameron was so tired, he replied with a grunt. She leaned over and kissed his forehead before leaving the room—he was asleep before she reached the door.

CHAPTER 49

'Taxi for Mr Black?' Imogen was standing in the doorway to Cameron's hospital room, full of excitement to be taking him home. He was on the edge of the bed, dressed in tracksuit bottoms and a hoodie. It was a far cry from his tailored jeans and shirts, but he still looked gorgeous. Imogen raked her fingers through his overgrown beard as Cameron pulled her in between his legs for a bear hug.

He breathed her in, 'Hello sexy, I'm pleased to see you. I can't wait to get home.'

'I can't wait to have you home. The place has felt empty without you—that, and your cooking is better than mine. Let's get out of here.'

Cameron stood up from the bed, refusing Imogen's help. He winced as he straightened up.

'Please, tell me you came in my car? I don't fancy folding myself into your Mini.'

'Don't worry, luxury awaits you. Are you sure you should walk? Aren't I supposed to be pushing you out in a wheelchair?'

'Absolutely not. I refuse to be wheeled out. The nurses have been trying to convince me all morning. Something about hospital protocol, but I refuse to be held down. I want to walk out of here, Imogen.'

She rolled her eyes at him. 'Well, I won't waste my time arguing with you. But we'll take it slowly, and I'll carry your bag. Understood?'

'Yes, ma'am.'

Imogen put her arm around him as they walked out. One of the nurses met them. 'Goodbye, Mr Black. Take it easy, won't you? You need plenty of bed rest. If you need anything, you can call.'

'Thank you, I intend to milk this for all it's worth. Don't worry—Imogen will take excellent care of me.'

'I think she fancies you. Very unprofessional if you ask me.'

'Are you jealous, by any chance?'

'Yes, I am, insanely. Don't think I don't know how many bed baths she gave you, and I'm sure they weren't all necessary.'

'I love you. You are so cute when you're jealous.' Cameron wrapped his arm around her shoulder.

'It's so good to be home. I've missed this sofa.' As he sank into the leather cushions, he let out a moan of happiness.

'I hope that's not all you've missed, Cameron.'

'Words can't describe how much I've missed you. The nights were the worst. I never want to sleep without you again.' She joined him on the sofa.

'I feel the same. I've slept in the same T-shirt while you've been gone because it smelt of you. Although, to be honest, it needs a wash now, so it's a good job you came home when you did.'

'Very sexy, Jen. Very sexy.' Cameron laughed and pulled her closer.

'You're meant to be taking it easy.'

'Okay, you can go on top then. How does that sound?'

'Oh my God, I can't believe you're horny already. You're recovering from being stabbed, Cameron.'

'Yeah, I know, but he didn't cut my dick off. See.' Cameron pointed to his impressive length.

The doorbell interrupted his antics.

'For fuck's sake, my balls are turning blue, and now there's someone at the door. Get rid of them, Jen.'

Jen laughed as she went.

'It's your parents, Cam—I think I'll need to let them in.'

'All right. Stall them, though. I think it's going to take effort to get this to go down.'

Imogen loved having Cameron back, and the stabbing hadn't killed his spirit. She was worried that he'd resent her for what happened to him, but he removed all concerns on that front. Imogen greeted his parents and showed them through.

Liz had brought flowers and champagne for Imogen and some Italian coffee beans for Cameron.

'Well, I was supposed to give them to you when we saw you on Saturday, but you got yourself stabbed. The beans were freshly roasted when we left Italy, so they should be perfect now. Imogen, shall we pop the cork? It's always time for fizz. Wouldn't you agree?'

'I certainly do.'

Liz and Imogen sipped champagne, and David made himself and Cameron a coffee. It was a lovely morning. You wouldn't know they'd all been through a horrendous week.

'Right, David. It's time we headed off, I'm afraid. We've got afternoon tea at Fawsley Hall booked with friends, and no amount of stabbing would get me to cancel those plans.'

'Cheers, Mum, I'm glad you're here.' Cameron rolled his eyes as Liz kissed his cheek.

As Imogen came into the kitchen, Cameron turned to her with his signature grin.

'So, is there any champagne left?'

'There is, yes, but you can't drink with your medication.'

'Oh, Jen, I have no intention of taking it internally.' He raised his eyebrows. 'Shall we take this bottle upstairs? I have an urgent medical need that only Nurse Taylor can help me with.'

'If it's a medical emergency, then it's my duty.'

Imogen grabbed the bottle and went upstairs, albeit slower than usual.

'Would you mind helping with my clothes?'

'I'd love to.' Imogen took her time removing his T-shirt. She peppered his chest with kisses as she pulled it over his head, releasing soft hums of pleasure as she did so.

'I've missed your touch so much. I can't believe I'll be out of action for a while. There are so many naughty things I want to do to you. I'm sorry.'

She looked into his eyes. 'We've all the time in the world to catch up on those. Let me take care of you for a while, okay?' Cameron nodded. She ran her fingers along the waistband of his trousers before pushing them to the floor. She ran her hands up his legs and repeated the process with his underwear. 'I'm just going to take a minute to squeeze these gorgeous butt cheeks— I've missed them.'

'Well, don't take too long—I could do with lying down.'

'Come on then, let's get you on the bed.' Cameron climbed up to the bed while Imogen plumped the pillows behind his back.

'Perfect, thank you. Now you can take your time reacquainting yourself with my body.' Cameron wiggled his eyebrows. 'I've often fantasised about you being my nurse. Maybe in the future, I should just buy you the outfit rather than getting stabbed.'

'That would be my preference—what did it feel like?' Imogen was tentatively tracing the edge of his dressing with her finger.

'I thought Mark had punched me in the stomach, but then it burned like hell. I don't remember much after that, just fear.'

'I'm sorry, Cameron. You're scarred because of my mistakes, and I can't forgive myself for that.'

'What? Please don't think like that, Imogen. This scar doesn't represent your mistakes—it represents my love for you. We're linked forever because of it. It's proof we can overcome anything that gets in our way. And it makes me look badass, so I love it. Now, can we get back to the fun?'

'I love you, Cam.'

'I love you, too. Get to work, Nurse Taylor.'

'It will be my pleasure.'

The following week flew by. Imogen worked from home to look after Cameron, and he milked it, just as promised.

'I'm not convinced you should work on the Walter and Holmes project.' Cameron stood in the doorway of their home office, leaning on the doorframe. Imogen took a moment to admire the view as he was only wearing his jeans. The scar didn't detract from his incredible body.

'I can't believe they asked us to continue with the plans, to be honest. I've asked that they make a generous donation to a women's refuge charity if Spencer and Black continue with their project. Mark isn't going to stop me from getting on with my life when his is over, so I'm going to rise above it and get on with it. Call it a final finger to him.'

'You're a strong woman, Jen, and I love you for it. And you did impress them. Have you heard any more about his funeral?'

Imogen was quiet. Unable to make eye contact, she cast her eyes downward.

'Jen? What's going on?'

'The funeral is in a couple of days. I've been thinking about it.'

'What've you been thinking, Jen?' Cameron's voice was steady but had taken on a deeper tone. Imogen sensed she had to tread carefully.

'I'd like to go to the funeral.' Moments passed in silence. Cameron clenched his jaw. 'Cam, please say something.'

'What the fuck do you want me to say? I hope you don't expect me to go with you?'

'No, of course not. Sarah said she'd come.'

'Right, so you've discussed this with Sarah. Were you planning to tell me at all?'

'Of course. I wasn't sure if I was going to go or not.' There was another long silence. 'Cam, please talk to me.'

Cameron's words were barely audible. 'I died, Jen.'

'I know. It breaks my heart that you went through that, but I must do this for me. I need to see it through to the end.'

'I died three times because of him, and you want to pay your respects to him? What respects, Imogen?'

'Cameron, please. You're tired, and I don't want to stress you out any further.'

'Too fucking right I'm tired, Jen. Your bloody ex stabbed

me. Look at the scar. Look at what he did to me.' Cameron snapped—all his pent-up anger was flooding out. Cameron lashed out before Imogen could respond and punched the wall next to him. The force of movement was too much for his body to cope with. He doubled over in pain, growling through gritted teeth. Imogen jumped up from her chair and went to him.

'Don't.' He held one hand up to her while his other rested on his knee for support. 'I can't talk about this now.'

'Cameron, please, you don't understand.'

'You're right—I don't.' He rose to full height, with adrenaline pumping through him. 'You had to end your life as you knew it—change your job, move house, move bloody county—to escape your abuser. He stalked you, did God-knows-what damage to Lucy, beat up Seth and stabbed me, all while building his sick shrine where he planned to murder you. I can't make love to you because of him. He's fucking dead, and he's still stopping us from being together. Have you any idea how angry that makes me? Fucking look at me—my traitorous cock has come to life at the thought of driving it into you, and there's nothing I can do about it.' Cameron leant on the doorframe, out of breath and trying to calm down. Perspiration left a sheen across his chest.

'I'm sorry. I had no idea that was how you felt. This is temporary—you need to take it easy for a few weeks, and then we can get back to normal and put it behind us.' Imogen walked over to Cameron and tried to undo the button of his jeans, 'In the meantime, I'll take care of that for you.'

'No, I don't want you to take care of it—I want to take care of you. I need to go. I'm sorry.' Cameron pulled away and stalked off. Moments later, she heard the slam of the front door.

CHAPTER 50

Song Choice: Better Days (Dermot Kennedy)

'Cameron, please answer the phone. I'm going out of my mind with worry. Come home so we can talk about this.' Imogen had been trying to get hold of him all afternoon. He'd walked out of the house, his car still parked in the drive. She lost count of how many messages she left him. She hung up, threw her phone on the desk, and put her head in her hands. Her panic was interrupted by her phone vibrating across the desk. She grabbed it, her hands fumbling to answer. 'Cam, is that you?'

'Imogen, it's James. Are you okay?'

'No, I'm not okay. I had a row with Cameron, and he walked out. I can't get hold of him. Have you seen him?'

'He's with me, Jen. Sorry I didn't call you sooner—I've had my hands full with him. I got a call from him earlier asking me to pick him up from the pub. He found out the hard way that pain meds and whiskey aren't a sensible mix—he's sleeping it off.'

'Oh, thank goodness—I've been worried sick. Apart from being unconscious, is he okay?'

'No, not really. I think it's safe to say he has some unresolved feelings about everything. He's been putting a brave face on it, but it scared him, Jen. I think he's struggling with the idea that, at the moment, he's not there for you. You know what he's like—the alpha male that must protect his woman, and he had to stand by helpless while you had a knife to your throat. I reckon I'd be pretty messed up if I'd been resuscitated three times. It's pretty fucked up.'

'What can I do to help him?'

'He needs time, that's all. He's tired and in pain and doesn't like it. Be there for him, and I recommend you stock up on greasy food and orange juice. He's going to have a brutal hangover tomorrow. I'll bring him home in the morning when I'm sure he's not going to vomit in my car.'

'Thanks, James. You're a good friend.'

'No worries. Get some sleep, and I'll see you tomorrow.'

'We need to talk, but we need to do it lying down. Standing up is killing me.' Cameron was standing in the hallway, smelling of stale whiskey and barely speaking. He wasn't looking very proud of himself.

'Come on, let's get you cleaned up and into bed.' Imogen led him upstairs and into their en-suite. She peeled his clothes off before turning on the walk-in shower, He closed his eyes as the warm water washed away the remnants of his drinking session with his shoulders slumped. She washed his body, massaging the suds into his shoulders, hoping it would help him relax. Two heavy arms wrapped themselves around her neck, holding her tight and halting her progress. They stood in silence, watching the bubbles slide into the plughole.

'Cam? Are we okay?'

'We're all good if you can forgive me for walking out yesterday. I don't know what came over me. I think it just hit me, and I needed some air. Unfortunately, that air turned into an exquisite forty-year-old single malt. My mind and body are at war with each other. One of them wants to pin you up against the wall, and the other won't let me. Can we get into bed?'

A few minutes later, Imogen settled into bed next to him. He was lying on his back, with an arm draped over his eyes. Propped up on one elbow, she lay facing him.

'Talk to me, Cam. What's going on in that gorgeous head of yours?'

'I'm sorry I lost my temper. I shouldn't have taken my frustration out on the wall. I hope I didn't scare you?'

'It's okay. You're only human, and you've been through a lot. I'm not going to think you're like Mark if you lose your temper or get cross about something.'

'I worry about saying or doing the wrong thing, so I've been bottling everything up. I want you to feel safe and loved with me, and I feel like I've let you down. Mark got to you and could have sliced your throat with that knife.'

'But he didn't. You took the knife for me. You fought for me until you couldn't fight anymore. Mark planned to take me away and do some unthinkable things in that room. The stuff the police found was horrendous. You saved me from a fate worse than death, and I'll never forget that. Never worry about saying or doing the wrong thing—you could never do anything wrong by me.'

'So why do you want to go to his funeral? Do you need to say goodbye to him?'

'It's not about me saying goodbye. Mark controlled me and took so much away from me. There are things I want to say, and he's taken away my opportunity to say them. I want to go to the funeral to tell him he didn't keep me down, he can't control me anymore, and I've found true love. I want to tell him I pity him. I need to have the final word, Cameron.'

'I understand. I hope you understand why I can't be there.'

'I do. I need to do this without you. This is between Mark and me.'

'I love you, Jen, more than you will ever know.'

'I love you too, Cam.'

'When I'm healed, which hopefully won't be too long, I'm going to show you how much I love you with every part of my body.'

'I look forward to that.'

'Now I need to lie in a dark room and not move, as I've already discovered that being sick with a healing stab wound is torture.'

'Muppet, take all the time you need—I'll be here when you feel better.'

'God, we thank you for the life you give us. It is full of work and responsibility, sadness and joy. Today we thank you for Mark Edwards and for what he has given and received.'

'What the bloody hell is this guy talking about? I am not thankful for Mark.' Sarah's whisper was too loud. They'd planned to arrive as late as possible and sit at the back. Imogen hoped to avoid the other attendees, but this was proving difficult. As they sneaked in, it was apparent that few people mourned his loss. Their footsteps echoed around the half-empty church, with only a handful of family and friends sitting in the front pews—it emphasised their arrival.

'Keep your voice down. I'm trying to be invisible. And if it weren't for Mark, I wouldn't have left London and met you guys, would I?'

'Oh, that's true—I'll give him that. But I still think he was an evil bastard.'

'Seriously, Sarah, you're in church—you can't talk like that.'

'Whatever.' Sarah rolled her eyes heavenward before facing the front. For the rest of the funeral, they sat eyes downward and stood to sing the final hymn. Imogen hung back while everyone else filed out of the church.

'I need to say a few last words to Mark. Can you give me a minute, Sarah? I'll meet you outside?'

'Yeah, of course—I'll see you in a minute.'

Imogen waited for the door to close before she lowered her eyes. 'Mark, I don't know if you can hear me, but it's the only chance I have, and I need to get this off my chest. For a time, I thought I loved you, and you loved me. I've discovered that what we had was not love. I stayed with you out of fear. Over the years, you chipped away at my soul until I was nothing but a shell. I wasn't strong enough to see you for who you were or leave you when I should have. You made me weak, and that's not love.

'I am so thankful that I found the strength and courage to leave you. My new life came along at the right time and has saved me. But most of all, Cameron has saved me. Because of him, I've found my soul. It's like he was the missing piece of my puzzle. I've felt overwhelming anger at what you put me through, but it was nothing compared to what I felt when you nearly killed Cameron. You wanted to take a piece of me away. Well, you can't take anything from me again.

'I feel sorry for you. You'll never experience what it's like to stare into the eyes of your soulmate and feel you could get lost in them forever. You'll never experience how your body crackles with electricity whenever your love is near, even if you can't see them.

'I can't forgive you for what you took or the damage you've done to Cameron and Lucy. But I'll always be thankful that you led me to where I am now. Because of you, I'm strong. I'll never take love for granted. I wake up every morning knowing I can take on whatever life wants to throw at me. Thank you for teaching me what I deserve and what I can achieve. I'm sorry that your actions led you to your untimely death. I believe there was good in you, somewhere, and I hope that part is at peace.

'Goodbye, Mark, may you rest in peace.' Imogen took a deep breath and cleared out any trace of the old life she left behind. As the breath left her lungs, a weight lifted. A sense of freedom came over her. She didn't need to look over her shoulder. She was free.

CHAPTER 51

'I've been thinking, Jen.'

'Oh no, that always worries me.' Imogen and Cameron were at the island eating dinner. Imogen prepared her favourite pasta, arrabiata, and Cameron was appreciative.

'Don't worry—it's nothing scary. I think our families should meet. I thought it would be nice for everyone to get together soon. What do you think?'

'I love the idea, but I don't want you over-stretching yourself when you're healing.'

'I've thought of that already. What's the point of me part-owning a restaurant if I can't hold a party there?'

'A party? What are we celebrating?'

'Life, Jen, we're celebrating life. I've invited the usual crowd. I don't think James or Sarah would forgive us for having a party without them. Lucy is bringing Tom, and Julian has asked Jess to come along. It's going to be great. Your sister will be there too, which is awesome.'

'I'm confused. It sounds like you've already organised it.'

'I don't know if you've noticed, but I haven't been busy of late.

I had to do something to keep me occupied, so I've organised it all. It's happening this weekend.' Cameron's words were met with stunned silence.

'Wow.' Imogen stopped in her tracks as she gave Cameron an appreciative once-over.

'What? What are you looking at, you dirty perv?' Cameron had walked into the kitchen, ready to take Imogen to the party. He was wearing tailored chinos, a crisp white shirt and, what looked like a new pair of tan leather John Lobb shoes.

'I'm delighted to see you've trimmed your beard and are looking like your old self. Is that a new outfit?'

'Might be. I wanted to make an effort for tonight, so James took me shopping. I can't wait to get behind the wheel of my car; being driven around like Miss Daisy is killing my street cred.'

'The fact you've just used the term street cred tells me you don't have any.'

'Cheeky—watch what you say, or I might take you over my knee. And with you looking the way you do, I'd enjoy that, and then we'd be late for our party. You look beautiful, as always.' Imogen wore a black, knee-length, figure-hugging dress with a Bardot neckline. Cameron had surprised her with a pair of black satin peep-toe Jimmy Choo shoes, and they were a perfect match for the dress.

'Thank you, and thank you for the shoes—I love them. Shall we get going? The taxi's outside.'

The Blacks and the Taylors were getting along well, and the conversation flowed. Izzy quizzed Cameron to within an inch of his life and gave him the seal of approval.

'Ladies, I've brought you a fresh glass of fizz.' Cameron had braved a visit to the group of women that had formed. Sarah led the conversation and had the rest of them in fits of giggles.

'Thank you, my love.' Imogen rewarded Cameron with a kiss, which was met with an "ah" from Jess and Izzy. The mood was carefree, and the champagne free-flowing.

'Everyone, can I please have your attention for a few moments?'

'Cameron?' Imogen looked confused. The room fell silent, and everyone turned to face him.

'I would like to take this opportunity to thank you all for coming. As you know, Imogen and I have had a rough few weeks, and we couldn't have got through it if it wasn't for all of you, so thank you. And if it wasn't for Lucy and James in particular, I might not have been here at all. I can't entertain the thought of what might have happened to Imogen. You fought for us without hesitation, and we will forever be in your debt. Please, raise your glass in a toast to the best of friends.' He raised his glass and nodded to James and Lucy.

In unison, the room repeated, 'To the best of friends.'

'Now, if you would be so kind as to entertain me for a little longer. I want to share something that I haven't spoken about before.

'I experienced something that few people get to talk about. I looked death in the eye. Those out-of-body experiences you hear about are real, and I saw the light.' Imogen began to cry—she had no idea that he'd gone through this. Cameron turned and took her hand.

'It would have been easy for me to die, but I decided I wasn't ready for that. What kept me alive was Imogen. I saw her face, and I felt the need to come back and keep her safe.' Cameron took a brief pause to compose himself. 'Before I get too cheesy and bring the atmosphere down, I'll wrap this up. I just wanted to say my final thank you to Imogen.' Cameron turned to face her. He wiped her tears away with his thumb.

'You often tell me that meeting me has saved your life, but you saved mine. I never want to lose you, and I'll do everything to keep us together for as long as we live, and I hope that is a very long time.'

Cameron reached into his back pocket and bent to one knee. Imogen, and the crowd of family and friends, gasped, but this time filled with hope and excitement.

'Imogen Taylor, will you do me the honour of allowing me to worship you, care for you and protect you for as long as we both shall live?'

Imogen was so stunned she couldn't process what he was saying. He opened the exquisite wooden box to reveal the most beautiful diamond ring she'd ever seen. It had a Phoenix-cut diamond in the centre, flanked by two smaller stones on either side, set into a platinum band. It was understated and beautiful. Imogen thought it was perfect.

'Yes, Cameron. My answer, without doubt, is yes.' Tears of joy were streaming down her cheeks as he put the ring on her finger. The diamonds caught the light of the spotlights on the ceiling, and rainbow-coloured sparkles danced on the walls.

'Three cheers for Cameron and Imogen.' Julian was shouting for joy, and the room erupted with cheers, glasses of champagne held high. There was barely a dry eye in the room.

Cameron dipped her for a kiss. This time, the room erupted with wolf whistles.

'You haven't stopped gazing at that ring all night. I take it I did all right with my choice?' They were getting ready for bed after getting home in the early hours of the morning.

'It's perfect. You're perfect. My cheeks hurt from smiling too much.'

'I'm glad to hear it. You deserve to be happy.'

'I couldn't be happier. I'm impressed you had all this organised without me knowing. Usually, I'm very good at sniffing out a surprise. I can't believe you even met secretly with my dad to ask for his blessing. I wondered why Mum and Dad weren't staying over until Izzy explained they didn't want to get in the way of us celebrating properly when we got home. Dad said it would be like sharing a room with a pair of newlyweds. Total cringe-fest. We'll have to save this feeling for when you're back in action.'

Cameron took her in his arms and ran his fingers through her hair before finding the zip on the back of her dress. He brought his mouth to her ear, nibbled on her lobe and then whispered, 'Consider me back in action.' He unzipped her dress before letting it drop to the floor.

'Have they given you the all-clear?'

'Signed-off and back in the saddle. I'll tell you about it later, but for now, I have a lot of celebrating to do.' His lips danced across her collarbone, and he made quick work of removing his shirt. Imogen closed her eyes, soaking in the warmth of his touch. Her hands roamed across his bare chest before he guided her onto the bed. His kisses worked lower over her breasts and to her navel. Taking her underwear, he pulled it down her legs before discarding it with the rest of his clothes.

Cameron had barely touched Imogen, but her body was ablaze in anticipation. They hadn't had full sex for weeks, and their bodies were crying out for that intimate connection. His gaze scorched through to her soul as he looked into her eyes. He kissed her at the top of her pubic bone before opening her thighs for him. He dipped his head and licked across her entrance.

'Cameron.' His name came out as a gasp. Knowing how this evening was going to end made the build-up more intense.

'I'm right there with you. I'm going to take care of you all night.'

He licked along her lips again before sucking on her clitoris. Imogen arched her back, unable to control her movements. Her hands reached down so that she could run her fingers through his hair and increase the pressure on her sensitive opening.

'I'm so desperate to feel you inside me, Cameron. I can't take it.'

'Don't worry, you'll get it. I'm savouring every moment of this, my beautiful fiancée.'

'Fiancée—I like the sound of that.'

Cameron licked through the folds of her opening, the tip of his tongue circling her engorged clit. He felt her clench as he pushed two fingers inside. She was wet and ready for him.

'Oh, Cameron, please. Please.' Imogen clawed at his shoulders to encourage him upwards.

'Patience, beautiful. Good things come to those who wait.' As he spoke, he thrust his fingers in again and drew her clit into his mouth for one long suck. Imogen's hips bucked as an orgasm ripped through her body.

'Cameron, please fuck me now.'

He crawled up the bed until he was over Imogen and nestled between her legs. Guiding his rock-hard length to her entrance, he nudged his way in.

'Oh fuck. I need to take it slow.' Cameron thrust into her as deep as he could go and stilled. 'You were made for me. We fit together perfectly.'

Lost for words, her eyes said it all. She wrapped her hands around his head and pressed her lips to his. 'I love you, Cameron Black, now and forever, but please fuck me before I explode.' Her hands swept down his back, and she dug her fingers into his arse, encouraging him to thrust.

Cameron withdrew to the tip, paused, and looked into her eyes. 'As you wish.' He drove into her, the air in her lungs rushing out with a groan.

'Ah, yes.'

He interlaced his fingers with hers and pinned her hands above her head, pressing them into the mattress. He slammed into her with perfect rhythm while bending to suck her nipples. Imogen tilted her pelvis and rose to meet his thrusts and deepen the connection. The friction on her clit drove her over the edge.

'Harder, I need it harder now.'

He increased his pace until he couldn't hold back. 'Ah, fuck, Imogen.' Cameron was growling. He came as Imogen climaxed around him. 'Bloody hell, Jen, that was incredible.'

'Well, I have no regrets about saying yes.'

CHAPTER 52

Song Choice: Falling like the Stars (James Arthur)

'When were you given the all-clear? I worry that you're getting good at keeping secrets from me, Mr Black.' She was cooking pancakes for brunch while Cameron watched TV with his feet up. The night-time activities had worn him out.

'Don't worry, I only found out the other day. The doctor phoned while you were getting your hair done. It impressed him how quickly I healed. I gave you credit for it—you tended my every need. I thought it was nice to surprise you after the party—I had a feeling we'd have cause to celebrate.'

'You assumed I'd say yes? That was brave, wasn't it?'

'I hoped you'd agree, but I figured if you said no, I could shag you into conceding. You do normally end up moaning yes to me repeatedly, so I was onto a winner.'

Imogen burst out laughing, 'Shag me into conceding. You're so romantic.'

'I know. You wouldn't have me any other way. I've more good news that I think you'll like.'

'Really? What's that?' Imogen joined Cameron on the sofa, holding two plates of pancakes in her hand.

'They look great. Thank you, gorgeous. My friend phoned and has found a farm for sale. The current owners are happy to offer it to Izzy and Miles before putting it on the market. I told Miles at the party, so they're looking at it today. I know the farm, and I think they'll love it and can move here soon.'

'That's fantastic news. It'll be easier planning a wedding when my Matron-of-Honour is close.'

'You're planning the wedding already?'

'Of course. Sarah, Lucy and Jess will be bridesmaids.' Imogen's face fell.

He turned to her with concern etched on his brow. 'What's wrong?'

'Well, that's everyone, isn't it? I don't have any other friends. I'm going to feel like a loser when my side of the church is empty, and your side will be full.'

'Nonsense. For starters, who said we must have sides of a church? People can turn up and sit wherever they like. My friends are your friends, so having sides would be pointless. I have no intention of inviting long-lost aunts, uncles and cousin fuck-knows, so don't worry, there won't be droves of family members filling the pews. I'd like a small wedding. Let's start the next chapter of our life with the people that matter, shall we?'

'You always know what to say to make me feel better. I think a small wedding will be ideal.'

'Perfect. I'd love a Christmas wedding.'

'Me too. That's a good idea, and it gives us a year to plan. That should be enough time.'

Cameron put his plate down and turned to her. 'I'm not waiting a year to marry you, Jen. I meant Christmas this year.'

'What? That's a matter of weeks away, Cameron. It can't be done.'

'It bloody well can be done, future Mrs Black. I've learnt a valuable lesson. Life's too short to wait around, and with you, anything could happen, so I should strike while the iron's hot.'

'Cheeky shit, but it's true—life's too short. Don't worry, I don't have any more crazy exes in the woodwork. I was hoping for some time to get used to being your fiancée before I become your wife, though, Cam.'

'What is there to get used to? You want to marry me, don't you? You didn't say yes because you felt pressured in front of everyone?'

'No. If I wanted to say no, I would've. I just didn't expect you to want to get married in a few weeks. What's the rush?'

'I can't wait to call you my wife. I don't see the point in long engagements. When a couple decides to get married, they should get married.'

Imogen stood up and put her half-eaten pancakes on the island.

'Where are you going?'

'I'm phoning Izzy and Sarah. I have weeks to sort a wedding dress and bridesmaid dresses. Oh, fucking hell, I need to sort wedding favours, order of service, invitations—the list is endless. You can arrange the venue—I'm not even going to try and sort that out.'

Cameron held her by the shoulders. 'Calm down, we're a team, and we can do this. We're going to do this.'

EPILOGUE

'Imogen, I give you this ring as a sign of our marriage. With my body, I honour you, all that I am I give you, and all that I have I share with you, within the love of God, Father, Son and Holy Spirit.' His words carried across the church with conviction as his thumb rubbed over the indent on Imogen's ring finger from her engagement ring. She'd moved it over to her right hand for the ceremony.

He slid the wedding band onto her finger. His smile as he gazed into her eyes could have stopped her heart from beating.

Cameron insisted on organising the wedding rings. His was a plain band of brushed platinum, and Imogen's, shaped to fit against her engagement ring, was set with a row of brilliant-cut diamonds. They caught the light from the mid-morning winter sun as it shone through the stained-glass windows.

She held Cameron's left hand and put his ring on the tip of his finger. She made sure she spoke with as much clarity as he did. She gazed into his eyes, her love for him clear.

'Cameron, I give you this ring as a sign of our marriage. With my body, I honour you, all that I am I give to you, and all that I have I share with you, within the love of God, Father, Son and Holy Spirit.' She slid the ring to the base of his finger. They exchanged smiles like giddy children on Christmas Day before turning to the vicar.

'In the presence of God, and before this congregation, Cameron and Imogen have given their consent and made their marriage vows to each other. They have declared their marriage by the joining of hands and by the giving and receiving of rings.' The vicar gave them a smile before looking up at the congregation. 'I, therefore, proclaim that they are husband and wife.' He joined their right hands before announcing dramatically. 'Those whom God has joined together, let no one put asunder.'

Cameron brought his lips down to hers. Cheers and wolf whistles from the congregation were silenced in their minds as soon as their lips met. It took all of Cameron's self-control to keep the kiss respectful. The wedding night couldn't come fast enough.

THANK YOU

'Thank you for reading this novel. I hope you enjoyed it as much as I enjoyed creating the characters. I would be forever grateful if you were to leave a review.

In 2015, I downloaded a book onto my Kindle called 'How to write your first novel.' I had, as they say, a book in me. Unfortunately, I had two things missing: confidence and time.

I met an inspirational woman who became one of my best friends. She taught me two valuable lessons—if you want something, you can make it happen, and it doesn't matter what anyone else thinks. Sheena, you have changed my life, and I am forever grateful to you.

Then I found myself in a pandemic, and like the rest of the world, I couldn't leave the house for swimming lessons, birthday parties and social engagements. So, I had time. During a virtual book club, I mentioned that I wanted to write a novel. They gave me the encouragement I needed to do it. With my newfound confidence and time, I wrote. Thank you, Swati and Gemma; your initial read-through helped me no-end.

Thank you to my husband. I know that love, at first sight, is possible because of you. Your love and support mean the world to me.

And thank you to all my friends and family that have joined me on my journey to share Imogen's story. You have encouraged me and supported me through what is a daunting experience.

Lucy, Sarah and Jess have their own stories to tell, so watch this space for the next instalment in The Book Club series.

To keep up to date with all things Ali Fischer, take a look at my Instagram and Facebook page, Ali Fischer Author.

ABOUT THE AUTHOR

Ali Fischer is a wife and mother of two boys living in the UK. Finance Manager by day, a hopeless romantic at night. Her path to finding true love is novel-worthy, and she is very happily married.

Ali had the idea for a novel but kept it to herself for many years. Then, during the Covid 19 pandemic, she found the time to write and discovered that she had an idea for four novels. The Book Club was born. She dreams that she can hang up her calculator and become a full-time author one day.